P9-CQG-068

DISCARD

For my grandmother

Vittoria Leone

who taught me how to love.

In memory of

Mary Sullivan, r.c.

ACKNOWLEDGEMENTS

I wish to thank the many people who helped bring this book to fruition. First and foremost I thank my husband Jim and our four children – Beth, Kathy, Jim and Noelle – for their belief in me to complete this endeavor, especially Noelle, whose writing skills provided expert editing throughout.

Many thanks go to my sister, Macrina Reed, who read the first drafts with engrossed interest; Bill and Mary Leverich for their early, insightful input; Dennis and Donna Esposito, Bob Caccamo, Joe Kelly and Don Bracken who provided invaluable networking opportunities; Florence Miller (my most enthusiastic fan) and her book club members – Corinne Carriero, Janet LaMantia, Barbara McLaughlin, Cathy Rocco and Barbara DiSalvo – who chose the book as their selection of the month and later invited me to hear their encouraging comments.

Thanks also to present and past members of my writing group, including Lillian Milazzo, Rose Milazzo, Anne Kerrigan, Marge McGullam, Mary Anne Dejewski, Helen Farley, Susan Kasper and Pat Zirkel who, in reading and critiquing the manuscript, buoyed me to persevere. Finally, special thanks go to Mary Sullivan, r.c., my life-long friend, writing partner and soul sister, whose eyes, ears and heart guided me and the book to a rightful end.

PROLOGUE

"You better not wait any longer," John said to his friend after an hour had elapsed. They've just posted another delay." The friend had driven John and his wife Marietta to Kennedy Airport. At the gate Marietta sank down with their one year-old baby in the only seat available while John went to check once more on the status of the flight to Los Angeles.

"The problem is mechanical. They don't know how long it'll be before it's fixed." John was clearly frustrated but Marietta didn't mind the extra time on the ground. She dreaded what might be in store for her once she was up in the air. Her first flight, when she was ten, had been traumatic, and she was afraid of the memories left within the clouds. Would they come to haunt her, knowing what she planned to do? Or would they come to her aid, give her the courage not to be afraid and not fail?

She also worried about the plane crashing. She cringed at the thought that her daughter might not have a full life. And the idea of dying before she saw her mother and sister again was too painful to bear. She'd never be able to ask the questions she'd been rehearsing for months, the ones that had plagued her ever since she was a little girl. They pestered her at every significant event in her young life. She knew it was no way to live – happy and sad at the same time. The vast emptiness she felt inside her was the worst. It masked the past where those questions lay buried like soldiers in unmarked graves. Someone had to come forward and identify them in order to grieve properly.

When Marietta married John he'd filled a part of that hole. But since giving birth to Anna, the questions surfaced with a vengeance. Hard questions. Not the kind you'd normally ask others, certainly not the kind you could ask your mother. How would Stella react when Marietta confronted her? They were family, but...

Family – Marietta smiled warmly at the sound of the word. In California she had the beautiful promise of family, *her* family. But then, family had torn her apart. She no longer trusted it. Would it betray her again as it had once before? Or would it welcome her back permanently, the way she had hoped for all these years?

The announcement to board finally came. The young parents gathered their sleeping child along with their belongings and entered the long corridor that led into the plane. With the engines roaring and the lights dimmed, Marietta leaned her head on John's shoulder and instantly fell asleep. She dreamed not of her mother Stella but of her grandmother handing her a slice of bread spread with olive oil, of her cousin Lucia waving her orange peel in the air urging her to come out and play. She dreamed of her lost childhood a world away.

Chapter One
Five Years Earlier

In the student lounge of St. Mary's College, Marietta's friend, Linda, pirouetted in front of the mirror, evaluating her attire for the spring dance that evening. With the point of her comb, she parted her shiny black hair in the middle and tied back the sides with two silver clips. Her chestnut-colored eyes gleamed, as though she awaited a wonderful surprise.

"Are you going to the dance?" Linda asked as Marietta swung in through the heavy wooden door.

"Not this time. The last one was a dud. Anyway, I'm not dressed for it." She pointed to her lab coat that smelled of formaldehyde. She'd dissected a female frog that very morning.

"That's no excuse. You live only four blocks away and you have two hours in between classes to go home and change. You've got to come. I can't sit home another Friday night." Her body turned rigid at the thought.

Marietta felt sorry for her friend. In fact, she'd felt sorry for her for a year and a half, from that very first Monday in September when they first met and she innocently asked how Linda's weekend had fared. The question was meant only as a conversation starter but Linda had burst into tears.

"My father drinks a lot," she began. "Every Friday night he stops at the local bar to cash his check and have 'a few' with the boys. 'What's wrong with a man relaxing with his buddies when he has the next day off?' he says. Well, there's plenty wrong," Linda moaned. "His paycheck shrinks and, with five children to feed, Mom needs the money to pay the bills. But that's not all. He staggers into the house three hours past dinnertime, bellowing Christmas songs for the neighbors to hear. When he's finally inside, he retches all over the front hall. It's disgusting! And as the oldest, it's my job to herd the younger children to another room and shield them from seeing what I see while Mom tries to steer him into bed to sleep it off." Instinctively, Marietta hugged her. The unexpected touch both surprised and warmed the girl. From that day forward, Linda confided in Marietta as if they'd been friends from childhood. At unexpected moments, in bits and pieces, Linda unraveled her life. Today was one of those moments.

"My father had another episode," she said speaking into the mirror. "I'm so angry with my mother. Why can't she admit he's an alcoholic and force him to get help?"

"Your mother doesn't want to believe there's anything wrong. Some mothers are like that," Marietta said, trying to console her friend, knowing how empty the words sounded. What did she know about mothers? Only that they can hurt you when you least expect it.

"I have to get out," Linda said, adjusting the skirt around her waist so the zipper fell directly in the middle of her left side. A Child Study Major, she felt she had all the qualifications to be a good wife and mother. She would choose carefully and not settle as her mother had, marrying the first man that came along in order to get away from her own alcoholic father. For Linda, every school dance provided the potential to meet Mr. Right.

Marietta had a different vision. She was majoring in Chemistry and Biology, pre-med to be precise. After medical school she'd establish a practice in Cardiology or Pediatrics. That's how she'd leave home and the ghosts that haunted her. Having spent the last eight years in a house devoid of children, of laughter and frivolity, she vowed that as an adult, her life would be different. She'd put the past behind her and not remember that day five years ago, when her mother, Stella, and sister, Pia, came to the Principal's Office and asked her to leave with them. Stella had separated from Marietta's father, Antonio, and was planning to go to California to seek a new life. Marietta had been a high school freshman when it happened, but it seemed a lifetime ago.

Uncle Paul and Aunt Teresa, who had adopted Marietta all the way from Italy when she was ten, had thrown a fit once they'd found out. Seeing the color missing from Marietta's face, Paul realized something awful had happened. A call to the Principal, a few questions posed to her teachers – they were nuns and couldn't lie – gave him the answer he needed to know. Dressed in his police uniform, he stormed into the school and yelled at the Principal as if she were a common criminal he'd apprehended on his beat.

"How dare you allow that woman to see my daughter? Don't you know I can have you arrested as an accomplice to a kidnapping attempt?"

"I realize now it was an indiscretion on my part. The woman had asked only to say goodbye to her daughter. Out of compassion, I…I allowed…I didn't think she'd want to take the child with her," Sister Augustine confessed.

"What you allowed was against the law. You had no right to do what you did. Why, if it wasn't for that nun's habit you wear I would cuff you and throw you in the slammer."

"You have my sincerest apologies," she cowered, fingering the rosary beads that hung from her waist.

"You should have seen how she hid her head in shame," Paul told his wife later that evening. "'You have my sincerest apologies,' my ass. Before I left, I made her refund me the tuition money for the semester. She had no leg to stand on," he smiled triumphantly.

From that day forward, Marietta was forbidden to have any further contact with her mother. However, several months later, a letter arrived from California. It had a post office box return address and, since it was from Pia, Paul and Teresa let her open it. Marietta read the letter with tears in her eyes. She learned that her sister was enjoying school. She missed Marietta but had some friends and a dog to play with.

Marietta was ecstatic and wrote back immediately. But when Pia's second letter arrived, it included a snapshot of her with her dog and another of Stella with the words, "Mom sends her love." When Teresa saw Stella's photo, she snatched it out of Marietta's hand and tore it in two.

"*Puttana* – bitch," she said, throwing the shreds in the garbage. "You no write no more!" she instructed in broken English.

"Can't I send one more letter to tell her I can't write any more?" Marietta begged.

"When I say no, I say no," Teresa shouted. Marietta knew then not to cross her. Her father Antonio, Teresa's brother, had crossed his sister once and paid dearly for it. One Sunday at the dinner table he made the mistake of admitting he was going out with Angelina, a divorced woman with a teenage son. Teresa didn't believe in divorce and told him to stop seeing her. He promised, but continued dating the woman on the sly. When their mother who lived in Italy died, Teresa, Antonio and their sister Sofia were left the house which had been in the family for years. Living in Brooklyn, the two sisters had no need for a primitive, two-room dwelling. Since Antonio planned to return to Italy, they were willing to give him the house to live in. But when they found out that their brother planned to bring Angelina along with him, they gave the house to a distant cousin who lived near their mother. When Antonio found out, he was so angry that upon his return to Italy, he vowed never to set foot in their hometown of San Demetrio again. He and Angelina settled in Trieste, where her family originated from.

With her biological mother, sister, and, now, her father gone, Marietta resigned herself to life as the only child of adoptive parents who monitored and restricted her every move. When she wanted to join the school chorus, Paul and Teresa said practice ended too late. When she asked to meet her classmates at the local ice cream parlor for an hour of fun on Friday afternoons, it was denied because it might not be safe. Even after she entered college, they limited most of her activities to just attending school.

Still, Mr. Right never entered Marietta's mind as a way of escape as it did for Linda. Yes, she'd dated a little in high school, even went steady with Ben, a freshman from St. Francis College. She'd met him at a friend's Halloween party during her senior year. Ben was tall and lanky, with a crop of thick red hair. More significantly, he was not Italian, an aspect that both pleased and relieved her even as it frustrated Paul and Teresa. On their first date he had surprised her with a corsage of gardenias, but she was attracted more to his piercing green eyes that hinted of the darkness he harbored. His parents were divorced, he said. With no extended family nearby, he and his mom had only each other to lean on. He talked about his dad a lot and how much he missed him. Marietta understood. She yearned for her mother in the same way.

But as the winter turned to spring, Marietta noticed a big change come over Ben. His eyes dulled and his face grew distant. He hardly talked about his dad anymore. Sometimes he'd let several weeks pass without calling, but then the phone would ring and he'd apologize. He'd been busy and would she like to go to the movies?

One April day, as they walked home from a date, he asked to have a heart-to-heart talk. Marietta beamed. Perhaps he'd snapped out of his gloom and the old Ben had returned.

"I've changed," he said. Well, Marietta knew that. "You wouldn't like my new friends," he acknowledged. He promised to take her to the Senior Prom, but after that, he said, she'd be better off without him. Oh well, Marietta thought. She had enjoyed his friendship, but she had not been in love

7

with him, and she certainly had never wanted to marry him. No, the key to her freedom, she believed, would be a career in medicine sometime down the road.

"Well, what do you say?" Linda snapped, shifting her weight from one foot to the other. "I mean about the dance,"

"I'd like to... but I have a big Anatomy test on Monday."

"If anyone doesn't need to study for a test, it's you. The dance committee needs people to set up. Come on, volunteer with me," Linda pleaded. "If after one hour, the dance looks like the 'old same-o,' we'll call it quits and go home. What do you say?"

On her way home to shower and change, Marietta smiled. Linda had a wonderful gift of compromise. She'd make a good wife to some lucky guy, she thought. She wished he'd hurry up and come along and make her friend's life less miserable.

"Wow! The auditorium looks like a garden in bloom," Marietta said as they hung the last paper Eiffel Tower across the ceiling. The theme was "Springtime in Paris" and the room reflected it.

"Now all we need is Prince Charming to arrive and rescue us from the prison of our lives," Linda said.

"You're a true romantic. Tonight may just be your night," Marietta vouched. Linda swallowed the words whole, hoping they'd come true.

A few classmates trickled in, holding hands with their boyfriends, positioning themselves in the middle of the dance floor since as couples they could take advantage of every dance. Linda eyed three or four single guys in sports jackets already settled at the food table. They were munching on pretzels and potato chips while ladling scoops of tropical punch into paper cups. The room soon filled with single girls who congregated in groups of twos and threes, their hands and heads bobbing gracefully in conversation, smiling, waiting for some single guys to ask them to dance. An hour passed and no one had yet approached Linda or Marietta.

"Something tells me you were right," Linda said. "Another dud of a dance."

"Oh, who needs men anyway? Let's have some fun and dance by ourselves before we call it a night," Marietta said.

Reluctantly, Linda agreed. They danced to Elvis Presley's "Jailhouse Rock" and "Blue Suede Shoes." Surprisingly, one of the young men from the food table neared and tapped Marietta on the shoulder. She smiled. Finally, she thought, someone has spotted Linda. She stepped aside, leaving him room to dance with her friend.

"No," he pointed. "I'd like to dance with you."

Marietta looked at her friend in apology and bewilderment, but Linda gave her thumbs up. That's what endears her to everyone, Marietta thought. Linda could rejoice for others even when they got what she herself wanted.

The young man was tall and muscular and his blue eyes twinkled against a face so pink and bright that Marietta thought the capillaries under his skin would burst. He had high cheekbones and his flat crew cut displayed a layer of blond hair that carried an aura of goodness around him.

The band was playing a cha-cha. Keeping pace with the one-two one-two-three rhythm of the dance, they moved in silence, smiling innocently at each other. When the music stopped, Marietta stepped back. A slow tune began to play.

"Would you like to dance again?" he asked. She nodded, examining him with her senses, the way she examined living tissue in Bio Lab. He smelled of aftershave, pine-scented and woodsy. His hand pressed her back gently. She waited to hear the sound of his voice again.

"My name is John," he said finally.

"John," she acknowledged, enjoying the sound of it. "Mine's Marietta."

9

"That's an unusual name. Do your friends call you Marie for short?"

"No one's ever called me that," she laughed nervously. "Marie" made her feel as if she were someone else. Maybe not such a bad idea, she thought, to be anyone but herself.

She hoped John wouldn't be like Vito whom she'd met at the last school dance. To her surprise, Vito admitted right from the start that he didn't attend college but had been working for four years and had saved most of his money. He must have thought she'd find him more desirable for having money. Vito had asked her out but she'd refused. They had nothing in common except that he was Italian and that was the last thing she wanted. She felt Italian men were two-timers who drank to excess, cheated on their wives and beat them at the slightest provocation. She didn't trust them. Why would she jeopardize herself as Stella had? She kept her vow not to date Italians, thus avoiding the possibility of falling in love with one.

"You're not Italian, by any chance, are you?" The words slipped out of her mouth as if they had a mind of their own. John threw his head back and roared with laughter.

Oh no, what had she done? She made a fool of herself, she thought. Don't let him answer yes too soon so she could enjoy his company a little longer.

"With a name like Sullivan, I hardly think so. But my sister married an Italian. Does that count?"

"No – yes – I mean, fine." He had misinterpreted her question. She was relieved.

"I'm a second year student at Columbia's Medical School," John said. Marietta's ears perked up. She'd visited Columbia once to hear a panel speak on the Collegiality of the Church, an academic subject that appealed to her philosophical mind, but the panelists had been so monotone in their delivery, it was hard to pay attention. The school grounds, however, had taken her breath away. The long

10

promenade flanked with trees leading to the center of the campus brought into focus the Library, an imposing structure with its many steps surrounding it. Inside, the books were stacked high along its walls. The heavy windows and large wooden tables in the middle of the room gave the building a charm that pulled her. Founded in 1754 as Kings College after King George II, the school was old. Like Marietta, Columbia had a history that dated back to another century, to another country, to another culture.

"I'm thinking of pursuing a medical career, too" she said.

"That gives us a lot in common. We'd have much to discuss." Then, out of nowhere, "How far away do you live?"

Here's the deciding factor, Marietta thought. If he thinks I live far, he'll thank me for a nice time and go his merry way. The scientist she was, she decided to test him.

"What if I lived an hour or more away?"

"Well, we'd have a lot of time to talk, but I probably wouldn't take you home. I have a study session early tomorrow morning, but I'd take your number so I could see you again." Fair enough, Marietta thought.

"Actually, I live just a few blocks away. My father is coming for me as soon as I phone him. So you're relieved of any responsibility."

"Call him and tell him not to come. I'll gladly escort you home."

"You're sure it won't detain you from getting your beauty sleep for the study session?" She looked up and his handsome face reflected back.

"Beauty is in the eyes of the beholder," he chimed. His eyes warmed her like two rays of sunshine. She wondered who the beholder was between them.

A full moon hovered over the empty street as John and Marietta left the school grounds. Its glow lit the pavement, brightening the brownstone stoops as much as the overhead lamps, making the concrete sparkle. A gentle breeze softened the air, promising warmth, while the smell of earth rose sharply with the dew. It was spring's first touch, bringing scents of honeysuckle ready to burst open. Neither John nor Marietta wanted to disturb the idyllic setting or for it to end. When they neared the familiar stoop of her house, she thought she saw the faint outline of a young girl playing stoopball past twilight. But that was her imagination of scenes from springs past, when day and night meshed, blending and confusing her memory of reality. If she strained, she could almost see Paul in years gone by, sitting in the twilight on the stoop landing. He held a flashlight, reading the Brooklyn Eagle that lay folded in half across his lap, one eye always planted on her as though someone would come and snatch her if he blinked. That was the girl she used to be, transformed from an earlier version still. She marveled how her thoughts naturally went back to the past, to the metamorphoses that determined her destiny. But now she wanted to hold them in check as it was well past twilight and she was out with a young man who had offered to take her home, a non-Italian who called himself John. Turning her back against the house, she faced him and the past suddenly erased.

"It was nice to meet you... and to dance. Thanks for bringing me home," she said, smiling.

"Can I have your phone number?" he asked. A thrill of adventure surged through her body, like the challenge she felt when her chemistry professor handed her an unknown compound to test and identify. The evening would continue. They might get to know each other, the way she'd know the compound, all its physical and chemical properties. She hesitated, her eyes searching his body for signs of pencil and paper to appear.

"Well, aren't you going to give me your number? Are you playing hard to get?" He laughed in the same hearty way as on the dance floor. It would take months, she thought, for her to hear as much laughter from Paul and Teresa as she'd heard tonight.

"I was waiting for you to jot it down somewhere."

"I don't need to jot it down."

Her heart sank. He was just being polite. He didn't plan to call after all. He was no different than the other boys she'd known who seemed interested at first, eager, but then they never called. She could have sworn he'd enjoyed dancing with her as much as she had with him.

Had he been just pretending? She wanted to tell him to forget it. Why make a charade of the situation? She'd had enough pretending in her family. If John couldn't match his actions with his words, "goodbye and thank you very much" would do. But then she made the mistake of looking into his eyes and melted. She had to give him the benefit of the doubt. Robotically, she recited the seven digits of her phone number, but expected nothing in return.

Chapter Two

By Thursday night, Marietta's memory of John erased from her brain as though she'd never met him. That's why, when Paul answered the phone and insisted the call was for her, she was sure it was Linda on the other end. They'd agreed that when either was absent from school, the other would collect the assignments teachers stuffed in their mailbox. Marietta never missed class, but Linda often did, especially when one of her siblings was sick or when her father mistook a day of the week for a Friday night. Obviously, Linda benefited more from the arrangement. Marietta didn't mind. It was the least she could do for her friend.

"It's a b-o-y," Paul spelled without bothering to cover the phone. Marietta turned red with humiliation. She hated it when he teased her so blatantly. He seemed to get a perverse sense of pleasure from seeing her squirm. She was about to tell him that picking on her wasn't funny but stopped herself in time. If the person on the other end was Vito, she knew she needed Paul to get rid of him.

"If it's Vito, tell him I'm not home," she whispered, covering the mouthpiece with her hand.

"If you're Vito, she said to tell you she's not home," he repeated. Marietta sighed.

"He says he's not Vito. He's J-o-h-n," he sang into the phone.

Her eyebrows lifted. She took the phone. "Hello." She kept her voice even, casual, without a hint of surprise.

"I hope I'm not calling at a bad time," he said, sounding confused. When Marietta didn't respond, he continued. "I was wondering whether you'd go out with me on Saturday night."

14

"*This* Saturday night?" she asked. Didn't he realize Thursday was too late to call for a date on Saturday? Had he exhausted the list of names in his little black book and she was his last resort? If she accepted, he'd know she wasn't popular. If she refused, he might be put off and not call back. She had to make a decision. "Well, this Saturday I have a previous commitment," she risked. With her books, she thought, so technically it was not a lie.

"Oh, I didn't mean this Saturday," he said, matter-of-factly. "I'm busy too. I meant *next* Saturday. Are you free next Saturday?"

"Y-yes," she said, relieved. "Next week would be perfect."

"I'll call again in a few days to know what time to pick you up," he added. "Well, until then…"

"Yes, until then. Goodbye."

At her desk Marietta couldn't contain her excitement. She saw John's face on each page of her notebook. Even the textbook had his name written in it. *John called. John remembered my phone number. I have a date with John next Saturday. John will call again.* Her mind played and replayed the conversation: *oh, not this Saturday. I meant next Saturday.*

Unable to concentrate on her work, she closed her book. Maybe some TV would settle her down. She walked into the living room and found Paul sitting on the easy chair and Teresa, on the couch, her legs across the cushion, her feet hanging off the edge so as not to dirty the upholstery.

"Well, to what do we owe the honor of your company?" Paul's tone was sarcastic and playful at the same time.

"No more books and studying, Miss High Hat?" Teresa chimed in.

"I study all week. I'm taking a break."

15

When *next Saturday* arrived, Marietta planned to dress early for her date. She didn't want to keep John waiting. Who knew what Paul and Teresa might say to him to embarrass her? When the appointed time came, she was ready. She sat at her desk where she had a good view of the street from her window and would be able to spot him as he climbed the stoop stairs. After fifteen minutes, Teresa walked by. "No here yet? Maybe he no come at all," she chuckled. Late in calling, late in coming – not showing up was precisely what Marietta feared. She pulled out a book to distract her. Ten minutes later, John appeared at Marietta's door wearing a gray woolen jacket and an open smile but no mention of tardiness.

"This is John," Marietta said to Paul and Teresa. "The boy who walked me home from the dance two weeks ago."

"How do you do," John said, offering his hand. Paul shook it without effort while Teresa eyed him from head to foot disdainfully. They don't like him, Marietta thought.

"Come back before *mezzanotte* or something bad will happen to you," Teresa warned.

Dating wasn't easy under Teresa's rules. The whole first year she dated John, Marietta was allowed out just once on the weekend and only for four hours. She had no problem keeping the midnight curfew. John lacked both money and time to stay out late. With their student ID cards, they paid discounted rates at movie theatres. They rarely ate out. More often they pressed their noses against a restaurant window and read the menu from the street.

"One of these days I'll have enough money for us to sit at a table rather than stand at the door," he promised.

"I don't mind waiting," she said, noting how the silverware glistened against the white tablecloths. A candle glowed next to a pink rose, creating an aura of intimacy and romance. Almost bridal in appearance, she thought. Yet she couldn't share her thoughts with John. She remembered how he'd tensed on their second date, when she had stopped in

16

front of a bridal shop and admired the five mannequins dressed in white. She loved the swirls of silks and taffeta that made up the Cinderella gowns, the pearls and sequins sewn throughout the white bodices.

"The store is closed," he'd pointed out, nervously, alerting Marietta that he wasn't ready for a wife. His focus was medical school, then setting up a practice. Marietta was surprised at his reaction. How could he think she was serious? It was too early in their relationship to talk of love, never mind marriage. And she'd never be the one to state her feelings first, in case John didn't feel the same way. She knew rejection all too well to risk it.

On subsequent dates, they were careful to refer to love only in universal terms. The way God loves all creation. Often they discussed the plot of a movie, where love or the lack of it played a part in someone's happiness. Love became an academic issue, as though she and John were students in a writing class or members of a Book of the Month Club.

John was unaware of the joy he brought Marietta. Not material possessions such as jewelry, clothes, or flowers that would delight most other girls. He offered Marietta intangible treasures like honesty, truth and goodness. Things you can't buy, things that last. She was afraid to tell him how happy he made her. If John knew her history, what would he think? Would he still grasp her hand? She shuddered at the confused look on his face when he came to her door and Teresa stared at his shoes. Was it too much culture shock to his American upbringing when he had to take them off? Would she ever be able to share her past with him?

"Can you guess where I was born?" she said one night as they walked out of the movie theater.

"A guessing game is it?" he chuckled. He never knew what to expect from her. "Hmm, I'll guess some exotic place. Especially after seeing how much you enjoy movies about Italy. I'm going to say Rome. Were you born in Rome?"

"No, not Rome," she said with a nervous laugh. He didn't seem surprised. He was sure that he'd be wrong.

"Let me take another stab at it. This time, I'll be serious. Brooklyn," he said, sure he was right. Suddenly the game seemed stupid to Marietta. It was the opposite of what she'd planned.

"Let's just forget I asked," she said, hoping to drop the subject. He agreed, but didn't forget. She'd piqued his interest and her request made her more mysterious. They finished the evening comfortable walking in silence, holding hands, listening only to the rhythm of their steps.

Their next date was to see Federico Fellini's *La Dolce Vita* in an artsy Manhattan theatre. John was amazed that Marietta understood the dialogue without having to read the subtitles. His eyes were having a difficult time trying to follow the action and read what was said. He couldn't keep up the pace. He fumbled with his glasses, pushing them back on the bridge of his nose. At the movie's end he turned to Marietta for her reaction.

"Did the characters seem as sad to you as they did to me?" he asked.

"Yes, completely sad, and so unnecessary." Her lips trembled. She was close to tears.

"Are Italians always this melodramatic?"

She sighed. "Italians wear their hearts on their sleeves, so hearts often get hurt and bleed." The image of her mother Stella bounced before her.

John touched her arm. "I don't see a heart on your sleeve." He saw her face, radiant and beautiful. Marietta managed a weak smile. The movie had worn her down. They rose from their seats, ready to leave, when they noticed the theater lobby had been transformed into a diner serving complimentary cups of espresso. A group hovered around the table where the smell permeated strongest.

"Let's have some," Marietta said, hoping to lighten her somber mood. She also wanted to introduce John to an aspect of Italy that was festive and happy, not fatalistic as the movie had depicted. They helped themselves to a cup each.

"Yuck," John said, spitting out his first sip. "You didn't tell me the coffee's bitter. What kind of cups are these? I feel like I'm drinking coffee from the tea set I gave my three-year-old niece for her birthday. Do people in Italy actually use these cups?" His hand looked gargantuan looped around the tiny handle.

"They do. But you must add sugar. Two or three teaspoons at least," Marietta instructed him. "Then the coffee is delicious."

"But there's too little coffee for three teaspoons of sugar."

"The teaspoon is tiny, too," she pointed out. They laid the demitasse cups on the table. Marietta's was empty but John's was still full. She noted the difference between them. She remembered the guessing game she'd started a few weeks earlier concerning her place of birth. Another difference, she thought.

They passed through the theater's glass doors into the street and the smell of coffee faded. As the cool night air ruffled a few leaves resting on the street curb, Marietta resolved to keep her past hidden. If she told John her own mother had sent her away, had given her up for adoption, he would surely think there was something wrong with her and her family. She'd wait. If their relationship never went beyond what it was now, sharing the past would be a moot point. She put herself on guard not to fall in love with him. Then, as if there had been no interruption of time from last they spoke of it, John asked the very question she was hoping to avoid.

"I'd say you were born right here in New York City," he ventured.

"Where I was born is not important."

"Then guess where I was born. I'll give you a hint. It's Brooklyn, Queens or Staten Island.

"Brooklyn."

"Right on the first try. Now you have to give me a hint with your birth place."

"I don't want you to guess where I was born."

"Why are you being so mysterious?" he asked, enjoying the suspense fully.

"You might leave." The words escaped her mouth before she could stop them. Not a fair game, she thought. He was playing…and she was serious.

"Why would I leave? Can't you tell I'm crazy about you?"

"I like you too, but…"

"There's a 'but'?" His shoulders dropped. He lost his smile.

"I don't want to like you too much and then…then," she hesitated, avoiding his eyes. He might see how frightened she was.

His face softened. His desire for her grew, as if she were forbidden fruit. He led her back under a canopy, near the doorway of a building. He placed both hands on her shoulders and kissed her passionately, first on her lips, then her neck, sliding his arms across her small back, pulling her nearer until she could feel his heartbeat. She had never been so close to anyone. She was his, entwined securely in his embrace.

"I would never hurt you or leave you. Unless you don't want me, unless you send me away." He said the words as if he were asking rather than telling her.

She laughed. Send him away? He was the spark that lit her world. She bit her lip at the realization of how much he meant to her already, how much she had allowed him to mean. She decided to share some things about herself.

"Well, I was born in a small town without electricity or running water. We had no phone, radio or television, but I was happy – happier than I have ever been." There. She blurted out the truth, but not the whole truth. She watched for signs. His face was warm and accepting, waiting in case she had more to say.

"I also have a sister and lots of cousins. We called one cousin *Peppino*."

"Why did you call him *Peppino*?"

"That was his name. What else would we call him?"

John burst out laughing. Why didn't you say 'Peppino was his name' in the first place?"

"Isn't it the same thing? You took French in high school. Remember how we learned to say our names? *Je m'appelle...Jean*?"

"Now I know you were born in some exotic place. Was it a remote island in the Mediterranean that no one knows exists?"

"You're right, John. Where I was born no longer exists, at least not for me," she said, her voice low and sad.

He cupped her face gently with his hand and turned her chin toward him. "Tell me about it," he offered.

She took a deep breath. "My parents were separated and my mother, sister and I lived with my grandmother in Italy. I called her Nonna...I mean 'Nonna' is the word for grandmother in Italian," she laughed for a brief second. "The parents you met aren't my real parents. They're my aunt and uncle, my real father's sister and brother-in-law. They couldn't have children of their own and adopted me... legally, I mean. I came when I was ten, by myself, on a plane." She gulped, alarmed that she'd shared so much and it amounted to so little.

"Thank God," he said. "I was beginning to wonder what's wrong with you that I can't see. I'm thrilled you're not their child. They're really weird."

21

She laughed again. "They're not so bad once you get used to them. They've done a lot for me. They're giving me a good education, one I'd never be able to get in Italy. They feed me and clothe me and they're there, every day when I come home, which is more than I can say about my real mother and father." Marietta was shocked at how she had defended Paul and Teresa. Yet, they had done good in their lives. Without them she wouldn't have met John.

"Where are your real parents now, still in Italy?" John asked. Marietta was forced to tell the rest of the story, down to the last detail of the confrontation in school.

"My mother and sister are gone. The only thing I have left is a letter from my sister with a post office box address from years ago. Who knows if it's still active? My mother and sister may have moved. I doubt I'll ever find them."

"You didn't try to write to them, reach them in some way?" he asked.

"How could I? I was forbidden to have any contact with them. I wasn't even allowed to write to Nonna. I thought of sending her my school address so she could write to me there, but I didn't want to implicate the school or any of my friends. Besides, Paul and Teresa would be sure to find out and I'd be in big trouble for disobeying them. Look at me," she laughed wryly. "I'm twenty years old and still under their spell."

"Don't worry. You'll find your mother and sister someday." The resolve in his voice was strong. It gave her hope.

"What do you do when you go out with John?" Teresa asked at dinner the next evening.

"We go to the movies," Marietta replied, a knot forming in her stomach.

"*Ma dopo*, but after, *che cosa facete dopo*? What do you do after?" Teresa pursued. Her tone was condescending, accusing.

"We come home. We talk. That's all," Marietta said. What brought this on? Where was it leading to? She looked at Paul for a clue, but he continued to eat his food in silence.

"What is this 'talk'? What do you have to talk about?" Teresa continued. She couldn't imagine how one could share feelings, hopes or desires with another. Other than "Paul, get me this" or "Teresa, where's my shirt?" Marietta had never heard intimate talk cross their lips. She wondered what kind of glue held them together for so many years.

"Well, what's your answer?" Teresa persisted.

"We talk about the movie. We talk about what we're learning in school and life in general."

"What do you know about life?" Teresa countered. More than you think, Marietta wanted to say, but she remained silent.

Teresa threw a menacing finger toward Paul. "It's his fault," she said. "He takes care of you like a baby. And this is how you pay us back? *Disgraziata* – Ungrateful one! Puhhh." She shaped her lips to spit, but only air puffed out. "Speak, you who like to talk," she yelled. "Speak!"

"For Christ's sake, leave the girl alone! Stop questioning her like she's a criminal," Paul finally interjected. Then in a kinder voice, he turned to Marietta and said, "Just how serious are you with this Irish Johnny-boy, anyhow?"

"He likes me and I like him. That's all. I don't understand why you're so upset." But she knew. John was not Italian. The problem was as simple as that. His being Irish undermined a sacred tradition so many Italians had followed for generations.

"He's not our kind," Paul admitted. "Why don't you go out with people of your own kind?"

"What's our kind – men who cheat on their wives and drink until they can't stand up any more?" Marietta blurted.

Paul's face turned red. He grabbed Marietta by the shoulders and lifted her off the floor. She stood eye to eye with him. "I... don't... cheat... on my wife," he said. Then he lowered her down to the ground.

"But many Italian men do," Marietta persisted, thinking about Antonio. It never occurred to her that Paul may have cheated on Teresa as well.

"Is that what you're afraid of?" he said, calming down. "We'll help you find a good Italian boy who doesn't cheat. We'll buy a nice two-family house. You can live on the top floor and we'll live downstairs." He touched his thighs. "These legs can't climb stairs when they're old. We'll make life easy for you and your husband. We'll watch the children when you work. We'll watch them when you go out. And we'll all live together. What's better than that?"

Everything is better than that, Marietta thought. She felt the bars of prison continue to strangle her. Marietta wanted independence. She wanted happiness. She'd never get it living under their wing. It was clear to her now that Paul and Teresa had adopted her to care for them in their old age. She was as much a commodity to them as she'd been to Stella. But she couldn't tell them. They would think her ungrateful. She'd have to let her actions speak, not her words. Words were never good with Italians anyway. Men promised to be true to their wives but had affairs with other women. Mothers promised to love their children but gave them away.

On their next date Marietta told John what had happened. She feared Paul and Teresa would forbid her from seeing him, the way they had forbidden her to write to Nonna and to Pia. If they tried, she'd leave home, she said. She was tired of being controlled by them. She was almost twenty-one. She wanted to live her life as she saw it, not as they did. John listened until Marietta finished.

"Don't fret. I don't think your parents will do anything. They just have big mouths," he said at last. "We'll work it out. My parents will help. They think the world of you."

Then, as if John had spoken to them, Paul and Teresa dropped the matter and the two continued to date without any disruption. They talked about the past and the future, never about the present. The present was too tempestuous.

"Why do you want to practice medicine?" John asked Marietta one day.

"I want to mend hearts and rid the world of pain." She laughed at how transparent she was, how shallow and naive.

"What about children? Do you see them in your future?"

"I love children," Marietta said. "I want to have twelve and raise them all myself. I'd never leave them to someone else's care. I want them to have a mother who's always there for them. If they have faults, I want them to be mine and not someone else's. "

"How are you going to accomplish that and practice medicine? They're both demanding jobs."

"I know. I've always seen marriage in the distant future."

"What if you fall in love before that distant future?"

"I don't know. It depends on whether the person I love loves me back."

"What if I told you I loved you?" His voice shook as if he were entering unchartered territory.

"Then you'd have to see if I loved you back."

"And if you did, then what?"

"You'd ask me to marry you. It's the logical thing to do."

"And then?" His eyes filled with hunger for her touch.

"You'll have to take the first step to find out."

He stared at her, seemingly lost. "I don't know what love is. I don't want to use the word until I'm sure. I do know I'm crazy about you." He swept her in his arms and their faces blended. He kissed her, their lips seeming permanently attached. Through their woolen clothes, Marietta enjoyed the solid feel of his ribs as they rubbed against her breasts until a fiery hardness jumped and pressed against her abdomen. Something released in her, bringing such elation all over her body, a desire that she had never experienced before.

"We better stop before it's too late," she said, pulling away.

"But I want you so. Don't you want me?"

More than you know, she wanted to tell him. She thought of what her father would say if they continued. *If you get in a family way, you're out of this family for good.* But that's not what deterred her. She knew she wouldn't stand a chance with John if she continued. After he'd had his fill, he wouldn't respect her. She wouldn't respect herself. He'd feel sorry for her. Then he'd leave.

"We have to wait," she said staunchly. She wondered what exactly she'd be waiting for and how long the wait would be, given their medical careers.

"I don't want to wait. I'm crazy about you," he whispered. Then he buried his head in her neck and kissed it in a circular motion, spiraling finally up her chin and lips.

"We have to wait," she repeated. "Crazy" was not the same as "love," she thought.

The following weekend they attended the marriage of John's good friend from college to his high school sweetheart. At the reception, they danced every dance. When they went up to the bride and groom to say good night and give them their gift, John agreed to help his friend bring the wedding gifts back to their apartment. It wasn't far. Marietta looked at her watch. 11:15 PM. It would take at least a half hour to get home from the reception hall. If John helped his friend, they'd miss the midnight curfew. She was concerned.

"Surely they'll see a wedding as more than a date to the movies. My friend asked for help," John said. "I can't refuse."

"You don't know my mother. She doesn't bend."

"Once I explain, she'll understand. Leave it to me," he said confidently. Marietta tried to stay calm. When they arrived home, it was 12:15 a.m. The lights were on. A bad sign as it meant that Paul and Teresa were up, waiting for her. Stiffening, she braced for the storm she knew would ensue. John took Marietta's hand to show he wasn't concerned. Once he explained the reason for the delay, he said, they'd have to understand. Anyone would. After all, this was the first time they were late.

When Marietta turned the key to unlock the apartment door, Teresa leapt from behind.

"What bad thing did you do to make you late?" she demanded.

"Mrs. Marino, it's not her fault. My friend needed me to help bring the wedding gifts to his house. We're only fifteen minutes late. Surely you can understand it couldn't be helped," John said.

"*Puttana.* Whore," Teresa said as if John hadn't spoken. "*Puttana* just like Stella," she spit. John was amazed to see how poisoned with anger Teresa was.

Paul grabbed his wife's arm. "Let the young man go home. This is family business."

"Please understand, Mr. Marino. I'm totally responsible for..." John began but Teresa interrupted him.

"She is *puttana* just like the mother," Teresa repeated vehemently.

"It's not true." Marietta shouted. "Don't talk about my mother that way. I am *of* her." She looked at John with resignation in her eyes. Did he see the insanity she lived with? Could he ever understand?

"Shut your fresh mouth or I tell this Ireesh boyfriend you have who you really are. I tell him you're not our daughter. I tell him about Stella," Teresa threatened.

"I already did. He knows everything" Marietta said triumphantly.

Teresa's jaw dropped. Realizing she lost her power, she turned away and entered her bedroom without saying another word. Paul followed her, quietly closing the door.

"It must be safe now," John said. "Go to bed but call me during the night if there's a problem. He dreaded leaving her alone.

She hoped he wouldn't detect her fear of walking past Paul and Teresa's bedroom in order to reach her own.

That night she hardly slept. Her mind was like a TV screen where the first ten years of her life played.

Chapter Three
Ten Years Earlier

Under the instep of Italy's boot, near the Ionian Sea just south of Bari, the medieval city of Castellaneta stood high above the land. Its ancient houses backed the precipitous edge of one of the most magnificent Apulian ravines, creating a protective wall from invaders. Within the cavity of the ravine, meandering paths pointed to a cleft of rock where the earth split in two.

One house in particular – that of her grandmother, whom she called *Nonna* – was dearer to Marietta than any other. It had only one window and it faced the cobblestone street. Suddenly, the shutters opened and Stella's head popped out.

"*Marietta, vieni a casa.* Come into the house. We're going shopping to buy you new clothes – a coat, dress, shoes, hat, everything. You're going to America!"

Marietta hardly looked up. She gazed at the numbered squares that she and her cousin Lucia had drawn in white chalk on the uneven pavement. Eying one of the squares, she aimed the top of her orange peel, which had been cut in a round shape for her by her uncle at supper the night before, and threw it forward. It landed exactly where she'd planned – dead center. Just as she had one foot up ready to jump into the first square, she heard her mother's voice again.

If Marietta hadn't recognized the familiar timbre, she'd think it was another child speaking, excited by a new toy or candy she'd just received. Yet Stella was not a child. Though only twenty-six, she was the mother of two: Marietta, 10, and Pia, 4.

Orange Peels and Cobblestones

"Didn't you hear me, Marietta? Come in this instant!" Stella repeated. "We're going shopping. *Zia Teresa e Zio Paolo* – Aunt Teresa and Uncle Paul in America can't wait for you to arrive and here you are wasting your time playing with orange peels."

Who cares about America? Marietta thought. Standing on the cobblestone street beneath the steps of Nonna's eleven hundred year-old-house, she was unaware that there was any other place to be. To her, Nonna symbolized the world and all that was good in it. No other person in the large family she had come to live with since her parents separated cared as much for the little girl as Nonna, the white-haired maternal grandmother whose name was Anna. She was the anchor on which the child rested, loving and guarding the child as if she might disappear at a moment's notice.

"Grownups like to shop. Children like to play," Marietta muttered under her breath. Why didn't her mother understand that? Who were Aunt Teresa and Uncle Paul anyway? She had never met them. They belonged to the *other* side of the family – her father's family. And they lived far away in America. What could they possibly want with her? But Stella's voice lilted with joy at the mention of these relatives, the way it did when she fingered money in her pocket or bought a new dress. When Stella spoke about America, her eyes grew big and her lips parted. To her, America was a land of wealth, of opportunity, of dreams coming true.

Not for Marietta. The cobblestones on Nonna's street contained more wealth than she'd ever dreamed of, all she'd ever want. Yet Stella persisted in talking about America with everyone she knew. Soon the whole town buzzed in conversation about it. People would spot the little girl as they passed on their walks for their daily *passegiata*. They pointed their finger. "Oh, Marietta, aren't you the lucky one! How does it feel to go far away to such a wonderful country, all

30

alone? And how old are you, just ten, no?" Marietta was confused. She felt lucky to be in Castellaneta, not anywhere else. She was determined to let nothing tear her away from the town she loved, the town that was close to the sea and the birthplace of Rudolph Valentino. Most of all, it was where Nonna and her extended family lived.

"You're wrong. It's just my mother's crazy dream. It'll never happen," a voice inside her finally emerged to answer, but it was a thought in the wind, one that flew over people's heads as they walked away.

Marietta felt safe within Nonna's house that dated to antiquity. She was happy to revolve her life solely around Nonna's narrow street that led to the piazza from which other narrow streets radiated like the spokes of a wheel. Her place was evident each school morning as Nonna braided the girl's hair into two thick ropes of corn silk that bounced on her back with every step she took. She felt secure also on Sundays and other special days when the grandmother combed the braids free, tying the sides together with a bow. Then her honey-colored tresses caught the sun's rays and sparkled like Italian gold.

Besides herself, Marietta knew of no other children whose mother and father didn't live together. It frightened her to stand out in such a way, apart from everyone else, as if she were branded with a terrible malady. To counteract it, she kept her shoulders back and her head high, both in school and at play, giving her the appearance of someone older, perhaps wiser, than her ten years. Every so often, however, a shadow crossed her brow, which she was adept at hiding. Only two people – Nonna and Lucia – could spot the darkness when it appeared. Her mother Stella never saw it.

This day that Stella summoned her daughter had been no different than the days preceding it. As Marietta played hopscotch with Lucia just below the steps of the old house, she stroked the orange peel in the pocket of her dress and savored the scent it left on her fingers. Its sweet aroma was second only to Nonna's homemade bread drizzled in olive oil that she ate for lunch every day. White, stone houses surrounded them. Their facades looked more Greek than Roman – like the pictures of Grecian homes in history books – and Marietta wondered if this particular region of Puglia had been unearthed and magically transported here to house Nonna's sons and daughters. Many of them were married and had children. All lived within steps of her presence as though they couldn't survive anywhere else. Except for Stella. She was restless all the time.

Marietta thought her mother's discontent stemmed from not having a husband and from having to go to work. But there were other reasons. Stella wanted greater rewards out of life, the finer things that only money and fame can bring.

Stella was a natural beauty. The women in town wanted to look like her and every man longed to possess her. She could have had her pick of boyfriends, but at sixteen she married Antonio, an out-of-towner twice her age. She had become pregnant with his child and, in Castellaneta, pregnancy before marriage was equivalent to "I do." After giving birth to Marietta, the couple moved in with Antonio's mother who lived in San Demetrio, a small mountain town in Calabria, a day's train ride away from Castellaneta.

The marriage had been rocky from the start and Stella came back to Nonna's house frequently. After a month or two elapsed, she found the courage to return to Antonio, hoping he'd change his ways. Perhaps he'd come home at night instead of going out with his friends. Or better yet, he'd agree to leave Marietta and Pia with his mother and take Stella with him on his many trips to Rome, Milan or Naples. Surely she would be discovered then. Some movie director would spot her sitting in a café sipping espresso or walking through the grand piazza. Poof! She'd be in movies. Just like that.

But Antonio didn't know how to be a husband and father – not after Marietta was born, nor when Pia came along. He and Stella would argue, often violently, and that was his cue to leave. And though she waited for the offer to go with him, it never came.

When her parents fought, Marietta's body vibrated with the bang of the kitchen utensils they hurled at one another. The fights lasted only minutes but she thought them endless. She'd crawl to the far end of the bed and hide in fear until she heard the door slam shut and the cold sound of her father's heels echo on the pavement below. After crying for a week, Stella would stuff the few belongings she had in a knapsack, fling it across her back and with a child in each hand she'd board the train back to Castellaneta.

The return to Nonna's house was the only part of her parents' arguments that Marietta liked. She could play with Lucia as she was doing this very moment and be as carefree as the breeze that blew from the sea.

Marietta retrieved the orange peel from her pocket and was about to hurl it again, when Stella's voice rang through the air a third time. She was tempted to ignore it still, but when she saw her mother at the front door with eyes glaring like two raging fires, she raced up the white stone steps.

"Mamma, dobbiamo andare al negozio proprio adesso? Possiamo andare domani? Puoi andare sola? Must we go to the store right now? Can we go tomorrow? Can you go by yourself?" she pleaded.

Stella fumed. Of course, she preferred to shop alone rather than be encumbered with a child. Marietta would pester her to go home as soon as they arrived at the *negozio*. But the clothes were for Marietta. She needed to try them on. Shaking her head in bewilderment, she recalled how when she was her daughter's age, she would have skipped meals to have new dresses. Every day she begged her parents to take her shopping. Instead they gave her the clothes her older sister

Maria outgrew. And now a bundle of *lire* burned in her pocket, money she'd received from America. But what did Marietta prefer? – The hand-me-downs from Stella's younger sister, Veronica.

But for Marietta, wearing Veronica's clothes was a visible sign that she belonged to her grandmother. Why couldn't Stella see this? At times Marietta felt a nagging suspicion that she wasn't Stella's daughter after all. Could Nonna be her real mother and somehow it had all gotten mixed up at birth? Nonna would never take her shopping when there was a perfectly good dress from Veronica's closet to wear. She would never discard something that still had value and could be used. Nonna would, also, let her finish a hopscotch game before she asked her to come inside.

"A letter from Uncle Paul – your new *Papà* – arrived," Stella said. "See, I've already replied to it." She held up a white envelope as proof. "We'll mail it when we go shopping for your trip."

What trip? What new *Papà*? Marietta had a *Papà* and he was never with her. She much preferred Nonno – her grandfather – as her *Papà*. He brought her figs and apricots and luscious peaches from his farm *in campagna*. What did these letters from America have anything to do with her? Why did they have to change her clothes or her home?

Though the war had changed many of the cities in Italy, *nel paese* – in town – nothing changed. Not the cobblestone streets. Not the white stone houses attached in a row. Not even the people. Generation after generation replicated the life of its predecessors. Castellaneta still had no running water, and people took turns filling buckets from the town well and carried them on their hips back home. They used candles for light, made pasta and bread by hand and cooked with coal. Everything remained the same as it had been centuries before. Why must Stella now turn the world upside down and insist Uncle Paul was Marietta's new father?

When would she stop sending him letters and signing Marietta's name so he'd think they came directly from the child?

Stella brought the envelope to her mouth to lick it closed. Marietta knew then she had to do something. Without thinking, she snatched the envelope right out of her mother's hands and began reading it aloud.

"Dear Papà,

I am very happy to come to America to be your adopted daughter. I can't wait for the paperwork to be completed. I think of you every day and hope that I will see you face to face very soon.

Baci,

Marietta"

"Why did you write this?" she demanded. "He isn't my father. I already have a father."

Stella's cheeks contracted and veins bulged on her neck like train tracks up a mountain road. "Where is that ingrate you call your father right now? Is he home with his family? No. He's drinking, gambling and carousing with other women! He prefers the life of the *Grand Signore* while we… we have to count on Nonna for food and shelter." Her lips trembled as if she were about to cry. Then her muscles softened and the veins disappeared. "Your Uncle Paul, on the other hand…he's like a father to us. He sent the doll you play with, the dress you wear to Church, even money for you to buy *gelato*."

"If having *gelato* means I have to go to America, I can live without it," Marietta shouted. "And toys and clothes too. I have enough from Veronica." Her mother should go to America, she thought. She seemed to want it so much. Stella could be Uncle Paul and Aunt Teresa's daughter. They could lavish her with clothes and fine jewelry, all the things she prized.

Suddenly Marietta felt guilty. She didn't really want her mother to leave. Despite their differences, she would miss Stella's vibrant smile, her childlike excitement through eyes that widened when people complimented her. Besides, the photos she'd seen of the American relatives frightened her. Uncle Paul dressed in black and Aunt Teresa in stiff organza, sternly posed and unsmiling as they sat on padded chairs of gold brocade. The chairs' curved wooden legs were engraved with figures of gnarling snakes, their mouths wide open. Marietta imagined them pouncing like a boa, devouring anyone in their path if they hadn't been frozen in the wood.

But the opulence energized Stella. Given the opportunity, she would easily trade places with Teresa. She felt she deserved the accoutrements of power and wealth. Why, she'd even been chosen "Miss Puglia" once – until the judges found out she was married and had a child and they disqualified her. Her beauty had so impressed movie scouts that they offered to send her to Hollywood. Stella couldn't contain her excitement. To be famous and admired by the whole world – what a coup! It had happened to Rudolph Valentino. It could happen to her. She ran all the way home to bring her parents the good news.

But Nonno would hear none of it. "What kind of life is that for a mother? You must make the best of your hasty marriage," he told her. He wouldn't let Nonna take care of Marietta while Stella gallivanted across the big screen. That's when Stella switched her dreams to amassing riches. Surely the connection with Antonio's family in America would prove fortuitous, the lucky break she needed...and Marietta, the key that opened the door.

"Wouldn't it be wonderful to live in a big house with servants who'd cook and clean for us?" Stella asked her daughter. No, thought Marietta. They were already rich. They never went hungry, never felt cold. They had a roof over their heads. Every Sunday and holiday, aunts, uncles and cousins – the whole family – gathered at Nonna's house. There was so much pasta and wine and fun. What better life could there be? Her dream was to grow up, marry and have as many children as Nonna had. She wished to extend Nonna's legacy.

But now the letter in Marietta's hand spelled a different scenario. If someone didn't alter the plans, her future was in jeopardy. Without a moment's hesitation, Marietta tore the paper in two.

Stella jumped, ready to lunge at the child.

"I'm sorry I ripped the letter," Marietta said, cringing. "It was an accident. I only wanted to read it. I'll write another and make it longer. I'll mail it tomorrow." Her words rushed out like lifeboats treading on treacherous water. Though she couldn't tell her mother what she'd write in the new letter, she planned to set the record straight. She would thank her uncle for all his fine gifts and good intentions and suggest that he and his wife have children of their own. Or, they could adopt an American child who, unlike Marietta, could speak their language.

"*Va bene. Andiamo al negozio un'altro giorno* – All right. We'll go to the store another day." Stella finally acquiesced. She was too tired to argue further. "How can you miss the advantages America offers?" she mumbled under her breath. But Marietta never heard. She'd already bolted out the door, back to Lucia.

"*Cosa voleva la Zia Stella questa volta?* What did Aunt Stella want this time?" asked the cousin.

"*Niente veramente.* Nothing really. It's that crazy dream of hers about America."

"But what if you really go?" Lucia's eyes widened with fright. "*Come ti mancherò!* How I'll miss you!"

"Don't be silly, Lucia. It was just a letter from America. Besides if we did go, we'd return often to see you and Nonna. But why would we go? We're happy here. I'd never leave you."

"*Ma tu non vedi? Se vai, vai sola.* But don't you see? If you go, you're going alone. We – your mother, sister, all of us – would stay here," Lucia cried.

"*Non è possibile.* It's not possible. Mamma would never send me away – not alone. How could she abandon me? She loves me. We've never been apart. We belong together. It is just talk, Lucia. Nothing will come of it. Like all the times Mamma said she'll get back with Papà. 'We'll be one happy family,' she promised. And it's yet to happen. We always return to Nonna," Marietta smiled.

Lucia smiled back weakly, wanting to believe her. She didn't see Marietta's fingers crossed deep inside her pocket, squeezing the orange peel to a pulp.

Chapter Four

Two years earlier, when Marietta was eight and Pia just two, Stella and Antonio had tried to reconcile their differences and bring the family together. Marietta remembered how her father had made a dashing figure knocking on Anna's door after a long absence. She first spotted him when he turned into her street.

"*Papà?*" she mouthed in shock, silently to herself. Her first reaction was to hide behind her cousins at the end of the jump-rope line, but as the lean, handsome man who was her father approached, Marietta gasped and a rush of air filled her throat. Would he recognize her? Would he lift her off the line and raise her into his arms as one half of her wanted and the other half feared? She stepped forward to see what he would do. To her surprise he brushed past her as if she were invisible.

Glad and disappointed at the same time, she decided to play the game her mother had taught her during the town's *passegiata*, a ritual every Italian engaged in daily. The *passegiata* had never been Marietta's favorite time. She had to quit her playing and dress in her finest clothes and parade up and down the promenade. After fifteen minutes of walking, she'd get bored. To keep her daughter occupied, Stella made up a game. She called it *Il Gioco dei Numeri* – The Numbers Game. The object of the game was to survey others on the walk and judge them by how well they were dressed.

"*Se la persona è ben vestita, ha soldi. Se no, è povera.* If the person is well dressed, it means he has money. If he's not, he's poor," she said with a wink. Stella even devised a rating system to judge from one to ten. Ten, of course, meant perfect clothes and much wealth.

Marietta loved games and she loved being with her mother who always dressed well and was pretty to look at. Once she scanned the crowd and rested her eyes on a young man wearing gray trousers, a blue sports jacket and highly polished black shoes, but no tie.

"L'uomo lì... quello è un otto o nove. Si, Mamma? That man... he's an eight or nine. Yes, Mamma?" Marietta ventured.

"Piu come un cinque. Le scarpe sono dal'anno scorso. More like a five. His shoes are last year's style," she answered. They'd continue up and down the promenade spouting numbers and, in no time, the walk ended and they'd head home to eat the evening meal.

Remembering the rules of the game, Marietta now used them to scrutinize her father from head to toe. She noticed the suit first. It was of brown tweed, one she'd never seen on anyone along the *passegiata,* and it smelled new like those in the store. The pants were neatly pressed with the crease evenly down the cuffs, and the jacket fit smoothly across his shoulders as if it were sculpted on. Stella had said that creases belonged only on pants, never on jackets. Marietta rated it a ten. It meant her father had money. If that were true, her mother wouldn't have to work anymore. She could stay home like her aunts and not be too tired to tuck her into bed at night.

But the game was no fun without Stella, so Marietta concentrated on her father's features instead. She saw him from the side, his head and eyes focused ahead, as if a heavy task lay before him and he needed to keep the task in view. With a fresh bouquet of wildflowers in one hand and a tight fist in the other, he bolted up the clean steps of Nonna's house two at a time. His red, wavy hair bounced across his forehead until finally he reached the top landing and knocked. Nonna stiffened as she opened the door. They stood on the platform for several minutes exchanging words in subdued tones. Then, as if he'd made his first conquest, Antonio walked in shutting the door behind him.

Moments later Veronica veered her head out the kitchen window.

"*Marietta, vieni sopra.* Come upstairs," she called. The little girl's heart began to race and she felt a bitter taste rise from her stomach to her mouth.

"*Vengo, Veronica.* I'm coming," she answered. She never addressed her as "Aunt" and no one minded. Veronica was only four years older than Marietta. At times they even played together.

Meeting her at the door, Nonna took the child's hand and caressed the top of her head. "Your father is here to see you," she whispered.

The minute Antonio caught sight of his daughter, he knelt on one knee. He spread out his arms, which were tanned and rugged, and opened both his hands. Marietta always admired his hands because they were capable of lifting her up into the air and she liked the rush she felt in her chest when he catapulted her above his head. But now she didn't know what to do. Her eyes turned to Nonna who nodded. Timidly, she walked closer into the circle of her father's arms.

"My little Marietta, oh how you have grown. Will you come live with your Papà?" he asked misty-eyed, as if he were the child.

"Will Mamma and Pia come, too?" she said.

"*Certamente.* Certainly. I've come to take all of you back home. I've just explained to your grandmother that I want us to be a family again." How Marietta wanted that! She didn't want to be the only one in school without a father. Yet the only place she had found family was here with Nonna.

"When your mother returns from her job at the florist, I'll explain it to her as well. I'll tell her about my new work in

San Demetrio. While I was away in Tuscany, I learned how to make the best wine and how to sell it. I was also lucky at cards," he added with a wink. "I'm a brand new man with money and a job." He smacked his hand across his chest and waved it in the air as if it were a flag. "Your mother won't refuse me now. Don't you agree?" he said, turning to Anna.

Marietta was surprised to see Nonna at a loss for words, although the look on her face showed she had much to say. Poor Stella, poor Marietta and Pia, Anna thought, shaking her head. Here he starts again with promises that he can't keep. When will Antonio grow up, get a permanent job and support his wife and children without leaning on either side of the family?

"Time will tell. Time will tell," she said, finally, with a resignation full of despair. By the tone of Nonna's voice, Marietta knew that she didn't believe him.

Once Stella's father and brothers learned of Antonio's return, they grew angry. The next day the family huddled in heated conversations that ended in a shouting bout. They shook their heads in disbelief. How dare he come back? There was no proof of a job, no amount of money saved, nothing that showed he'd changed – only words that meant nothing. Words don't put food on the table or clothes on the children's backs. Why, Stella should throw the bum out as quickly as he had come, they felt. They weren't afraid to voice their opinions. Each time Marietta entered the house, Nonna placed her finger on her mouth to hush her sons. She didn't want to upset the child. But the tension in the house created a thick web and Marietta felt caught in it.

"Good for nothing, bum, drunk, gambler" hurled around the room shamelessly. Marietta knew that the words referred to her father when her uncles spewed them out. "Deluded dreamer" described her mother. The name-calling flew across the air like arrows, piercing her. As much as she tried to shake them off, she couldn't.

"What about the time he threw the loaf of bread and hit you right in your pregnant belly? The child you lost – have you thought of that?" Pasquale reminded his sister.

"Yes, but he'd had too much to drink then. He'd just left his third job in six months. He was desperate. You drink, too," Stella pointed at him with her finger. "I've seen you drunk at Mamma's table many times. It's not his fault he lost at gambling. He thought he could make some money for us," she explained, her chest heaving up and down through tears.

"But he never will and what little he makes he spends," Nonna shouted. Then, in a gentler voice, she added, "Stella, no one wants your happiness more than I do. You've made a mistake. You should have listened from the beginning, when we told you to stay away from Antonio. Instead you sneaked off together. Don't keep making the same mistake. Start a new life for yourself. You've got the children to think about."

"Remember the knife he kept at your throat the last time you were with him?" Nonno added. "You escaped in the middle of the night and have been with us ever since. How can you be so naive to trust Antonio again?"

"Stop it! I can't stand it," Stella screamed. "I can't live here anymore. You're always telling me what to do, how to run my life. He's changed," she said. "Can't you see he's changed? I've got everything to gain if it works out and nothing to lose if it doesn't. What do I have right now? I'm miserable and poor, dependent on your charity. I'm tired of your charity. I want my own life!"

Marietta felt sorry for her mother. After dinner she stirred the sugar in her coffee. She helped take care of Pia instead of playing with Lucia. That night she prayed, the way the priests in Church had taught her.

"Caro Gesù – dear Jesus," she said, "Please make Mamma and the whole family happy again." But the end of the week brought no change. The tension in the family hung like fog.

Zio Vittorio, the oldest uncle, was the most upset. He had opposed the marriage from the start. Now he threatened to "muscle" Antonio to scare him away so he'd never return. Nonno tried to keep reason in the forefront. "Let's see if we can talk to Antonio and Stella more calmly. Perhaps they'll wait until he actually earns some money from the wine venture he claims he has," he said.

But Stella was unwilling to wait. All efforts to dissuade her proved futile.

"There's nothing we can do," Marietta overheard Nonna say to Nonno. "And who knows? Perhaps Antonio has turned a new leaf. Who are we to deprive Stella of another chance at happiness? Doesn't a wife belong with her husband after all?"

The next morning before dawn, Antonio gathered the suitcases as Marietta's aunts, uncles and cousins assembled at Anna's door. They planted sleepy kisses on both sides of Stella's cheeks. They hugged Marietta and Pia goodbye.

"*Buona fortuna* – Good luck," whispered Nonna.

"Have a safe trip," Zia Maria said.

Marietta began to cry. She didn't want to leave in the middle of the night to walk the two miles to the train station. She wanted to stay in Nonna's warm bed and wake up to her smile. Castellaneta was home. Her grandmother and her cousins were her family now. Why did she have to give them up again and again? Except that she was fatherless, she was content.

"We'll write to each other," Lucia said, trying to buoy her own spirits.

"*Ritorniamo.* We'll come back," Marietta whispered. "Just wait and see."

At the train station, Antonio cautioned his wife. "Stay here while I purchase the tickets. I won't be long." One hour later, he was immersed in deep conversation with a group of men near the newspaper stand. Baby Pia's wet garments had

44

been changed and with closed eyes her mouth searched wildly for Stella's nipple. Marietta marveled each time her sister found it.

"Pia is like your father," Stella told her. "She has an independent spirit. She wants what she wants when she wants it. Not like you. You're like Nonna, gentle and easygoing. The world can fall apart and you adjust." Marietta didn't understand. When had the world fallen apart? How had she adjusted? If her mother meant coming back to Castellaneta, how could that not be the easiest thing to do? Nonna was wonderful. It pleased her to know she was like Nonna, but she also wanted to be like Pia. They were sisters. Wouldn't it be natural for them to be alike?

She looked up and studied Pia more closely. Her hair was wispier than Marietta's, but the same shade of honey, and it curled below her tiny ears. She had a Roman nose, already defined on her baby face, and her brown eyes were big when she opened them. She lay in Stella's arms, sucking loudly, maintaining a tight grip on Stella's breast. Marietta wished she could be as carefree as Pia who was too young to know where she was going or whom she was leaving.

Marietta already missed Nonna. In the darkness, there was no Lucia to play with. There was nothing to do but stare at Pia and her mother, who seemed exceptionally radiant against the moonlit sky. Her almond-shaped eyes, the color of chestnuts, contrasted sharply with the long, black curls dancing on the sides of her ivory face. She'd worn a black dress with white polka dots, Antonio's favorite. It revealed the slim, curved torso that was her trademark. She truly had the makings of a model or actress, Marietta thought. She wondered why her mother hadn't pursued her dream with more determination before marriage. And why hadn't she married someone in town, as did her brothers and sisters? Then they'd never have to leave the family in the middle of the night. But the courage to ask eluded her.

"How did you and *Papà* meet?" she asked instead once they were settled comfortably on the train. Stella sensed that her daughter needed a distraction, a game or story to make the long ride bearable.

"Oh," she began, lifting her eyes away from Pia and out into the darkness. "It was during the war. Nonno and Nonna lived in Tripoli then. That's a city in Libya, in northern Africa. It's not too far from here. Mussolini, the ruler of Italy – you'll study him in school – gave large tracts of land to those who supported him." Marietta's eyes grew big when she heard the dictator's name. She had heard her uncles talk about him and was glued to her mother's face the way she was glued to the blackboard when the teacher wrote on it.

"Nonno didn't like Mussolini's politics or his way of thinking, but fate brought the two together. Once, Mussolini received a superficial wound on the leg. Nonno, who was nearby, saw him fall and hit the ground. He immediately ripped off his shirt and bound Mussolini's leg to stop the bleeding, as he would for any man, for Nonno is honorable and brave. He lifted Mussolini and carried him on his shoulders to safety. Mussolini was indebted to Nonno for the rest of his life. When he became the leader of Italy, he wanted to make Nonno a governor of state, a captain in his regime, but Nonno didn't want any part of his government. Without sounding ungrateful, he asked if he could have some land instead, a place where he could farm and quietly raise his family. He was granted three thousand acres in Tripoli. We had a beautiful house, fine clothes. We were rich." Marietta pictured her mother flouncing from room to room in expensive dresses and leather shoes finer than she had seen on any *passegiata*. But somehow she couldn't place Nonno and Nonna there. They belonged in Castellaneta, in the house in town that she had grown to love as her own.

"Then when Mussolini lost the war, we lost our house and our farm," Stella continued. Her mouth drooped with

46

sadness. "We had to run away like criminals. It was then I met your father. He was a soldier helping people return safely back to Italy. I was just fifteen and he was twenty-eight, so brave and handsome in his uniform. I fell in love with him the minute I saw him. He'd traveled everywhere. He even had family in America. He told me how beautiful I was, beautiful enough to go to Hollywood!"

"You must have been the prettiest bride ever, with lots of flowers and everyone watching," Marietta said, recalling the town custom where people flank the streets admiring the bride and her procession of family and guests as they walk to the church. "Our family must have celebrated with *una festa grande* – a big party," Marietta added, wishing she could have been there too.

Stella lowered her eyes. "No, Marietta. We had a small wedding. Nonno and Nonna almost didn't come. They never liked your father. They wanted me to wait and marry someone from our town." Marietta wondered whether that "someone" was one of Stella's many admirers. She fell asleep guessing which man it may have been and the *grande festa* that would have followed.

The sun was setting when the four reached San Demetrio, a town high in the hills of Calabria. They trekked up the rough mountain road in silence. As the wind bit into their faces, they crisscrossed their hands and arms against their chests to keep their coats closed. Finally, the church steeple lay behind them. Adapting to the cold, unfriendly air of this environment was always a challenge for Marietta.

Nonna Filomena, Antonio's mother, and her house loomed ahead on the first flat track of land up a few hundred feet from the village square. The house was dark and gray, not bright and inviting like Nonna Anna's. Its only sign of beauty was the black wrought iron balcony on the second level facing the street. The floor below, parallel to the street, served as a basement for storing wine and foods and sealed boxes whose contents were a constant mystery to Marietta. Above, the sparse, windowless kitchen was furnished with a small stove and a wooden hutch on one wall and a table with four chairs against the opposite wall. The only source of light and air emanated from the front door and the balcony. Empty space formed the middle.

The bedroom was equally stark. It contained two double beds, one for Filomena and the other for Stella and Antonio. A cot was placed beside their bed for Marietta, but she never slept on it. Since her father was rarely home, most nights she slept with her mother. And Pia slumbered in the same cradle that Marietta had used as a baby. It had been borrowed from relatives who lived further up the mountain.

Filomena resented the family's return. Though only five feet tall, she was feisty, naturally cantankerous and subject to no one.

"Perché non ci vuoi? Ti abbiamo offeso? Why don't you want us? Have we offended you?" Marietta asked innocently the first day back.

"Mi piace stare sola. I like to live alone. I have nothing but death to look forward to," she grimaced as if she'd just chewed the flesh of a lemon, her long skirt hung down covering the top of her shoes, the hem sliding across the stone floor as she walked.

"Why doesn't Nonna Filomena wear short dresses like Nonna Anna?" Marietta asked her mother when the grandmother was out of earshot. Stella answered with one word: tradition.

"What's tradition?" said Marietta.

"As a bride Nonna Filomena insisted on following the town custom of wearing clothes dating back to medieval times. A young girl in San Demetrio has two options on her wedding day. She can wear the traditional long, white wedding gown of the West, or her ancestral garb, which consists of a long, dark skirt heavily embroidered with gold or silver thread, a matching high-necked blouse and a vest equally decorated with swirls of gold and silver thread. These clothes are priceless heirlooms handed down from mother to daughter for many generations. By choosing the dress of her ancestors over that of the West, the bride commits herself to wearing similar clothes the rest of her married life. Although the daily ancestral clothes are not as heavy or as decorative as those on the wedding day, they are, nonetheless, dark and confining. After the war, the American soldiers ridiculed this medieval attire and most of the women, weary of the weight, stopped the practice. Not your grandmother. I told her she'd be more comfortable in the cotton dress her daughter Teresa sent her from America. 'I was married in these clothes and I'll die in them,' she told me."

As a result Marietta decided to avoid her crabby grandmother as much as possible. But Stella attended to her like a daughter. Marietta couldn't understand why. Stella had to explain again.

"Nonno, Nonna Filomena's husband, left for America shortly after their wedding. He then sent for his wife to join him. But Nonna was stubborn. She wouldn't leave Italy. She said it was the land of her birth, where her family lived. Up to that day, no wife had defied her husband, so she was the talk of the town. Nonno was forced to return to Italy each year and, for a few weeks, they would pretend he never left. She bore him three children: Teresa, Sofia and your father, Antonio. She raised them alone, only to see the two girls join their father in America when they turned eighteen. Only your father remained. And since he's rarely home and the two daughters live far away. I must do what I can to take care of her."

Though she was an ocean away, Teresa did not forget her mother. She sent a letter every month.

"Cara Mamma,
We are all fine here. I hope this letter also finds you in
good health. *I'm sending you thirty thousand lire, as usual,*
for you to buy what you need. The sugar, coffee and cocoa
you love should arrive in a few days.
I remain your daughter,
Teresa"

True to her word, a cardboard box arrived each month, much to Marietta's pleasure. The package was wrapped in heavy muslin and hand-sewn tightly along the folds. Besides coffee, sugar and cocoa, it contained clothes. Once, there was a pair of pants for Marietta, which Stella told her to wear to school on a bitterly cold day.

"Only boys wear pants," Marietta pointed out. No girl had ever been seen in pants, not in Castellaneta and definitely not in San Demetrio.

"But these are the latest styles in America," Stella said. She insisted her daughter put them on.

That day, when Marietta arrived at school, everyone glared at her legs as if they were covered with sores. Even the teacher reprimanded her. She pulled the little girl to a corner of the room so the other students wouldn't hear.

"Are you trying to be one of the boys?" she whispered. But they heard anyway and snickered, stopping only after the teacher threatened them with a cold stare. After school let out, the teasing escalated.

"Marietta is a boy... Marietta is a boy," they sang. "Show us your *campanello,* you know, the little bell that hangs between your legs. Then we'll know for sure you're a boy." She sprinted home as fast as her legs would allow, but the other children followed in pursuit, chanting the same words all the way home.

"They wouldn't leave me alone, Mamma. Even the girls made fun of me. What is a boy's *campanello?* Is it true they carry one between their legs?"

50

Stella gasped. *"Ma che caffoni sono questa gente!* What low class people they are! They'll never rise from the dirt they walk on." She took the pants from her daughter and packed them away.

Unlike the pants, the item in Aunt Teresa's package that Marietta loved was the cocoa. Unfortunately, the cocoa was also very dear to Filomena. Either out of a sadistic amusement or greed, she rationed it out sparingly. When Marietta could not squelch the temptation to have more, she waited for her grandmother to take a nap. Then, quietly placing one of the kitchen chairs in front of the cupboard, she'd climb high to reach the second shelf where she knew the cocoa lay in a canister. With spoon in hand, Marietta helped herself to what she felt was a more equitable share, licking her lips and spoon clean. It didn't take long for Filomena to notice that the precious cocoa had dropped in level.

"I'll teach you not to steal!" she yelled swinging her cane in the air like a wild woman. But Marietta was too fast for her. One day, however, Filomena devised a scheme to teach her granddaughter a lesson. She pretended to fall asleep. From the corner of her eye she could see the child climb up to the cupboard and just as she was about to place the delicious cocoa in her mouth, the grandmother sprang up like a fox disturbed from its lair. Sensing the swift movement, Marietta immediately stuffed a mouthful down her throat, jumped off the chair and dashed under the double bed, crouching into the furthest corner possible.

"I'll get you, you little thief," Filomena threatened in hot pursuit. Her cane swished back and forth but still could not reach where Marietta hid. Disgusted and tired from bending over, she went to rest on her chair in the kitchen where she eventually fell asleep for real, allowing Marietta to crawl out from under the bed without fear.

When Antonio returned from his job picking grapes, not making wine as he had told Stella, the house came alive.

He entered through the unlocked door and, like a gust of wind, caught everyone off guard. Marietta had learned to expect him only at odd times. Where he ate and slept when he wasn't home, she couldn't imagine. But when he chose to show his face, she'd usually be setting the table while Stella stood in front of the coal stove stirring pasta in a pot of boiling water. Nonna Filomena rocked in her chair, warming herself by the fire while Pia cooed in a blanket on the floor. Suddenly, Antonio would appear and lift them out of the stupor of their daily existence. He always brought presents.

"For the most beautiful woman in the world," he'd say to Stella, keeping one hand hidden behind his back. Marietta watched her mother fall into his arms, instantly gratified with whatever was in it – perfume, a comb, a silk scarf. Then Antonio would turn to his mother. He'd bend forward and gallantly kiss the back of her hand. Turning it palm up he'd fill it with a box of Perugini chocolates, her favorite. She'd groan, lifting her short, round frame from the chair and immediately proceed to hide the box.

"Oh, and what do I have here?" he'd say next, his hands roaming and searching his jacket pockets. A false frown hid his smile.

"What, indeed, do I have here?" he'd repeat with a twinkle in his eye, pulling out shiny pink, blue and red ribbons.

"Who could be pretty enough to wear these lovely presents?" He held the ribbons high in the air, looking left, looking right, in every direction but Marietta's. She rushed around him, turning every which way to catch them.

"For me, Papà, could they be for me and Pia?"

"Pia is too young for ribbons. When she wakes up, she can have a chocolate. But these," he explained, "These are ve-ry spe-cial." He stretched out his arms pulling the ribbons as if they were dough. "The shopkeeper said they're fit for a princess. Only those whose name begins with M are worthy enough to…"

"Mine begins with M. Mine begins with M," Marietta shrieked. Antonio released the ribbons and they floated through the air, dancing between father and daughter. When they landed on her palms, Marietta closed her hands and felt their softness. Though they were hers, she made a mental note to share them with Pia. Then Antonio bent down, grabbed his daughter by the waist and lifted her high in the air, squeezing her against his muscled chest.

The next morning he was gone for good.

Within a month, Stella was back in Castellaneta, as if the reconciliation had never taken place, as if she and her two daughters had never left. Nothing could have pleased Marietta more. The joy of returning to cousins, aunts and uncles and, most of all, to Nonna Anna was intoxicating. After dinner the bedroom filled with portable mattresses that seemed to materialize out of nowhere. One came out of a closet, another from inside a wall hidden by a curtain and yet another from under Nonna's high four-poster bed. In the morning, these same beds would return to their hiding places as magically as they'd come out. Two beds only – Nonna's and the cot that Marietta slept on – stayed in full view twenty-four hours a day. Sometimes, to Marietta's delight, Anna let the child climb into her giant bed and encouraged her to jump on it. "Have fun, *cara*, before I make the bed," she said. She gazed at the leaping child and their eyes locked. Rays of love emanated from Nonna's eyes. Marietta felt them envelop her. With each jump, the straw flattened and the bed sank, but Nonna's love grew higher and higher.

"Nonna, can I make a wish, the way you told me you did when you were a little girl?"

"Yes, a wish with each jump so you can hope for many things."

Marietta closed her eyes and wondered if Nonna could read her mind. Did she know that her first wish was to live with her forever and that every other wish she made was a carbon copy of the first? Marietta stopped wishing only when she was out of breath from jumping and Nonna kissed her on the forehead as she helped the child down to the floor. Then, as if it were a ritual, the child bent down under the bed and emerged with a long stick, which she gave to Anna. Marietta watched how easily Anna found the hidden hole in the mattress, inserted the stick and thrashed it to and fro until the straw fluffed full of air and the bed rose like leavened bread. Nonna's patience accomplished that, thought Marietta.

"Nonna, where does patience come from?" she asked one day.

"It may be from years of waiting or years of loving. I'm not sure. The only thing I know for certain is that some people are more patient than others. And it's easy to spot who's who."

Yes, thought Marietta. It is easy. She wished her mother and father could be more patient and love one another the way Nonno and Nonna did. But then she retracted her wish. It might mean she'd have to live far away. It was enough that Nonna was patient. She had love and patience written across the lines of her forehead and in each strand of her white hair.

Each morning Marietta watched as Anna braided her own hair in one long rope and then twisted it in a tight bun. She held it together by inserting long pins at the back of her head. At night she removed the pins and the braid unraveled. The hair spread out on her shoulders like a waterfall. Some evenings, when Anna's body ached from kneading the dough for the family's weekly supply of bread, she'd ask her granddaughter to undo her hair. The child jumped at the chance to run her fingers through those long white tresses.

"What happened at school today?" Nonna would ask as Marietta swept the hair into a gentle arc.

"Signorina Notalli told me to read my composition out loud."

"What was it about?"

"I wrote about a wonderful person who had twelve children and how the children grew up and lived near each other after they got married. When the children had children of their own, the cousins became best friends. I called it "One Happy Family."

Anna's eyes misted. "And did Signorina Notalli like it?"

"She gave me an A and the class clapped."

"Read it to me, *cara*. We have time."

The sheet of paper crackled as Marietta retrieved it from the pocket of her dress and unfolded it. She guessed Nonna would want to hear the story word for word and had placed it there in preparation.

"...by Marietta Bollina," she said, finishing the recitation, looking directly at Nonna, hungry for her reaction.

"*Brava, brava,*" Anna said, giving her a big hug. It was times like these that Marietta forgot her parents' differences, whose daughter she was, that her name was Marietta Bollina, not Marietta Santangelo like Nonna's. When people asked her, she only gave her first name, never the last one, hoping to be lumped in with her cousins.

Those times when the word "America" reached Marietta's ears and other's glances traveled in her direction, she pictured her cot at the foot of Anna's bed and felt reassured of her permanence. She was a part of Nonna's house as much as the stones that framed it.

But in the end her last name gave her away.

Chapter Five

"We can't delay any longer," Stella said the week after her fateful pronouncement to buy new clothes for the trip to America. "I'll dress you in the finest clothes from head to toe. You can't arrive in America in rags."

There she was with crazy talk again. Couldn't she just forget about America for one day? And what was wrong with Marietta's dress, a lavender frock that had belonged to Veronica? It was smocked at the chest and flared from the waist down. After Veronica outgrew it, Nonna had washed it and wrapped it in one of her new cotton sheets to protect it for the two years it took Marietta to grow into it. It was all the dearer since it had belonged to her aunt.

Yet Marietta knew she couldn't stop her mother from going shopping this time. At the store Stella had eyes only for the latest styles. Other shoppers peered in store windows, but none were as mesmerized as Stella.

"Look how pretty this dress is... Oh, what a stunning shade of pink! ...I love these shoes." As Stella chatted with the merchants, Marietta became more aware of what the other shoppers were wearing. She began to play the Numbers game. Seven, ten, three...

"Suede is the rage this year," said the bald storeowner standing at the door of his shop, his steamy eyes roaming up and down Stella's body.

"Suede it will be," she said. Stella pointed to a red dress and belted, camel-colored coat that hung high on a rod near the ceiling. The salesman used a long, hooked pole to get them down. When Marietta tried on the clothes, she flinched.

"Che cosa? What is it?" Stella asked.

"Voglio ritornare a casa. I want to go home."

"Andiamo. Andiamo. Non puoi godere pure un poco questi vestiti? We're going. We're going. Can't you enjoy these clothes just a little?" After she paid the salesman, her hands carried two bags: one contained the dress and coat; the other, a pair of two-toned brown suede shoes and matching suede beret.

Walking back in silence, Marietta wondered how her mother's dream could have progressed this far. And more importantly, how was she going to stop her from carrying it through? It can't happen, she told herself. Nonna would never let her go. Wouldn't Stella have to listen to Nonna the way Marietta had to listen to Stella?

When a week went by without the mention of America, Marietta relaxed. "See, Lucia. There's no more talk of it. I told you it would pass," she said, joining her cousins who were outside playing a game of hide-and-go-seek. But the next day, while they were in school, two packages arrived for Stella. One was from the Italian Consulate office with Marietta's passport, the other, a letter and money from Uncle Paul.

"I overheard Mamma tell Papà," Lucia confirmed.

"Are you sure?"

"Marietta, I know what I heard. I told you it was real. You didn't believe me but it's true." She burst into tears.

"Stop crying, Lucia. I'm not leaving and that's final!"

"You can't disobey your mother."

"I'll think of something." Then, as if the solution lay somewhere else and she had to go find it, she ran down the street, across the piazza, down a dozen stone steps that forked in two directions. She turned right and descended more steps until she stood in front of the two large wooden doors that opened into *la chiesa di San Domenico*, the church of St. Dominic. Marietta entered the dark interior and walked straight down the center aisle in front of the marble altar rail and knelt. She wanted to get as close to God as possible.

"Dear Jesus," she prayed, looking directly into the tabernacle. "Don't let this happen. Don't let Mamma send me away. You have to do something to help me." She squinted her eyes to show the depth of her fervor and waited for God's answer. Ideas swam through her head. Maybe a storm would come and wash away the passport and her new clothes. Or a fire could sweep their street in the middle of the night and burn the contents of the houses. The people would be saved, of course. They'd smell the smoke, gather their children and cough their way out of the house, but all their possessions would be gone, including the new clothes and passport.

"San Domenico," she continued. "This is your house. Can you keep me in mine? Dear Blessed Mother Maria, talk to your Son and to God and speak for me if they don't hear. I want to stay here. I don't want to leave. Help me, please!" She recited the same words, going back and forth from one person to the other. She didn't see that Lucia had followed her and was kneeling in the last pew, praying the same prayer as vigorously as she did.

The priest in charge of the vestry, a Franciscan, spotted the two lone girls in the empty church. He'd never seen them sit apart, but always together in the same pew and side-by side at the altar rail when receiving communion. He tapped Marietta on the shoulder.

"*C'è problema?* – Is there a problem?" he said. She looked up. Her eyes were wet and red from crying. His face blurred. Was he an angel, the messenger God sent?

"Whatever it is, my child, talk to me. I can help."

"My mother is sending me to America. I don't want to go. I don't want to leave my family." The tears gushed out, despite Marietta's resolve to hold them back.

"Ah, I know all about it," he said. "I heard it discussed in the *piazza* many times. But it may not be as bad as you think. America is a wonderland. You might grow to like it."

"I'd rather die. All that I know, all that I love is here, not in America."

"That may be true for now," he said, bobbing his head as though it were on a spring. "But you will adjust. You're young. You'll make a new life there."

"No," Marietta screamed. She covered her face with her hands. She didn't want to adjust. This was not why she came to church. She leaned forward against the pew in front of her and sobbed.

The priest gently touched the child's head with his hand. Placing his thumb on the top of her hair, he blessed her with the sign of the cross. He put his hand inside his cassock and pulled out a piece of paper neatly folded.

"This is for you. I've kept this with me for twenty years, since I entered the Seminary. Now I see it's time for me to let go of it." He placed it in Marietta's pocket. "Go with God," he said and disappeared behind the altar.

Still crying, Marietta unfolded the paper and read it out loud. *What appears to be the end may truly be a new beginning.* What does it mean, she thought? Was this God's message? She sat as still as the statues that surrounded her. The smell of wax burning from the devotional candles wafted under her nose but she was no closer to understanding the words on the paper. Confused, she thought of Nonna, the only person that she knew would understand the message. As she rose to leave, she spotted Lucia. Grateful to see that familiar face and exhausted from her crying, she walked home with Lucia in silence. Marietta decided to table all thoughts about America until tomorrow. She went to sleep, the note crumpled in her pocket.

In the middle of the night, Marietta felt the firm touch of a hand on her shoulder and awoke. It confused her to stare into Stella's face, her black hair tightly arranged in a bun behind her head. Two strands of ringlets fell out of their hold. They bounced on Marietta's cheek, tickling her. Was her mother leaving and wanted to say goodbye? Her lips were bright red, full and creamy, but they didn't lower for a farewell kiss. Wisps of her perfume floated in the air. Marietta's head shook to make sense of the situation. I must be dreaming, she thought, her eyes closing, giving in to sleep once more.

"Wake up! Wake up!" Stella shouted. "We'll be late for the train!"

Could it be her mother had made up with her father again? She rubbed her eyes and forced them wide-open to make sure she was still in Nonna's bedroom, sleeping on the cot, a few inches away from her bed. What she saw frightened her. Nonna was there, but not in bed. The whole family was present in the room. They stood a few feet behind Stella: first Nonna, then Nonno, then aunts, uncles, Lucia and her other cousins. Even Pia, latching onto Veronica's hand, was awake, pale-faced and looking just as frightened as Marietta. Red and teary-eyed, they stared at Marietta as if to get a long look, one that had to last a lifetime.

"Please, let this be a dream, God. Let this be a dream," Marietta moaned.

"This is a dream," Stella said, pulling Marietta's arm to get her out of bed. "You're going to America, the land of dreams."

"No, no. I won't go. I don't want to go."

"Fool! You don't realize the opportunity you have," Stella shook her daughter with all her strength. "It's all decided. You can't undo it." At those words Marietta's will to live left and she turned limp. Stella was forced to dress her daughter as if the child were incapable, as if she were two, not ten.

"We can't be late for the train. It takes us to the plane that will bring you to America." There was such a singsong quality to Stella's words that Marietta had to fight hard not to think it a nursery rhyme and fall sleep again. But the word "America" hit a nerve and her spirit bolted.

"I don't want to go," she said. "I want to stay here with you and Pia, with Nonna and Lucia."

"You will love America," Stella continued as if Marietta had assented to go. "Aunt Teresa and Uncle Paul will love you as a mother and father would. You'll finally have a father. You'll be their special child. Then your sister and I will come too. We'll be together again."

"I don't want to be special. I want to be ordinary. I don't want to leave Nonna." Marietta flailed her arms like a baby. One of them came out of the sleeve of her dress.

"Mamma, Papà, tell Marietta this is for her own good," Stella pleaded with her parents. When neither moved, Marietta filled with hope.

"Please, Nonno, Nonna, can't I stay with you? I promise to be good. I haven't done anything wrong, have I? Please make Mamma change her mind. I love you. Don't let her send me away!" Marietta lunged toward her grandparents and uncles, hoping she could hide in their circle, safe from Stella's clutches.

"How we wish we could! But your parents have custody over you. We can do nothing. The papers are already signed," Nonna said.

Marietta's heart sank. She scanned the room for anyone who could persuade her mother. So many people and no one to help her. Better she were dead, she thought. You can't send the dead to America. Aunt Teresa and Uncle Paul wouldn't want a dead girl for a daughter. Then, as if to make death's hold easier, Marietta fainted. Anna gasped, her face writhing with pain. She pushed her daughter aside and caught the child before she fell, embracing her and planting kisses all over her face. Marietta felt Nonna's touch. She recognized her smell – the scent of love she had come to treasure. She opened her eyes and smiled at the familiar face she loved.

"Tu sarai sempre nel nostro cuore. You'll always be in our hearts," Nonna said with tears running down her cheeks.

Once Marietta was fully dressed, the relatives took turns to hug her. They spoke her name, as if it were the necessary password to preserve her identity in their lives.

"Marietta, ricordati che ho bevuto il latte della Zia Stella, l'ostesso latte che hai bevuto tu. Siamo come sorelle. Remember that I drank Zia Stella's breast milk, the same milk you drank. We are like sisters," Lucia said, her voice cracking from crying.

"Ti tengo sempre con me, Lucia. I'll always keep you with me, Lucia," Marietta said.

Walking down the cobblestone street with the shops on either side was totally different at night than during the day. The noise of shoppers and shopkeepers was missing. Only an eerie silence pervaded, making the rat-tat-tat sound of their shoes seem unnaturally loud as they hit the pavement. The moon hung high and full, lighting the way.

On the eight-hour train ride Stella chatted with anyone who came near. Her daughter was going to America! Wasn't it wonderful? She would live with a very rich aunt and uncle. Could you believe their good luck? Eventually, she, too, would go to America and be rich and famous. Marietta sat stone-faced, staring out the window. She'd lost the power to understand and her mother's words trailed off like empty ghosts. But the news opened people's mouths. They thought how brave the girl was. Why, not a whimper! On such a long trip! What a pretty face! Just like her mother!

Stella turned to the two women beside her. "My husband...the bastard...he beat me and cheated on me. Once he left me for dead. If it weren't for a neighbor coming to see what the screaming was about, I would have died. My daughter doesn't understand the sacrifices I'm making for her to go to America, to have a better life than I've had. It's for her good."

"Yes, her life will be better," said one of the women as the other nodded in agreement.

Oh, but you don't make my life better. Not all the riches in the world would make me want to leave Nonna, Lucia, and even you, Mamma. I want to stay. Even if I have nothing to eat!

Is this what happens when you die? Where are God's hands to welcome me home? Did the priest lie? I see only your hands, Mamma, sending me away from everyone I love.

No one heard Marietta's thoughts, not even the wind.

Chapter Six

There was a bustle of activity at the Rome airport when Stella and Marietta arrived. They were both tired from the long train ride. The noise of people talking all at once echoed through the large waiting room and unnerved them. Marietta looked especially pale. Normally, she loved the boisterous, simultaneous conversations from her aunts and uncles around her grandmother's table. At Nonna's table sounds of her family blended as symphony to her ears. She could play guessing games with her cousins or talk about school under the cacophony of adult voices that hovered above them like an umbrella shielding them from harm. But at the airport men and women scrambled in all directions. They seemed as lost as she.

Raising her head, she read the sign above her. *Ciampino Aereoporto di Roma.* The loudspeaker came on and a male voice, strong and deep like that of the principal in her school in Castellaneta, announced that American Airlines flight 905 to New York would depart on schedule.

"*Credo è nostra.* I think that's ours," Stella said. She searched her purse and pulled out a sheet of paper that had been folded in half. Her lips moved as she read it silently to herself. "Yes, it is our plane," she confirmed.

Marietta stared at her surroundings. She couldn't believe so much had happened in so little time. Was the voice overhead really that of her principal? Was she at school imagining this airport scene so that she could describe it more vividly in her essay? Or was the airport really an airport and the whole school had come to say goodbye?

She remembered the train ride. It had seemed interminably long and short at the same time. How did they get from the train to the airport? Did they walk? Did they take a taxi? Why did these events blur when in school she

64

could remember even the smallest detail of grammar and history and geography?

Sensing her daughter's distraught state of mind, Stella took the child's hand and led her inside a small restaurant where the rumble of the airport subsided. They neared an empty table and sat. Stella reached for the menu.

"What should we order?" she asked cheerfully.

"*Non voglio niente.* I don't want anything," Marietta said in a voice barely audible. But Stella was hungry. She ordered *penne bolognese* – pasta with meat sauce – for both of them. After the waiter left, Marietta became aware of the metal seat that stuck to the back of her legs. It felt hard and cold just like she did. She wondered if she'd ever feel warm again. Everything inside her had grown rigid, as if her body was wrapped in folds of linen. How could she eat?

When the waiter returned, he placed two steaming hot plates on the table. The vapor rose in menacing swirls like thunderclaps ready to burst. Marietta eyed the white tubes starkly laden with only a dollop of red in the center and longed for Nonna's golden fare drenched with cheese and laced with her delicious sauce. In her mind she asked: what was she doing in this cold restaurant when she could be eating at Nonna's table? Strangely, she felt the pasta read her mind and sneer. It can't be, she thought. Pasta is not alive. But if the penne could speak, her mind went on, what would they say? Dare she let her imagination roll as Signorina Notalli encouraged when she assigned essays in class? She granted it free rein. To her surprise, she saw the penne move on the plate.

"Why are you not fighting back?" they said in unison. "You know you don't want to go to America." Marietta was too shocked to answer. She was convinced she was hallucinating. "Why did your mother hold your hand?" the pasta continued like a Greek chorus. "Does she think you'll run away? You should. Let her see how it feels to lose someone you love. But it won't equal your pain for you lost everyone, not just one person as she is about to do now."

Marietta rubbed her forehead. She wanted to chase away these visions. "I can't hurt Mamma," she whispered, lowering her head nearer to the plate so Stella wouldn't hear the awful conversation.

"Don't you get it? She doesn't love you. She doesn't want you," the pasta persisted. Marietta was horrified. This pasta must be from bad flour, she decided. Nonna's pasta was always warm and inviting to eat. It had never said a bad word about anybody. Perhaps letting her imagination run wild was not as good an idea as Signorina Notalli espoused. But now she couldn't stop it

"She has to make sure you get on that plane. Ask her. What is she getting in return for giving you away, for abandoning you? Is it money, a trip to Hollywood, more freedom? Ask her. Just ask her! Don't be a coward all your life, for heaven's sake."

Marietta's head pounded. Could the pasta be right? She was tempted to do anything that saved her from her fate, to dissuade Stella and bring them both back to Castellaneta. But she couldn't accuse her mother of these dreadful things. If they proved true, she'd be devastated. Who was the authority leading her on, she reasoned? Ribbed penne?

This was *pazzeria*, insanity, she told herself. She closed her eyes and prayed for a miracle. She believed in them. Didn't Jesus feed a multitude with just a few loaves and fishes? He cured lepers and gave sight to the blind. He even raised Lazarus from the dead. Certainly Jesus could tame this delinquent pasta and change it to the one Nonna cooked. He could transform the small table before her into the larger one in Nonna's kitchen. Then the people around her would become her aunts, uncles and cousins. She wouldn't mind the noise. She'd welcome it. Her eyes opened searching for the miracle to have occurred. But all she saw was Stella devouring her meal.

"*Mangia,* Eat. They say the food on the plane is not so tasty," Stella said. Marietta picked up her fork and swirled the pasta until the sauce mixed and lost its deep, sanguine color. "Don't be sad. I have a surprise for you," Stella added.

Marietta's heart jumped. She was going home, back to Nonna and Lucia. The miracle had happened! Wide-eyed, she turned to her mother with love. What a fool she was to have doubted her. How can a mother abandon her child? Never could it happen. Exhaling a sigh of relief, she waited for the words she longed to hear, the words that would plant her where she belonged.

Stella dug into her large handbag and pulled out a white, two-inch square box. She opened her daughter's hand and placed it in it.

"*Apri.* Open," she said. Marietta lifted the lid and found a pair of yellow earrings and a ring inscribed with the letter "M." The 18-carat gold caught the light in the ceiling. Dozens of sparkling circles immediately formed on the wall.

"Aren't they beautiful? I was saving them for your birthday, but I decided to give them to you now while we're together rather than send them," Stella said. Marietta was dumbfounded. This was no miracle. Gold was worth nothing in comparison to her family. Stella removed the ring from its snug depression in the box and slid it on her daughter's finger and, leaning closer, inserted the earrings in her ears. She cocked her head to admire them. "When you arrive in New York, they'll think you come from royalty," she beamed. "We do have royal blood, in case you forgot, from our French ancestors." Royal blood? It was the first time Marietta had heard of it. As far as she was concerned, her royal blood was left on the cobblestone street below Nonna's house.

The principal's baritone voice on the loudspeaker told them it was now time to board. A group of people immediately stood up and formed a single line. Stella, clutching her daughter's hand, got up as well. They inched their way forward, until they reached the attendant inspecting the tickets. *"Ti amo.* I love you," Stella said in a loud voice, draping both hands on her daughter's shoulder. "Write to me every day so you'll never forget me." She embraced the child, then, released her.

Marietta felt numb. Walking side-by-side with the stewardess down the long plank, she turned and saw Stella's form shrink smaller and smaller as they neared the steps of the plane. With one turn Stella and the life Marietta knew and loved were gone. She wondered if she would ever see her mother again.

On the plane the stewardess took a maternal interest in the child. She buckled the strap of her seat and brought her peanuts and soda. At lulls in her work schedule she noticed the girl's lifeless body and sat beside her. She recounted stories of her own daughter, just about Marietta's age, who was thousands of miles away. To help pass the time she handed the girl a deck of cards and a silver-colored flight pin that had the words "Junior Pilot" engraved on it. Marietta accepted the gifts silently. She fingered the pin but didn't touch the cards. They lay on her lap next to two books. She couldn't remember who had given them to her. She had no luggage. Not even a purse. Could her mother have placed the books in her hand when they were on line? Or did the stewardess give them to her along with the cards and pin? Her mind went blank, the way words and numbers erased from Signorina Notalli's blackboard.

Marietta touched the cover of the larger book, spreading her hands across the title as if it were written in Braille. Pinocchio by Carlo Collodi. The pages felt cold and stiff, unyielding like the wooden puppet. She fingered the second book, which was smaller and fatter. The Sunday Missal for Mass. Its black leather binding was soft and pliable. Its pages, thin and white except for the black print, offered no resistance as she thumbed through them. They felt smooth and gentle like Nonna's hands. Marietta noticed the familiar Latin on the left next to the Italian translation when several holy cards fell out and landed on her dress. One was of the Sacred Heart of Jesus. She picked it up and saw how red Jesus' heart was, how exposed. "From your cousin Vittorio," it read. "*Ciao, Marietta. Ti ricordo sempre. Non ti dimenticar di me.*"

"Of course, you'll forget," chided the harsh pasta voice again. You'll want to forget. It hurts too much to remember."

How ridiculous that the voice still tugged at her, she thought. It was only her imagination that had made the pasta talk. Why did the voice seem so foreign and yet it came from inside her? She felt terribly small and alone, compromised in such a big world. Gathering the holy cards from her lap, she placed them inside the pages of the Missal, burying her feelings among them. When she closed the book, the pain abated.

A man across the aisle glanced in her direction. He was tall with thinning brown hair and wore a gray business suit. Seeing the playing cards still in their jacket and the little girl unaccompanied by any adult, he carefully folded the newspaper he was reading and placed it in the back pocket of the seat in front of him.

"*Vuoi giocare con le carte da gioco?* Would you like to play a game of cards with me?" he asked, pointing to the deck on her lap. Marietta looked at him, then at the deck, but said nothing. Interpreting her silence as assent, he sat in the empty seat next to her and took the cards out of the jacket, shuffling them. "Is this your first trip to America?" he asked, hoping conversation would bring a smile to her lips. Marietta, again, said nothing. "Do you go to school? What grade are you in? Where are you going in America?" he persisted. Marietta responded only with empty, searching eyes that lowered as soon as she felt them blur with tears. With bowed head she put one hand over her trembling mouth and shook her head "no."

"*Ah, non puoi parlare.* You can't speak," he said, giving her a graceful way out. She nodded. It was true. If she spoke, she'd have to say words that she dared not utter, words that hurt too much. She'd have to say her mother had given her away, discarded her like an old pair of shoes. How could Marietta not unravel and fall apart? And as to where she was going, how could she know? She'd never been there.

Marietta had never felt such intense isolation. A myriad of feelings – fear, love, hate, anger and betrayal – stewed in her heart, emotions which, except for love, she didn't understand. The events that took place in her young life left her shocked. Do mothers and children separate often? Where do children go when their mothers no longer want them? America must be the place, she thought, or else, why would she be going there? In school she had learned that America was a land of immigrants, but were these immigrants all children sent away by their mothers? Were they wrenched from their native homes as she was? There was much she didn't know and no one to ask.

The man beside her sensed how distraught she was. He wanted to calm her with his gentle voice. But her mind spun like the wheels of a racecar stuck in a hole. Everyday events flew by in a flurry of frames trying to make sense of where she was and why. Stella must not love her the way she loved Pia, she concluded. Or, was it possible that Stella truly made the ultimate sacrifice to give her daughter a better life? That she didn't really despise Marietta? If so, why did it hurt so much?

Or, did Stella send her far away because the child had done something bad? She must have done something bad, she reasoned. No mother would punish a good child. What possible offense might she have committed? She thought hard but couldn't come up with one. Unless it was the times Stella called her to come in from playing hopscotch and she delayed, choosing to play with Lucia instead. But Lucia didn't always listen to her mother either. And Zia Maria had not sent her away, nor would Nonna – not for this or for any other offense. Nonna! The word warmed her heart. "That's it," Marietta said almost out loud. Her mother must have guessed she loved Nonna more than anyone else. No wonder she gave her away. Stella knows she didn't come first. What an ungrateful child Marietta must be, for mamma is the most cherished word in Italy, second only to God. And Marietta, with Nonna and Lucia in the picture, had relegated her mother to a lower place. Suddenly Marietta felt sorry for her mother. How could she not have put her first? Poor Mamma, she thought. She tried to do the best she could without Papà and without money. "It's my own fault," she whispered sadly. "I wasn't a good daughter."

But her love for Nonna would never change and Lucia was her second skin. If only the kind man beside her and the stewardess who checked in on her could have been her father and mother. Then she would have them here with her and all would be well. Exhausted, Marietta fell asleep dreaming of cobblestone streets and orange peels. She awoke just as the pilot began his descent.

When the plane finally touched American soil she had no clue what to do. Her mother hadn't said how she would meet Aunt Teresa and her new *Papà*. Where would they be? How would she recognize them? People stood up and deplaned but Marietta remained strapped in her seat. When the line of exiting passengers finally ended, she noticed that the man beside her, also, stayed back. He rose when the stewardess came near. Then, as if they were her parents, each clasped Marietta's hand and led her out. The three of them walked across wide corridors until they reached a large, well-lit room full of people and strong with the smell of coffee.

The stewardess scanned the area. Not finding what she expected, she bent down and hugged Marietta.

"I wish I could stay and wait with you but I must get back to work," she said. She pointed to an airline employee behind a tall desk who was answering questions in front of a long line of people. The woman waved. "She'll watch over you until your relatives come. Sit here while you wait."

The man in the gray business suit also bent down and kissed Marietta on the forehead. *"Forse ci vediamo un'altra volta.* Perhaps we'll see each other again," he said. He handed her a piece of paper with his name and phone number. *"Se hai bisogno di qualche cosa, mi telefoni. Si?* If you need anything, you can call me." They turned and in a blur blended with the crowd, leaving Marietta alone in a sea of strangers.

Outside, just steps away, snow gently laced the streets of New York City. Light, powdery flakes danced in the air, suspended, almost refusing to come down. Eventually, the snow yielded to gravity and made a quiet landfall. Like angel dust it filled the ruts and holes of the pavement. It covered the imperfections and smudges on houses and streets. The landscape took on the clean appearance of newly painted walls.

The snow had caught people by surprise. Beneath this blanket of white, the first day of spring dawned. Forsythias were ready to bloom, anxious to burst their delicate yellow flowers like stars in the night. Daffodils had already broken ground and risen to their golden heights. They stood proudly, haughtily against the snow. Marietta was unaware of the birth around her. Like an orphan, she waited for someone to claim her, someone who wanted her, someone to whom she could belong. For a place to call home.

A mile from the airport, Paul sat in his car cursing at the traffic caused by an overturned car in front of him. He and his entourage – Teresa, Sofia with her fiancé Sal and a neighbor child named Ellen – had calculated an extra hour on account of the snow, but had not anticipated the accident. And now they were late to meet the newly adopted daughter. Paul was angry. He had wanted to wait for her at the airport in anticipation of the wonderful gift that life was finally handing him. Marietta was the miracle that had come true. In his twenty-five years of marriage to Teresa, they had endured five miscarriages and no live births. After the last failure, the doctor had said, "Enough. Your wife's body just can't carry a child to term."

This was fine with Teresa. She didn't want children. Children were work, she said, and with the cooking and cleaning already burdening her, she didn't want to add to it. Children caused problems. They grew up, moved away and disappointed you. All she had to do was to take one look at herself and her sister Sofia and know it was true. Look how far away they were from their mother in San Demetrio. Even their brother Antonio, Marietta's father, who could be near their mother, hardly was. Children tore the family apart.

"Son of a bitch," Paul said. "Even my badge won't get me through this time. He banged his right hand on the steering wheel and the horn accidentally blew. A few heads turned. He didn't care. "Goddammit, let's go," he ordered. As his fingers closed around the curve of the wheel, Teresa glimpsed at the scar on the back of his hand where he had been knifed while stopping a young hoodlum from robbing a cash register. It had taken place right in Giovanni's Market, where she bought her meat every week, where she painstakingly chose the pieces of beef, pork and veal behind the glass counter and told the butcher how to grind them for her meatballs. The pork store had been part of Paul's beat for twenty years. If he hadn't instinctively used the hand as a shield, the thief he apprehended would have sliced his heart. She drew a deep breath at the memory.

"*No* be in such a hurry. We get there," she said in her broken English, annoyed that he was making such a fuss. "*È*

73

bambina. She's just a child. She *no* go away." The others sat in the back seat, tight-lipped. They knew nothing would appease Paul except arriving. When the firemen on the scene finally allowed Paul to drive on the grass, around the other motorists, past the area that was now bordered with tape, he sped as if his life depended on it.

"Dear Jesus, *finalmente!"* he said as they pulled up in front of the airport terminal. He displayed his policeman's parking sticker on the dashboard and gave the guard a wave to indicate he was here on official business. In the waiting room he searched for the little girl who might be searching for him.

When a smile broke over Paul's face, Teresa knew he had spotted the child. Reluctantly, she followed his lead, the others trailing behind. As he drew near, Marietta immediately rose to attention, the way she did when Signorina Notalli or the principal entered the classroom. She had been waiting for an hour and the number of people in the giant hall had dwindled. It was easy for her to examine the group in front of her. A short, well-dressed woman moved to one side. Marietta thought that must be Aunt Sofia, Aunt Teresa's sister, who was of small stature. She didn't know the man who held her hand. She quickly spotted a burlap of a man about fifty years old, big in all directions, with tanned skin and black curly hair that lay in short, cascading waves on top of his head. He wore a long, navy-blue coat with big buttons. She was tempted to count them but at the last minute decided there wasn't time. The coat lent an air of elegance and gentility to his rough demeanor. When her eyes rested on his face, she noticed that he smiled the way Nonno often did when he thought she wasn't looking. He let out a deep sigh of contentment, as if a mission of his had been fulfilled. That must be Uncle Paul, the *"Papà"* in Stella's letters, she guessed. Next to him was a woman wrapped in a black lamb's wool coat with a silver fox collar and cuffs. Fidgeting, moving her handbag from one arm to another, she looked so uncomfortable that Marietta wondered if she, too, had been abandoned as a child and the airport held painful memories. Could she be Aunt Teresa?

Suddenly a girl with long black hair framing an olive complexion emerged from behind. For a moment Marietta thought she was Lucia. Her cousin could have boarded the plane in secret to keep their vow of never being apart. If Lucia were here in America, Marietta felt she could survive. But a blink of an eye convinced her otherwise. She blinked several times more, wondering what was real and what wasn't, imprisoned in this cavernous room thousands of miles away from home.

The girl stepped forward and offered Marietta a doll the size of a newborn. It had blonde hair braided in two long ropes down her back the way Marietta often wore her own hair when the mercury soared. The doll wore only a pink, cotton dress. It had no coat and Marietta wondered if it were cold. The American girl moved her lips and muttered words that sounded strange. With effort, Marietta pieced the rough dialect together: *"Buona venuta all'America.* Welcome to America."

"Ah, grazie." she said finally, accepting the doll, surprised at the sound of her own voice. Wanting to hold something soft and close, she pressed it against her chest. But the doll's body felt cold and hard. She pulled it away and inspected its plastic face, perfectly sculpted, with pink dots for cheeks. It was different from the soft, cuddly dolls Nonna had taught her to make by folding a towel in half and rolling it across its length. She hoped she wouldn't harden like the doll in this strange new land.

The adults immediately rushed at her. *"Bona venut,"* they said in imperfect Italian. Paul reached for Marietta's hand and led her and the others out the door into a sea of white.

"*Nevica.* It's snowing," Marietta said, stopping to catch some of the falling flakes with her free hand.

"*È la primavera.* It's spring," Paul said with a smile, as if the irony explained everything. He opened the doors of his oversized Oldsmobile, sparkling black against the white snow. Directing Marietta to the front seat between him and Teresa, he took the wheel and drove. Everyone spoke at once. In improper Italian, they conveyed how sought after Marietta had been and to what pains her "*Papà*" had gone to experience this moment. Someday, they said, she would understand what it took to allow her to enter the country as the legally adopted daughter of Paul and Teresa Marino. Yes, Marietta nodded. Someday, she hoped to understand what had happened, but not today. Today was full enough. It could hold nothing more.

Without warning, the car came to a halt in front of a group of brownstones, all attached and exactly alike. Marietta couldn't tell them apart. She searched for clues: a balcony, a different colored wall or window, a door with a red plant in front, anything that would distinguish one from the other, like the houses in Castellaneta. But, she reminded herself, she was no longer in her hometown.

Paul took her hand again and led her up the steps of the stoop. Taking a key out of his pocket, he unlocked the door. It led into a small vestibule. Suddenly, the inner door opened and the tenants in Paul's four-family brownstone rushed at them in greeting. They had heard so much about Paul's great prize and couldn't wait to feast their eyes on the girl. When she walked in, the tenants divided in half, some going to the left, others to the right, as though they were a wave parting in the middle. Retreating against the walls of the corridor, there was plenty of room for her to pass. Then Paul proudly led his daughter up the creaking stairs to the second floor in front of the door of her new home.

Before entering, Teresa took off her shoes and lined them neatly on the brown mat against the hallway wall. She motioned for Marietta to do the same. Marietta looked down lovingly at the suede shoes Stella had painstakingly bought her to match her coat and hat. They'd endured the trip. She bent down to unbuckle the strap that held them to her feet and slipped out of them. The doll, still in her arms, bent with her, and its eyes promptly shut. Just like the first ten years of her life.

Chapter Seven

Upon entering Teresa's Lilliputian kitchen, Marietta's eyes landed on the white linoleum floor speckled with silver dots. It reminded her of the colorless hospital floor in Bari where she'd had her tonsils removed a few years earlier. The wall on the left housed a giant refrigerator as white as the newly fallen snow. A small Formica table with three matching chairs pushed snugly under crunched next to it. The stove, a square metal box where four silver knobs protruded like buttons, completed the wall. Barely five feet separated the opposite wall. At one end stood a sink with two white, deep wells: one left uncovered for washing dishes and one covered with a pleated, metal washboard for washing clothes. A silver faucet in the center moved from side to side converting to each task. Beside the sink another chair adorned the bare wall. The only inviting piece of furniture, Marietta thought, because the seat faced out. A glass door dressed with off-white sheer curtains led into Paul and Teresa's bedroom. Of the two remaining kitchen walls, one held a long, curtained window that opened onto a fire escape. The other was the front door through which Marietta had entered.

Marietta shivered at the kitchen's cold complexion. It didn't matter that the room had conveniences she'd never seen, such as running water and a gas stove or a massive refrigerator and freezer stocked with more food than she could imagine – steaks, veal cutlets, lamb chops, chopped beef, sausages, milk, bread, fruits and ice cream. What struck her was that the room had no place for people. Except for its miniature size, Teresa's antiseptic kitchen reminded Marietta of Nonna Filomena's house. She longed for Anna's simpler, spacious kitchen that could seat twelve, the splash of red geraniums on the windowsill, the brown shutters that spread out like the wings of a bird when they opened, and the music that the wind blew in through the closed slats. On the table, she saw no brown-crusted bread like the kind Anna made with her own hands, nor straw-covered bottles of red wine made from homegrown grapes. What had become of the terracotta stone floor that rouged Nonna's kitchen, the one she'd cleaned with a rag and a pail full of water just days before?

"Come, I will show you the rest of the house," Sofia said. She ushered Marietta through the sheer curtained door, exposing an ample-sized bedroom. The double bed, covered with a thick, green, damask bedspread lay opposite a heavy, cherry mahogany triple dresser and chest-on-chest, giving the room a somber tone and shrinking its size. Heavy drapery obscured what little light struggled to enter through the two long windows. The bedroom, in turn, opened to a narrow hallway with a bathroom on the left and a closet on the right before enlarging into the living room. A French provincial couch with matching end tables on each side flanked the big wall while an easy chair protected by a throw cover sat on a ninety-degree angle on the shorter wall. Straight ahead two windows ran from ceiling to floor, each heavily draped and fronted by a wing chair. Marietta gasped when she recognized the chair legs with gnarling snakes frozen in wood. She turned away immediately. Her eyes rested on a covered candy dish in the center of a mahogany coffee table. She wondered whether it was filled with chocolates or caramels. When she saw the lid sculpted in the form of a naked woman, she blushed and gave up on the candy.

"*Perché la casa è così scura?* Why is the house so dark?" Marietta asked.

"*Troppo luce da mal di testa a mia sorella.* Too much brightness gives my sister a headache," Sofia said. She pointed to a large piece of furniture in the shape of a rectangular mahogany box. Marietta thought it held clothes, perhaps some for her. Sofia put her hands in the center of the cabinet and pulled the doors open. A glass screen magically appeared.

"*Questa è la televisione,*" she said. Then pointing below, "*Qui è la radio,*" she added. Marietta eyes widened. In school she had heard that rich people owned television sets right in their homes. And radios, too. On Nonna's block, only one family had a radio. The father, a traveling salesman, had brought it home from one of his trips. Marietta remembered how she and her cousins used to gravitate in front of that house when the radio was on. The owner obliged them by turning up the volume.

Sofia then led Marietta to a gold, wrought-iron table. "*Questo è il telefono,*" she said pointing to a black object. Just when she thought the tour was over, Sofia brought her through an opening in the living room wall into another room about the same size as the kitchen. It was crowded with a double bed and nightstand with a lamp on top. A small dresser sat at the foot of the bed. A Singer sewing machine catty-cornered the window and the doorway. Marietta was surprised not to see a curtain hung across the opening for privacy, as in Nonna's bedroom.

"*Questa è la mia camera dove dormiamo insieme. Sarà la tua dopo che mi sposo.* This is my room where we'll both sleep. It'll be yours after I get married." Seeing the bed, Marietta's eyes almost closed. Leaving Nonna's house where everything was done by hand and arriving into this mechanized confine, she felt the weight of a hundred years pass by. She'd venture another hundred years if she could wake up in Nonna's arms, she sighed. But no, she must put the past behind her or the pain would return, then the tears. She couldn't let her heart continue to break. It had been a long day and she was exhausted. She would have fallen and slept on the floor if Sofia had not caught her and maneuvered her body gently on the bed.

The next morning Marietta awoke to outdoor sounds and sunlight peeking through Venetian blinds. She could make out the shrieking and laughter of children, but the words she heard made no sense. For a moment she thought she'd died and gone to heaven with the two children that Nonna had lost during birth and a third, Graziella, through a tragic accident when the child was nine years old. She remembered Anna's account vividly, as if Nonna was there with her and had just finished telling the story.

"Graziella had a passion for climbing high places," Anna had said. "She loved to count the stars and trace the moon as it moved in the early evening sky. Since there were no trees in the street, she would climb to the flat roof above the porch landing and look up. I made her promise never to go there without first telling me so I could guide her steps and not fall. One evening, while I wasn't home, Graziella couldn't control the urge to visit her favorite place. As the moon rose in the sky, she, too, rose to follow its path. I was returning home and saw her step too close to the ledge. I called out to her to step back. When she saw me, she slipped and fell onto the cobblestone. She died in my arms with a smile on her face. When I die someday, Graziella and the babies will come greet me. And when you die, we'll rush down to take hold of your hand so you won't be afraid."

Marietta looked around for Nonna and her dead children, but to no avail. Instead, the smell of brewed coffee reached her nostrils. She listened more acutely and heard undertones of conversation in broken Italian and recognized the strange voices of her American relatives. Suddenly a head popped in the doorway.

"She's up! She's up!" Paul shouted. Two more heads, Sofia's and Teresa's appeared, gaping as if Marietta were a specimen in the zoo. Sofia walked in and rolled down the bedcover. Paul stepped forward and offered his hand inviting her to get out of bed. He led her through the apartment back to the tiny kitchen. On the table lay two glasses of orange juice, one cup of tea, and one of coffee near a plate of English muffins toasted and buttered.

"*Mangia,*" Teresa said dutifully. "Your *Papà* wants you to eat." Paul sat beside Marietta while the two sisters stood and watched. As the child lifted the glass to her lips, Paul smiled. The juice tasted sweet on her tongue. She took a bite of the English muffin and, surprisingly, it slid down as easily as Anna's piece of bread drenched in olive oil. Then she sipped the tea and welcomed its warmth.

"Well, Marietta," Paul beamed when she finished chewing her last bite. "Today we're going shopping to buy you new clothes." Marietta tensed. Not again, she thought. Her last shopping trip had produced traumatic results.

"But first," Teresa interjected, "we have to get you all cleaned up – wash the dirt from Italy off your body and deal with the clothes you have now."

"I'm not dirty," Marietta said defensively. "I took a bath and washed my hair before I left. And all my clothes are new. Mamma bought them for me to wear especially for America," she added, remembering with a tinge of guilt how much she hated them the day they were bought.

"We're throwing them out," Teresa said firmly.

"Why? They're brand new." Marietta felt violated. The clothes were her last link to the past.

"You'll have American clothes now," Paul said, trying to appease her. "Your Italian clothes make you look like a foreigner."

The two sisters led Marietta to the bathtub. Much to her embarrassment, they washed every part of her as if she were a baby. "We have to get all the dirt out, especially the lice. Everyone that comes from Italy has lice," Teresa said. They dressed her in a stiff crinoline dress that was a size too large. Thankfully, they let her keep the shoes. She'd wear them until they bought new ones at the store. They sent her into the living room with Paul as they scoured the tub and bathroom floor. Marietta couldn't help think how, with all their wealth, fine furniture and clothes, her aunts worked as hard as Anna. So much for the servants that Stella had claimed they had.

Paul removed his newspaper from the footstool and motioned Marietta to sit. He took his seat on the throw-covered easy chair opposite it, removed a cigarette out of his shirt pocket and lit it.

"Papà," she said, timidly using the word for the first time. "*Dove è la piccola ragazza che mi diede la bambola?* Where's the little girl who gave me the doll?" Marietta had not seen her since the airport and would have liked to play with her.

"*Elena è a scuola.* Ellen's in school, Marietta. That's where all smart girls go." He stooped closer, leaning to her ear, letting her in on a big secret. "Next week you and I will go to St. Margaret Academy. This is an even better school than the one Ellen attends."

"Will I live there?" she said, her voice trembling, the new clothes finally making sense.

"Why would you?" He placed his hand on her shoulder. "You'll go to school in the morning and return here in the afternoon like the other children," he said. Marietta was hesitant. She didn't know whether she could trust him.

When the two women finished their cleaning, they nodded to Paul that they were ready. He rose and instructed Marietta to follow. The four went through the kitchen, out the door, down the one flight of stairs. Paul leaned over the banister and called Ellen's mother below. "Susie, are you ready?"

"Just a second," she answered, but no one waited for her. Instead everyone walked out the vestibule door and down the stoop steps. Marietta was surprised to see Susie come out the basement door below the stoop.

"Susie knows what to buy. She picked out all the clothes we sent you in Italy," Paul explained. Susie was plump and short, hardly taller than Marietta. With narrow lips and hair severely pulled back in a tight comb across the top of her head, she was a ganglion of nerves, chewing gum with ferocious intensity all the way to the store and back. Every half hour her hands removed the spent piece of Spearmint from her mouth, rolled it in its original wrapper and dumped it in her handbag as though it were a garbage can. Robotically she pulled another stick from its pack and flicked it in her mouth. The scent permeated the air.

"The child needs party dresses and everyday clothes," Sofia said. "We'd best go to Macy's."

"A&S is cheaper." Teresa countered.

"She has to look good," Sofia cautioned.

"You pay for it, if you care so much," Teresa said.

Paul ignored his wife's conversation with her sister. He turned to Susie. "Where should we go first?" he asked.

"I'd go to Mays' Department Store." she said. Paul drove in that direction and parked the car. They returned with three different colored plaid dresses for every day, one blue chiffon party dress with lace that was so lovely Marietta couldn't believe that it would be hers, a pair of brown penny loafers for play, and one pair of black patent leather Mary Janes for Sundays. Susie also insisted on a straw hat with a wide brim and white ribbon for attending Mass, a matching child's purse that looked like an Easter basket and two pairs of white gloves exactly alike because children have a tendency to lose just one, she said, and the pair gets saved. For cold days, she favored a brown tweed cloth coat with a Peter Pan collar that would double for school and play. Teresa and Sofia spent thirty minutes picking out six pairs of socks. Teresa chose four plain cotton ones for everyday; Sofia, two nylon pairs trimmed in lace for special occasions. Marietta felt as though a puff of wind blew her from place to place as she tried on each outfit. No one bothered to ask what she liked. It didn't matter. She liked everything.

Paul glowed at her pleasure. Except for a brief period when he disappeared, he had been at Marietta's side guarding the clothes-shopping process carefully. After each selection, he stood on line in front of the cash register, pulled a billfold of money out of his pocket and paid the bill. Everyone went home feeling satisfied.

After dinner Paul took Marietta aside. "There's something I want to show you," he said. His hands held a large stack of papers bound together by a thick rubber band. "Do you see these? These are only the last six months of paperwork that had to be done for your passage to America." He pulled out one sheet from the bunch. "This one in particular is the most important. You can't read it now because you don't understand English. I will tell you what it says. It's a Congressional bill that was signed allowing you to enter the country as my legally adopted daughter. See here," he pointed with his finger, "here's your name. You can read that. I spent a lot of time and money to get you here. A Bill of Congress, for Pete's sake! That's what it took to bring you here."

"*Mi volevi, veramente?* You really wanted me?" she asked, surprised.

"For a long time I wanted you. God knows how long I have wanted a child. And now you're finally here."

"Thank you, *Papà*." Marietta's heart warmed and she felt more secure.

"*Papà*," she hesitated. "Where did you go for those fifteen minutes you left when we were shopping?"

"I sent a telegram to your mother. I told her you had arrived safely." At the mention of her mother, Marietta's body stiffened. She hadn't thought of her since she'd arrived. There was no room for her anymore.

85

Chapter Eight

The following week Marietta noted that Paul was dressed differently when he sat down for breakfast. He had shed the tan cotton shirt with the cigarette burn in the breast pocket, where he routinely stuffed his pack of Philip Morris. Gone were the loose, brown pants shiny in the seat from wear. Even his slippers went missing. He'd worn these clothes – house clothes, he called them – every day since Marietta's arrival. Today he wore his policeman's uniform. Everything shone, from the brimmed hat down to the highly polished shoes. The uniform transformed Paul, Marietta thought. He looked taller and slimmer and very important, reminding her of the policemen in Italy. When she walked toward the piazza, hand in hand with Anna, she often saw the *carabinieri* strutting down the streets, their guns and sticks swinging at their sides, their eyes and ears alert for prowlers and thieves. When families walked by, the officers lifted their plumed hats in greeting. They patted children on the head. They'd touched her head once and she imagined them strong, brave and superior to most men.

She looked up half expecting the same pat of the hand from Paul. Instead, he knelt on one knee. He took off his hat and placed it on her head. The hat was too big for her small frame and angled to the right, making her look like a child model posing in a magazine. He smiled.

"Would you like to hold my policeman's stick, too?" he asked. Marietta nodded. Lifting it from its holster, he put it in her hand. The wood was smooth and shiny like the hallway banister. She balanced it on the floor and held it at arm's length.

"Don't move," he instructed. Running into the next room, he returned with the camera he'd bought especially for her coming. "Smile," he said and then he snapped the picture. He removed the finished roll from the camera and put it in his pocket. "Would you like to go with me to the drugstore? I have time to drop it off and bring you back before I report to work."

"Yes, Papà," Marietta smiled again. The two were halfway down the stairs when Teresa called from the kitchen, speaking half in English and half in Italian.

"Paul, pick up a quart of milk and a loaf of bread for dinner on your way home."

"*Latte e pane*," Paul reiterated in Italian, so Marietta could understand. "These are your first days in America," he said as they walked hand-in-hand down the main avenue. "What would you like to know? What would you like to do? Think, and tell Papà. I will do my best to show you."

Marietta didn't have to think long. "In Italy, I was told I'd see things I had never seen before. People with dark skin and trains in the air high in the sky and deep underground. How do trains stay up and not fall down, Papà? And those underground, how do people get inside them? Aren't they afraid to go below the ground? And I have never eaten a banana or even seen one except in books."

Paul laughed, relishing her excitement and innocence. "Today, I'll show you some of these things," he said. Marietta believed it was the uniform that gave him the power. "There," he said, pointing up to what looked like metal on stilts. "There are your trains up in the sky." Marietta's eyes widened. Several charcoal-colored train cars, linked together like people holding hands, came to a loud stop. Doors slid open. Men, women and children got off and descended the stairs. Others climbed up the stairs and boarded the train. The doors banged shut and the train rolled on all within a matter of minutes. Underneath, cars and people whirred about, oblivious to the activity above. To Marietta, it seemed as if she were seeing heaven and earth close together. It disturbed her to see the iron stairway leading to the platform littered with candy wrappers, apple cores and bird droppings. The streets and trains she'd seen in Italy were spotless. Also, there were no sides to the rails on these train tracks, even though they were about thirty feet above the road. Was it safe?

Paul sensed her concern. "When you're careful, nothing bad happens." Then he leaned down to her ear and whispered, "Don't stare, but behind us is a family with dark skin." Marietta turned and saw a man, a woman and a little girl about her age. She was surprised to see they were dressed in clothes just like hers. Having never seen any other race but Italians, she had expected them to wear long robes, the way the ancient Egyptians did or no clothes at all if they truly came from the jungles of Africa, the way they were depicted in her history book. Except for the dark skin and fuller lips, they looked and acted just like her.

Paul stopped in front of a store with colorful sidewalk displays of every fruit imaginable. There was no need to go inside. Scales, bags and storeowner were all outdoors. The customers touched and tasted as much fruit as they wanted before loading it in bags and giving them to the vendor to weigh. The owner pulled out a pencil from behind his ear and in seconds computed the cost on the back of a brown paper bag. He placed the bills and coins he received from customers inside the large pocket of his apron and pulled from it any change that was due. Many customers spoke Italian, which made Marietta wonder whether America was simply an extension of Italy. Paul brought her in front of the large bin of bananas nestled between the pears and apples. He broke one off its bunch, peeled it half way and offered it to her.

"Taste it. Tell me if you like it." She took a bite.

"It's sweet," she said. Paul grabbed a large bunch and took out his wallet. The owner put up his hand.

"No charge for you. A gift for the *bambina*."

"*Grazie*," Paul said, putting away his money. They walked into the small grocery store next door and picked up the quart of milk for Teresa. They crossed the street and entered Gino's Bakery where he worked the ovens and his wife, Serafina, managed the cash register. She, too, refused payment.

"So tell me, how do you like America?" Gino asked, smiling at Marietta.

"*Mi piace. Papà mi fa vedere tante cose marvelose.* I like it. Papà is showing me many marvelous things."

"Your Papà, a very good man he ees...ees very important. Steeck with him and you do bene," Serafina said, patting Marietta on the shoulder. They started to head home when Paul remembered the roll of film. He pulled it out of his pocket, holding it in his hand until they entered the drugstore. Marietta wondered if that, too, would be free when it was time to pick it up. Once home Paul handed Teresa the milk and bread and bananas and kissed her goodbye on the cheek in one continuous motion. He bent down and gave Marietta a tight hug.

"Don't go," she said.

"I have to go, Marietta. It's my job. How else can I buy you all the things I want to give you? I'll rush right back at the end of my shift, I promise."

Marietta couldn't imagine what more she could have. All she wanted was his time and love. Standing at the kitchen door she watched him descend the hallway stairs. Then she ran back into the kitchen, through the bedroom, into the living room, finally reaching one of its long windows that faced the street and with one jerky motion pulled the drapes apart. From the street, Paul turned toward the house and looked up as if he knew she'd be there. He waved, then opened the car door and drove off. With Paul no longer in sight, Marietta returned to the kitchen.

"Sit here," Teresa said. "Now your Papà is gone, I can clean the house. He makes the place a pigsty, leaving a mess everywhere he goes." Marietta didn't like hearing the bitter tone in Teresa's voice. Didn't three people, now four with her coming, live here? Didn't they all contribute to the mess? She wasn't comfortable mentioning this to Teresa. She was as afraid of her as she'd been of Nonna Filomena. She sat in a corner, quietly watching Teresa gravitate to the dust rag as though it were a magnet. Once the tan flannel cloth was in her hand, Teresa swirled it across the mirror above the triple dresser. Holding the mirror firm with her left hand, she stretched her right arm up until her hand reached the top corners. She circled and buffed the same spots as if she could increase their luster. Marietta caught the vengefulness with which she moved, the vigorous pressure she applied stripping the parquet floors of their natural glow, as if she drew something from them, and the resignation in how she spread shellac on the wood to bring the shine back.

If Teresa would only sing like her cousin Rosaria while she cleaned, it'd put her in a better frame of mind, Marietta thought. She knew a song with the name Teresina in the lyrics but couldn't remember all the words. The ballad was about a young man who went to serenade his sweetheart, Teresina, under her window. When the girl ran down the stairs and out the door to be with him, her mother stuck her head out the window and called the daughter in. Some lyrics went through Marietta's head: *Sali sopra, Teresina. Lasci'andar quel mascalzon.* Come upstairs, Teresina. Let that scoundrel go. To which the young man replies: *Non sono un mascalzone. Neanche un delinquente. Son un figlio di un Tenente. Son venuto per far l'amor.* I'm not a rascal. Not even a delinquent. I'm the son of a lieutenant. I've come to woo you.

While Marietta enjoyed the memory of the song's upbeat rhythm, she wasn't sure Teresa would. To pass the time away, she delved further into her memories. She recalled what Stella had told her how it was that Teresa and Paul met and married. Apparently, when Teresa was eighteen years old and still in Italy, she'd received in the mail a notice of a marriage contract her father had signed with a family in Brooklyn. Within six months she came to America and married Paul. The only family member to attend the wedding was Teresa's father, as much a stranger to her as her new husband.

Now, watching her aunt move with such fury, Marietta wondered if Teresa's heart was broken at leaving her mother. Was she angry with her father for forcing her to marry a stranger, especially if she had someone else she loved? Suddenly, she felt sorry for her aunt. She got up from her chair.

"Can I help you with something, Aunt Teresa?" she offered.

"And have you do it wrong? Don't bother getting up. I'd only have to re-do it and make double work for myself. You'll mess up the house more than you've already done since you've come."

Marietta froze in her spot.

"Those damn cigarettes. He burns something all the time. Someday the whole place will go on fire. How I hope it does. It'll teach him good!" Marietta jumped from her seat as if the fire had already started. She was tired of hearing Paul criticized.

"Where's Aunt Sofia?" she asked meekly, thinking she could spend time with her.

"At the factory making men's pants," she said. That's why she has men on her mind. First she brings home this one, then that one. Each one's more awful than the last. *Madonna mia*, they don't even take off their shoes when they come into the apartment. She wants to get married and won't stop bringing 'the pants' home until we say yes. *È pazza.* Crazy she is. What does she want to get married for anyway? She doesn't know that it's better alone. Men always want what you can't give them. She's too old for children, anyway. *Ha quaranta-cinque anni. Mi fa schivo* – She's forty-five years old. It's shameful." The sides of her mouth curved down in disgust. "All the money we spent to bring her to America, to feed and clothe her. For what, so she can get married and leave us? A fine way to repay us! Ha, I should have stayed with my mother in Italy. Mamma warned me it would come to this."

Three hours later, Marietta's stomach began to growl but she knew enough to keep quiet. She had to wait for Teresa to finish the housework before lunch would be served. When she was finally done, Teresa slapped several pieces of salami between two slices of Wonder bread. She called it American bread to differentiate it from Gino's Italian loaf. Marietta had barely put her last morsel in her mouth when Teresa scooped up the plate.

"That's the trouble with eating. It makes more work," she said. After lunch Marietta thought Teresa would rest. Instead, she took a bundle of clean clothes, wet her fingers under the kitchen faucet and sprinkled drops of water over them. Then she plugged the iron in the wall socket. As the steam hissed, she pressed three of Paul's shirts, two housedresses, four handkerchiefs and the dress Marietta wore that week. Then she ironed the newly washed muslin sheets and pillowcases from the beds. How different this silver, electric iron was from Nonna's black one filled with hot coals! As different as Nonna and Teresa themselves.

The afternoon wore on too slowly. Marietta grew tired of doing nothing. She yearned for Paul. "Aunt Teresa, may I go and sit on the porch and wait for Papà?" she asked.

"And get your shoes dirty? Stay where you are. He'll come home soon enough." Marietta didn't know what to make of Teresa's preoccupation with shoes. After everyone's shoes were off their feet and neatly arranged on the small rug in the hallway, Teresa knelt down in front of them and scrubbed them clean. But a few days earlier, when a group of police officers from the precinct came to congratulate Paul and Teresa on the arrival of their new daughter, the men walked in without removing their shoes. Teresa's eyes immediately jumped to their feet, then their faces, then back to their feet several times in succession. She was torn between asking them to shed their shoes or let the dirty shoes stay in her clean house. Paul shot her a warning glance. She knew it was better to risk the dirt, which she could remove, rather than Paul's wrath, which she could not.

Marietta walked to the living room window, instead, in search of Paul's automobile outside. Within five minutes, it arrived. He got out of the car and saw Marietta's tiny face against the pane. He hoped she hadn't waited there all day. Running down the stairs to greet him at the vestibule door, she felt the blood rush through her body at Paul's bear hug.

After dinner Paul retired into the living room to read the newspaper. Marietta was sent with him. She could hear the water splash against the sink and gurgle down the drain. She was glad to be on the couch next to Paul rather than in the kitchen. She noticed how the couch had a throw cover on it just like Paul's chair. Then she saw Paul open the cabinet drawers and turn on the TV to the evening news. The screen was only twelve inches, but to Marietta it was large and magical. Soon Perry Como came on. The song "Wanted" was Paul's favorite and when he heard it, his eyes misted.

"Wanted," Paul said at the song's end. "That's what you are."

"Thank you, *Papà*."

"So, tell me. What did you do all day?" A curve formed between his lap and open arms, invitingly. She crouched comfortably in it.

"Aunt Teresa cleaned the house. I offered to help but she said no. I enjoyed seeing how the iron worked as she pressed your shirts." She left out the parts in which Teresa complained about him.

"Marietta," he said with a trace of sadness. "You call me *Papà* so easily and I love it. But if I am your *Papà*, then Aunt Teresa is your Mamma. How does it look to others when you refer to me as *Papà* but call her 'Aunt Teresa?' I want you to call her Mamma from now on."

It was easy for Marietta to refer to Paul as *"Papà."* Her own father had hardly lived with her. But for Teresa to be called "Mamma," something lay in its path. That something was Stella. "I can't, *Papà*," she said, finally.

"It would make me so happy," Paul urged.

"But my mother in Italy, what do I do about her? How do I explain her?" she countered.

"You haven't even written to her."

It was true. *Write me every day when you get to America.* The words echoed in Marietta's ears. *Si, Mamma.* She had promised, mechanically, not knowing what "when you get to America" meant. Now that she was in America, Marietta felt cut off from her mother, from Italy, from all that had gone before, as though the umbilical cord had been severed again, this time by Stella herself. No number of words on a piece of paper traveling miles across the Atlantic Ocean could bring them back together or restore what they had before. And what would Marietta say to the woman who threw her away? What *could* she say? – Only, *why, Mamma, why did you give me away?* How can gold, clothes and a dream called America be more important than a mother's love for her daughter? No, she had no mother. Not Stella and certainly not bitter Aunt Teresa who didn't want her.

Marietta began to cry. Paul reached in his pocket for his handkerchief and handed it to her.

94

"If you really love me, you must call her 'Mamma,'" he repeated.

She nodded, but her thoughts were not with Teresa. They were with Stella.

Chapter Nine

The next morning Paul once again dressed in uniform, which meant another day of sitting and watching Aunt Teresa clean. Marietta didn't know how she would bear the slow passing of the hours. Worse, she was expected to call her Mamma. She decided to forestall it as long as she could. If she eliminated the words "Aunt Teresa," the ones that apparently bothered Paul, no one would notice she wasn't calling her "Mamma." Especially Paul. And if she spoke to her aunt only when spoken to, it would reduce the number of mistakes. Today would be a good day to stay out of her way, she told herself. She would pretend she was back in Signorina Notalli's class and had to write about her adventures in America. She'd omit the whole mother issue and recount only the things Paul had shown her: the baker, the fruit man, the black family, the elevated train and bananas. But Paul had different plans.

"Put on your Sunday dress. We're going to see Mother Superior."

"You're not going to work?" Marietta said, pleased yet fearful at the sound of the word mother.

"Don't be frightened. She's the principal of St. Margaret Academy, the best private school in Brooklyn. Politicians' children go there. You're too smart to waste your time at home." His eyes inadvertently went to his wife. He retrieved them quickly, realizing his indiscretion. Teresa was clearing the breakfast dishes but caught the slip. She turned her back to him and spat in his plate. Marietta was appalled to see the arched trajectory of white mucous leave her aunt's mouth and land into the dish. Paul had to have heard the loud puff of air that propelled it forward even if he hadn't seen it. Her body shook in fear lest they'd argue. But Paul's attention stayed fixed on Marietta. "Don't you want to go to school?" he asked in mild frustration.

"Oh yes," Marietta said. School was the very thing she wanted. In school she wouldn't be with Aunt Teresa. She could get lost in the extraordinary life of learning, and be as ordinary as the other students, hidden behind books. She felt years, not days, had passed since she had last touched a piece of chalk or saw the black stain of ink on her fingers, and she longed to return to a world that exhilarated her mind and made her forget pain.

Parking the car directly in front of the school's main doors, Paul opened the glove compartment, pulled out his Patrolman on Duty sign and displayed it prominently on the dashboard. Marietta looked out the window and stared at the school name written in bold letters on the face of the building, a massive four-story brownstone.

"Are you sure I won't live here?" Marietta asked, not knowing whether she should be alarmed or relieved.

"No," he assured her. "The nuns told me that at one time rich families lived here. When they moved away or died, they donated their homes to the Sisters of St. Joseph for the purpose of building a small, private school that would stress academics. The nuns had the interior gutted to make classrooms and hallways from first grade through twelfth. The two houses in front of you are for the high school. There are two in back for the elementary school, where you will start."

"Why don't we go in the other side, then?"

"This is the entrance for visitors," he whispered, knocking on the high wooden doors. A tall, slim nun dressed in the Order's black and white habit answered. Her round, white bib, strongly starched, bobbed up and down under her neck. She swung open the door and leaned back to let them in. Paul removed his police cap and held it flat across his chest. He introduced himself. The nun stared at the cap more than his face.

"Mother Superior is expecting you," she said with an admiring smile. "Follow me." Walking through the entrance hall she climbed the three steps to a larger landing, then four stairs to the right until she reached a wide hallway with highly polished wooden floors. The nun stopped in front of closed door where the words "PRINCIPAL'S OFFICE" were carved on a slab of wood. She gave the door a soft knock, opened it and motioned Paul and Marietta to enter. Behind a giant desk stood a wisp of a woman, frail and wrinkled, dressed exactly like the young sister who'd ushered them in. The desk glistened under the ceiling light.

"Sister Augustine, this is Officer Marino," the young nun said. She bowed her head slightly as if to apologize for the intrusion and, closing the door behind her, slid out of the room as effortlessly as she had entered it.

"Good morning," Sister Augustine said. With a shaky hand, she pointed to the two chairs directly in front of her for them to sit. "What can I do for you today?"

"Pleased to meet you," Paul answered, swirling his hat in his hand. "I'm not a learned man," he began. "A sixth grade education hardly counts. But when I was twelve my father died and I chose work over school. I got a job at the Brooklyn Navy Yard where I unloaded packages from boats that docked there. Every day I delivered them from store to store. I soon came under the watchful eye of Officer Murphy, a strapping, six-foot Irishman who patrolled those streets. Officer Murphy took a liking to me. Knowing that my mother was widowed as his mother had been, he often gave me fatherly advice. 'Go back to school. Make something of yourself. Get a job with a higher purpose than just making a living.' I can't tell you how often I heard these words from Officer Murphy's lips. I didn't listen to him. I copied him instead. As soon as I was of age, I took the policeman's exam.

I wasn't a good student as you might guess, but while I didn't score high, I passed. Had my father lived, he couldn't have been prouder of me than Officer Murphy! That's thirty years ago." He shook his head and fingered the band of his hat, as if he, himself, couldn't believe how quickly the time had passed.

"Take the last few years, for example. I've been studying to become captain. The position would get me off the streets, where it can get pretty dangerous even when you're careful. I've taken the test four times. Four times I've failed. That's because I didn't stay in school. But am I giving up? No, sirree! I mean no, ma'am! Oh, excuse me, no disrespect. I mean, no Sister! I'll take the test again when it comes up later in the year. See, I don't give up – just as I didn't give up wanting a child."

He turned toward Marietta and sighed. "My wife and I haven't been able to have children of our own, but God knew how much I wanted one. He answered my prayers by sending Marietta. She's my wife's blood so she's like our own. And now I want nothing but the best for her, including her education. That's why we've come to your school, because of its fine reputation."

Marietta understood none of what Paul had said. But he and Sister Augustine looked in her direction. They nodded their heads and smiled. She knew she was very much the center of the conversation.

"Officer Marino, you must understand that it's the middle of the term and your daughter doesn't speak English. Wouldn't you rather wait until after the summer and she knows our language better?" Sister Augustine explained.

His eyes held hers. "I'm willing to make it worth your while for the three months left in the school year," he said. His hand touched the large clip that clasped the stack of money in his pocket. He took it out and, counting one bill at a time, piled it on the principal's shiny desk. Marietta had never seen so much money. She didn't know it equaled a year's tuition. Sister Augustine looked up at the ceiling for guidance. Paul immediately added three one hundred dollar bills to the pile. She smiled. He smiled back and Marietta knew that whatever Paul had tried to do succeeded.

"Welcome to our school," Sister Augustine said, patting Marietta gently on the shoulder. She wasn't much taller than the child, and had to look up at Paul when speaking to him. "Bring her tomorrow morning at 8:30 sharp. We'll put her in first grade to see how quickly she learns the language. From her progress, we'll determine what steps to take."

The next morning, before he went to work, Paul and Marietta were back at the school, this time on the elementary side. Sister John Francis met them by the schoolyard gate. Paul spoke to the Sister in words Marietta couldn't understand and then he bent down and kissed his daughter's cheek.

"*Ritorno alle tre*," he said to Marietta and then to the nun, "I'll come back at three." Marietta watched him drive off, waving goodbye. The sound of a girl's scream made her turn toward the middle of the playground. She'd caught the ball her friend had thrown and was no longer the "monkey in the middle." A bell rang and Sister John Francis took Marietta's hand. She brought her to the front of a line of chatting six-year-olds. At the teacher's presence, the children grew silent. Marietta noticed that she stood a head taller than the rest. With hands clasped, the two led the line into the building and entered a large classroom much like the one Marietta had experienced in Castellaneta. The nun walked Marietta to the first seat in the center row, directly in front of her desk. She motioned for her to sit. The rest of the class found their places but never took their eyes off the strange, new girl. They imagined her important, sitting so close to their teacher and being bigger than they were.

Sister John Francis began to check homework. She walked around the room to each desk while the class wrote their spelling words five times each in their notebook. Left with nothing to do, Marietta examined her surroundings. The four windows were opened wide and she could hear robins chirping. At the center of the wall above the blackboard, behind the teacher's desk, was a large crucifix. The words, "For God So Loved the World That He Gave His Only Son" scrolled in italics across the corkboard to the left and right of the crucifix. Marietta liked the way the letters swirled although she didn't know what they meant. Nor did she understand anything of what was said in class. But the familiar smell of chalk and the blackness of the board vitalized her.

Her thoughts traveled back to the only school she knew, the one in Castellaneta where the building was a large, rectangular, two-story structure that served the neighboring towns as well. She pictured Signorina Notalli, slim and still green from university, at the front of the room. Her enthusiasm made up for what she lacked in experience. Marietta remembered that writing compositions had been her favorite activity. Inside the covers of a marble notebook, she could be a princess living in a palace with the king and queen who loved her and wanted her trained to rule the realm after they passed on. Sometimes she was a child who fell down a deep canyon full of wolves. Lions found her shivering and hungry. They brought her berries and carried her to a stream to drink the water, their warmth and strength restoring her. When she was healed, the lions led her up the mountain where she could spot Nonna's house and return safely home. Other times, she was a mother raising twelve children while her husband worked on the farm, or, she was the town doctor healing all who got sick.

Signorina Notalli taught the class to compose stories in their minds before putting them down on paper. Students had to fold the page in half, lengthwise, with sentences starting on the left side and stopping at the crease until they reached the bottom, then, continuing on at the top right of the crease, like the columns of a newspaper. "Never write on the back of the page, or the ink will penetrate and mar the beauty and visibility of the words. The Italian language is poetry," she said. "We must not do anything that takes away its music." Marietta excelled at writing compositions, bested only by a new girl named Dora who, when she read her stories, dramatized them as if they were plays. Even Marietta enjoyed listening to them. She envied Dora, not just for her writing, but also for the poise and confidence she exuded, as if she owned the ground she walked on.

"Marietta," the teacher said. "There's room in the class for both of you. We want everyone to write as well as you and Dora."

"Marietta," she heard again, only this time it was Sister John Francis who spoke. With the palm of her hand, Sister motioned for her to stand. She put both hands on the child's shoulders and gently turned her around to face the class. "Boys and girls, I'd like you to meet Marietta Marino who has recently come from Italy. She doesn't speak our language. I'll be working with her until she learns it. How many of you would like to help me teach her?" All hands went up. "Let's first give her a big hello."

"Hello, Marietta," the class chimed in unison. Marietta smiled. That word she knew. She couldn't help but notice how young and angelic these faces were. Their fine hair and soft features reminded her of Pia. About half the class had blond hair. A few had hair the color of rust while the rest had brown or black. Their eyes so transparently blue or green shone like precious jewels, their skin soft and tender and full, like a baby's. Instead of the four-year difference, Marietta felt decades stood between them. They were innocent, untouched, and she... she'd already been half-way around the world.

The class sat in seats alternated by gender, the girls in maroon jumpers and white blouses and the boys in navy-blue pants and white shirts. Suddenly the pink dress Marietta wore stood out. She wanted desperately to look like them. But her uniform would not arrive for another week. Had she stayed in Italy, she'd be wearing Veronica's black satin uniform. It didn't need to be ordered. It was already there with Nonna.

The class was given a ditto of simple arithmetic problems, about thirty of them. Marietta could compute them in two or three minutes. From the way the others fidgeted in their seats, she knew it would take them longer. She wanted to help but Sister John Francis pulled up a chair and motioned her to sit beside her. She pointed to herself, then, to Marietta, then, to her lips and back to Marietta's lips, and in sign language explained how the English lessons were to be conducted.

"Book," she said, touching the dictionary on her desk. On a piece of paper, she wrote the number "one," then the word "book," spacing and pronouncing each letter. "Book," she repeated, enunciating slowly in front of Marietta's face, forcing the child to note the curvature of her lips, each distinct sound falling unhampered on the girl's ears. Pointing to the book and her lips, she instructed Marietta to mimic her by touching the book and saying the word at the same time.

"Book," Marietta said, fingering its spine, her own spine tingling with nostalgic pleasure. She repeated the sound and motion three times. They continued the same pattern with as many objects as they could touch from where they sat. When they had exhausted their supply, they rose and circled the room. Window, glass, wall – Sister John Francis named every object she could find. Marietta repeated each word three times, until finally they returned to their starting point. Then the teacher pointed to the words she had written on the sheet of paper on Marietta's desk. She drew a descriptive sketch for each word. She waved an imaginary pencil in the air and held up five fingers. Marietta understood she was to write each word five times.

Orange Peels and Cobblestones

When it was time for lunch, the class formed two lines and, in silence, Sister led them to the cafeteria. There she picked up lunch for Marietta and herself, then clasped the child's hand and together they walked back to the classroom. In sign language, she explained that they would eat in the room and continue to learn more English words. She twirled her finger around Marietta's sandwich, pronounced it and wrote the word on a clean sheet of paper. She pointed to the white slices of bread. Then, to what lay between them. She did the same with the milk container she had brought for Marietta before she bit into her own food. With the same twirl of her finger, she delineated "sandwich, bread and ham." She wrote the words on paper. Marietta identified the items by pronouncing the English words once more. After they ate the objects they identified, that part of the lesson was over. They reviewed the morning's words until they heard the loud shrieks of children at play.

"Recess," Sister John Francis announced. She pointed to Marietta and herself. "We'll go, too," she said. Outside, children's voices thundered as if they had been pressurized in a bottle and suddenly opened. Sister brought Marietta near a group of girls jumping rope, hoping she would mingle. Marietta stood apart, amazed at the variety of activities taking place in the playground. To the left, girls were tossing a pink ball to each other. Some bounced it off a penny. Others played hopscotch and, to her surprise, threw rocks in the boxes instead of orange peels. To the right, boys swung balls with wooden bats. Others shot a basketball into a hoop. Some simply stood together in a circle and talked, laughing heartily at what was said – all under watch of their teachers who fingered their rosary beads and crucifixes hanging from their waists.

For four weeks Sister John Francis and Marietta worked together naming every piece of matter they could find. Marietta pronounced the words flawlessly almost the first time she heard them. Sometimes she hesitated, stammering, trying to recall words they had already dealt with. Sister seemed incredibly patient. Just like Nonna, Marietta thought. When enough weeks passed and it was time for Marietta to face the Principal to prove her proficiency, Sister Augustine took a book off her bookshelf and randomly opened it. "Can you read the first paragraph?" she asked. Marietta read the words flawlessly. "Why there's not even an accent!" she beamed. "Sister John Francis, you have done a fine job. Now it's time for Marietta to finish the school year in the fourth grade. And at recess, leave her free to mingle with the other children."

Sister's face fell. "A little more one-on-one instruction would help her greatly." She wasn't ready to let go.

"No. I have heard her speak and read. It is time."

In the month of May, Brooklyn bloomed. As Marietta walked the five blocks to school, she noticed that the oak and maple trees were past the budding stage. Like a newborn baby, they had shed their blood-colored birth coat. Roses surrounded the life-size statue of the Blessed Mother in the corner of the school grounds near the front gate. They stood stiffly closed in the morning chill but gently open in the afternoon sun. Marietta grew more comfortable in her environment. With a renewed sense of security, she fought hard to forget her past and forged forward.

"Hi," Marietta said one morning to a girl who stood at the entrance of the school building. She had smiled the day before as they bumped into one another in the hallway. Their classrooms were next to each other.

"Aren't you the new girl from Italy who couldn't speak English?"

"Yes," Marietta blushed. "But I can speak it now. Sister helped me." Her eyes instinctively turned toward the spot where Sister John Francis often stood. Sister was there and met her glance, half expecting her, waiting, just in case she was needed. Marietta turned her attention back to the girl.

Line-up was fifteen minutes away and she didn't want to stand by herself. "Do you want to play hopscotch?" she asked. "I've got chalk."

"I can't. I'm waiting for Annette. We always play together," the girl said. Marietta tried not to show her disappointment. "I can talk to you until she gets here, though. What's your name?"

"Marietta."

"Mine's Jean."

"That's a pretty name. When I grow up and have children, I'm going to call one of them Jean." The name seemed very American, Marietta thought.

"I never liked it much. It's too short. I always wished for a longer name like Elizabeth or Kathleen. They're my sisters' names. I like it when my mother gets mad at my sisters and calls them Eeeeliiizabeth or Kaaaathleeen. With me it's Jean if she loves me and Jean if she's angry with me. I can never tell how she feels when she calls me." Then she pulled up the sleeve of her blue cardigan and looked at the round Mickey Mouse watch on her wrist. "It's almost time for the bell. I guess Annette's going to be absent today. Let's walk together to the line and be partners, okay? By the way, do you have any brothers or sisters?"

"I-I-I, yes, w-w-well," Marietta stammered. She hadn't expected this question. Jean looked confused. Marietta saw how foolish she must have sounded. She had a mental flash of her life with Paul and Teresa and saw no children but herself. She wanted to explain but didn't know where to begin. "No," she said finally. Immediately she knew she'd betrayed Pia. The line-up bell rang and Marietta couldn't have been more grateful. She hoped Jean would blame the language barrier for her inability to answer such a simple question more directly. How could she explain something she didn't understand?

Yes, she had a sister. But at home where she lived with the two people she now must call Mommy and Daddy, there was no one but her. If she said she had a sister, someone might ask if they slept in the same room or if they got along or fought a lot. She couldn't answer those questions. She didn't want to answer them. It hurt too much to think about them. Where she lived Pia didn't exist. So, yes, she was an only child.

Without knowing how she got there, Marietta found herself inside her classroom, sitting at her desk, pencil in hand, heading her paper, ready to copy the morning's arithmetic problems that served as review. She didn't remember lining up outside or walking into the building and climbing the three flights of stairs, or entering the classroom. She didn't remember morning prayers or the salute to the flag. She thought only of Pia whose existence she had just denied.

Chapter Ten

In September, Sister Augustine placed Marietta in the fifth grade. When Paul heard she'd remain there for the rest of the year, he wasn't happy with the news. She'd still be a year behind. He wanted her on grade level.

"I don't want the other students to torment her the way they tormented me when I repeated fifth grade. They called me retarded because I was bigger than they were. I hated school all the more," he explained.

"Nonsense. Everyone can see she's bright. And she's about the same height as the girls in fifth grade. No one will suspect she's older. The stability of being in the same class for a full year will allow her to establish some friendships with other girls. In school, she's very quiet. She keeps too much to herself. You must be aware how lonely and withdrawn she is. She'll benefit more by staying in one place than moving midstream just to be in the right grade. We'll tutor her with some sixth grade math, science and history two days a week. Next year she'll start seventh grade, just where she should be, and will again complete the year. The continuity will give her a sense of belonging."

"But if she's not happy there, you'll reconsider, right?" he persisted.

"Yes. We'll reevaluate. We'll do what's best for Marietta."

To her surprise Marietta adjusted well in fifth grade. The girls still played with dolls and didn't put on airs the way the sixth graders did. The more she observed them, the more she found she didn't like sixth grade behavior. They wore nylon stockings and constantly flirted with the boys in class. In the morning, as they waited in the schoolyard for their teacher to arrive and tell them to line up, they no longer played jump-rope or monkey in the middle. They preferred to huddle in groups of four or five in remote corners of the schoolyard. They never talked to fifth graders. Their eyes were on the boys. It seemed they couldn't wait to grow up.

Marietta, on the other hand, felt she had grown up too quickly. The move from Italy to America weighed heavily on her shoulders. Gone were the carefree days under the hot sun with Lucia beside her. Now she found herself alone. Why did she feel so guilty much of the time? Problems plagued her. Was she betraying Stella and Pia? Would she call Teresa "Mom?" Paul had demanded it. No, it was Stella who'd made it happen in the first place. Had Stella not given her away, she would not be in this predicament.

If only there were someone like Nonna or Lucia that she could talk to. Then her mind wouldn't be in such a jumble. What Marietta wouldn't give to be back on the cobblestone street with an orange peel in her pocket! She longed for it like parched earth yearns for rain. In America whom could she trust? Paul? If she let her guard down, he might abandon her, the way Stella had. No, she couldn't risk it. She wasn't capable of trusting anyone anymore.

As a result she avoided the sixth grade girls whenever possible. One brisk Monday morning, however, she was thrown in their midst when the fifth and sixth grade classes were detained outside the school building due to a false fire alarm. While on line, Marietta overheard a sixth grade girl talk about a party she had hosted in her basement over the weekend. Boys had been invited as well as girls. They had played spin the bottle. Not familiar with the game, her ears perked up. From their conversation, she gathered that it was played with a friend. She leaned her ears more closely, hoping to learn the rules so she might play it with her own classmates during recess. Her eyes almost popped out of her head upon hearing what they said: *Boys and girls sat on the floor in a circle with an empty soda bottle in the middle. A girl spun the bottle. When the bottle stopped spinning, and its mouth pointed at some boy, that girl and boy had to kiss. Not only that, the kiss took place in a dark closet.*

"Thank God, Mom and Dad never came down the stairs to check on us. We would have been mortified," the sixth grade girl exclaimed.

"And grounded," added her friend.

Boys and girls, kisses in dark closets? Marietta couldn't believe it. Didn't they realize that playing "grownup games" was dangerous? Stella tried to be grown up while still a child. If she had remained a child a little longer, she might have married someone more dependable, someone in her hometown, someone that would have kept Marietta in Castellaneta.

Marietta had much to sort out before she could think about boys. She couldn't socialize with the sixth grade girls. Instead, she made friends with two classmates - blue-eyed, blonde-haired Susan O'Rourke and green-eyed, red-haired Terry Ryan. Each morning before class, Susan, Terry and Marietta met in the playground and compared homework. If they disagreed, they'd go over their pages to find out who had made the mistake and then they fixed it. Not until every response matched, did they talk about other things. The girls, to Marietta's delight, were rich in brothers and sisters, grandparents and cousins, aunts and uncles as she used to be. Weekends boasted of Saturday picnics, family dinners and birthday parties. Marietta envied them. There wasn't much she could tell them. Paul and Teresa's house lacked all semblance of extended family. And of course, she couldn't share the intimate details of her life in Italy. If she did, how would she hide the fact that her mother didn't want her anymore? How could she tell her friends she had a sister when there were no signs of her presence at home? How could she recount fun times with cousins when they had strange, non-American names and they were now erased from her life? She knew she was lying by omission but, she felt, her life in America was a lie. She should be in Castellaneta, with Stella and Pia and with Nonna and Lucia.

When the closing bell rang and the girls packed their books to go home, Marietta felt a great sense of loss. She pictured Susan and Terry walking in the door into the welcoming arms of their mothers and younger brothers and sisters. Upon entering her house, on the other hand, Marietta went straight to her room where she started her homework. When it was done, she read from one of the five novels she took out of the library every week until it was time for dinner or bed. The books filled the holes in her life. They helped her avoid thoughts of Italy and they kept her out of Teresa's way. It was only when Paul returned from work that Marietta sparked. She'd hear him come in from his beat and walk directly to her desk where she sat. He kissed her hello and her lights turned on. Then he left her to complete her work.

"Don't go, Papà," she wanted to tell him. "Stay and talk to me. Tell me about your day. Ask me how mine was. I need to know I matter to someone the way I mattered to Nonna." But he never stayed and she never had the chance to tell him. She watched him go into his bedroom and close the door so he could change his clothes. Then he retreated to his chair in the living room with the newspaper and read it cover to cover until Teresa called him for dinner.

But at the table he was full of words. "If I could have worked at school the way you do, I would have passed the Captain's test years ago rather than still hope to pass it someday," Paul said cutting his steak.

"Don't give up, Papà. I'll help you study for it. You'll pass."

"It's not as easy as you make it sound."

"When you study it's very easy to get a good grade on a test."

"You like learning. I never did. When I was your age, my friends and I used to pass the bakery on the way to school. We stopped with the excuse that we were hungry even though our mothers had given us a good breakfast. We'd go in the store and buy doughnuts. Jelly ones and sugar ones and cream-filled ones, and crullers of all shapes and sizes. Boy, did I love those crullers! Jesus, we could get three for a nickel then! We'd go to the park and not come home until school was over. By the time my parents found out how many days I'd missed, it was too late to make up the year. School was always a struggle. It left a sour taste in my mouth. How could I like it when I didn't do well?" He patted Marietta proudly on the head, as if to insure she was really there and not like the cruller that was gone after he ate it.

Sofia and Teresa shook their heads when they saw Marietta's report card. They thought their eyes were tricking them. They couldn't understand how she came home with hundreds on her tests. One Saturday afternoon, after Marietta had finished reading *Little Women*, Teresa challenged her. "You read the whole book?" she asked.

"Yes, I just finished it."

"*No, impossibile.* It has too many pages."

"But I did. I read every page, from beginning to end,"

"*Impossibile,*" she insisted. "You must have only turned the pages."

Marietta gave up trying to convince her. She knew even if the truth stared Teresa in the face, she wouldn't rejoice in anything the child did. She'd only criticize.

"I have something to say," Sofia said suddenly changing the subject. "Sal and I set our wedding date." Marietta was all set to smile at the news when Teresa violently pushed her chair back and got up from the table.

"If you get married," Teresa told Sofia, "don't expect me to come."

"I'm not getting any younger," she snapped back. "You've nixed all my previous boyfriends. I won't let you stop me this time. I'll elope if I have to." She ran out of the room angry. Marietta followed her. She'd rather face Sofia's angry mood than Teresa's testy demeanor.

"Are you really going to elope?" she asked.

"No. I said that to scare my sister. We've already booked the church with the local priest and put a deposit on a hall in Bay Ridge. I need her. Who else but Paul can walk me down the aisle? My father's dead and my mother's thousands of miles away." Her lower lip quivered. She looked afraid.

It struck a chord with Marietta. "Aunt Sofia, why do marriages bring problems?"

"They always do," she said. "But this time, I'm going to get my way."

The next evening, while Teresa stepped outside to throw out the garbage, Sofia approached Paul as he sat in the living room reading the evening paper. She took a deep breath. "I'd love it if you'd walk me down the aisle and give me away," she said. She waited, hoping her brother-in-law would be honored, hoping he could sway Teresa. Paul dropped his paper on his lap, patiently. He looked across the room into the distance, past Sofia, as if he could see through her, beyond the years that had occurred since her coming to America. Sofia had always been more like a daughter in his eyes. She'd lived in their house since she stepped foot on American soil. Paul had spoken to the owner of the sewing factory on his beat to secure a job for her. Though he couldn't help her study when she was applying for American citizenship, he drove her to the Court for each of the three attempts it took her to pass the exam. Without him and Teresa, Sofia had no one in America. How could he refuse her? Where else could she go? But with Teresa so adamantly opposed, his hands were tied.

Marietta could see the struggle going on in Paul's head from the way his eyes moved. The long silence alarmed Sofia. She feared he'd side with Teresa. She decided to play the only card she had left, the one she had saved for last. She didn't want to use it for it would mean sharing the limelight on her special day. "I would also like Marietta to be the flower girl at the wedding."

Paul's face instantly brightened. "Leave it to me. I'll find a way to get your sister to agree," he said. The image of Marietta dressed in a long gown with a bouquet of flowers in her hands as she walked down the church aisle filled him with delight. He knew he had to use all the skills his marriage brought him plus the diplomacy of a policeman to sway Teresa.

"How will it look if we don't show up at the wedding?" he said to his wife that night. "People will say we have no heart. We have to go for our own sakes, to show that we're generous enough to give Sofia a fine wedding as if she were our own child." Each night he alternated the order of the sentences but basically reiterated the same message so that every morning Teresa woke up with a pounding headache. After five days, Teresa could stand it no longer. She caved in, as long as he stopped talking to her about the wedding.

"You'll have a beautiful long dress and be the first to walk down the aisle. All eyes will be on you. Then, on to the football wedding," he said privately to Marietta.

"Football wedding?" she didn't get the connection.

"It's not a sit-down dinner with waiters serving food as they do in a restaurant. At the reception, the table is filled with rolls and sandwiches of different cuts of cold meats such as roast beef, ham, bologna and salami. The sandwiches are already prepared and wrapped. You can ask another guest to throw you one if he's closer to the table before the kind you like is gone. Just like a football," he explained.

When the wedding day arrived and the vows finally were taken, it was hard to know who beamed more, Sofia or Paul. Despite Teresa's predictions that it might rain and that Sal would definitely leave her stranded at the altar, Sofia looked radiant in a princess-style gown as she walked out of the church, arm in arm with her new husband. But it was Marietta who got all the attention. She wore a long voile dress of pink organza and carried a white basket of matching rose petals with pink and white streamers hanging from the sides. A crown of fresh roses lay on her head. As she floated down the aisle, she carried the eye of every guest.

"There she is. That's the adopted girl," they whispered to each other when she led the wedding party into the reception hall. When Paul twirled her across the dance floor, everyone ooohed and aaahed.

"She came from Italy not quite a year ago. You'd never know it to hear her speak," they shouted above the music as Paul made his rounds at each table with Marietta at his side.

"Why it's unheard of to learn a language so quickly," said another.

"Say something so I can hear whether you have an accent or not," one guest asked. Marietta's mouth went dry. She could speak volumes to answer Sister's questions in school, but here she couldn't think of one thing to say other than "hello."

"Well then, say something in Italian. I heard you don't speak a dialect, but the Italian spoken in Rome. Is that true?" asked another.

"Non so che dire. I don't know what to say," she said, hoping it would satisfy her audience. She looked up at Paul. Her eyes begged him to take her away. She didn't want to be on display. But Paul reveled in the attention.

"She's shy," he explained.

Later that night, with the wedding over, Marietta reflected on the day's events. She didn't like how uncomfortable the guests had made her feel. She wasn't a museum piece for them to stare at, half Italian, half American with a foot in both worlds. She was different from Teresa who blended Italian with English, creating a language of her own. For the aunt the word *is* became *ets*, *cake* turned into *kekera* and *tomato sauce* was *ragu*. She usually communicated with fingers, arms and body parts rather than with words, a style that so embarrassed Marietta, she didn't want to ask friends to her house. Also, Teresa was not discreet. No matter who was present, she nagged Marietta about writing to Stella. Her friends didn't know about Stella. What would they think if they heard Teresa say, "Why you *no* write to your mother?"

It was pointless to explain anything to Teresa, much less why Marietta still hadn't been able to bring herself to write to Stella. Yet she realized that the price for not writing was steep. It meant she had no contact with Nonna. And for Marietta, that was heartbreaking. Finally, one day she screwed up the nerve to write. *"Cara Mamma,"* she began. The Italian language unearthed like an ancient relic. *"Come stai? Io sto bene.* How are you? I am fine. *M'imparo tanto a scuola.* I learn a lot in school. *Ho certi amici.* I have several friends. *Mia sorella come sta?* How is my sister? *La mancho tanto.* I miss her very much. *Mando baci alla Nonna, il Nonno, Lucia e tutti i miei cugini, zii e zie.* I send kisses to grandmother, grandfather, Lucia and all my cousins, aunts and uncles. *Baci a te, Marietta.* Kisses for you, Marietta."

She left the envelope on the kitchen table. She knew Teresa wanted to add a few lines herself even though, with the limited formal education she'd received, it would take her an hour to write them. She'd boast about the new bike Paul gave Marietta on her birthday, the new furniture and curtains for her room now that Sofia was married and had moved into the

116

apartment downstairs. *Le cose che tu, Stella, non potevi dare mai-* the things you, Stella, could never give.

"*E* you *Papà?* Why you no write him, eh?" Teresa surprised Marietta the next day.

"Why would I write to *Papà* when he's right here?" Marietta looked confused. Teresa laughed snidely as if she were privy to secret information. "I *no* mean him." She pointed to Paul. "He *no* your real father. I mean my brother, your real *Papà.* You know he come soon."

"Come soon? Here, to America?" Marietta turned white. She remembered Stella telling her she and Pia would be coming and she hadn't believed it. Her father was the last person she expected to see.

"*Ma, si.* But, yes," Teresa nodded. "Why you think I say okay to the wedding? I make the one you call "*Papà*" do for my brother what he did for you."

A chill ran through Marietta's body. So that's how Sofia's wedding went on smoother than expected. Paul had to trade off something he wanted for something Teresa wanted. And she wanted her brother in the United States.

The thought of having two fathers in America terrified Marietta. How would she differentiate between them when they were both in the same room? Would she call each one "*Papà?*" Real *Papà* and adopted *Papà?* First *Papà* and second *Papà?* In the end, she decided to use the two languages to tell them apart. Antonio was "*Papà*" and Paul became "Daddy." One thing was certain, though. She still couldn't tell anyone in school.

Six months later, Antonio's plane landed at the same airport where Marietta had arrived. Paul, Teresa and Sofia went to meet him. Marietta had begged off. She had a unit test in math and her teacher had said no one would be excused unless there was a grave reason and if she had to devise a make-up test, it would be twice as hard as the original.

Orange Peels and Cobblestones

Marietta decided that going to pick up a father who'd been absent much of her life did not constitute a grave reason. "How will it sound to my teacher if I say my father is arriving from Italy when my father is already here?" Marietta reasoned with Paul. "She'll be confused." He agreed.

Coming home from school that day, she entered the kitchen afraid of what she'd find. Teresa, Sofia and their brother sat together talking, animated like the three children they once were. The kitchen smelled wonderful. The fragrance of garlic, onion, parsley and meat marinating in tomato sauce wafted through the air. Teresa had outdone herself. She'd cooked a batch of her ragu with meatballs usually reserved for Sundays. There were pieces of beef and pork so tender that the meat fell off the bone when the fork touched them. Teresa had eyes only for Antonio, and she stood over him protectively as he sat comfortably at the table. With a large spoon, she poured a generous portion of sauce over the ziti. In the meantime, Sofia pulled out the silver espresso pot to make the demitasse coffee. Marietta was always fascinated by how the boiling water defied gravity by passing through the middle compartment that held the dense coffee grinds and landed in the upper chamber, dark and delicious. Sofia lit the burner and waited. Its aroma intoxicated the room. The two sisters offered their brother every food in the house. He dined with gusto, as if he hadn't eaten since they last saw each other thirty years before.

Teresa finally noticed Marietta with her schoolbag in one hand and a note from the teacher addressed to her parents in the other. *"Ecco tuo Papà* – Here is your father," she said. She had one eye on Marietta and the other on Paul, who had emerged from the bedroom. For a moment, Marietta deliberated which father she should give the note to. She gave it to Paul. He could read English.

"Marietta earned 100%- a perfect score- in this morning's math test. She is a pleasure to have in class," Paul

118

read. "And you said she'd be stupid. How wrong you were, Teresa!" He took Marietta in his arms and almost lifted her off the floor. Seeing his daughter, Antonio rose and kissed her on both cheeks. Teresa frowned. Her celebratory mood vanished. Antonio shifted his feet, confused, almost as if he thought the note had been about him.

"*Grazie mille,*" he said pointing to the food. And to Teresa especially, "*Grazie per farmi venire a l'America. Commincio la vita di nuova.* Thank you for bringing me to America. I'll begin a new life." Teresa's smile returned.

That night Marietta slept on the couch while Antonio slept in her bed. "It's only temporary, until we find him an apartment and a job," Paul said. One month later, Marietta was still sleeping on the couch. She had the use of her desk in the afternoon since her father was out. While she was in school, Antonio's job was to find a job. Paul gave him money each day for the bus and a quick lunch, but Antonio pocketed the money and spent this time hanging around the neighborhood. He came home for all evening meals. He ate the main course upstairs with Teresa, then, he descended to Sofia's apartment for espresso and biscotti. He lauded his sisters on their cooking. "Meat is expensive. I only ate it once a week," he said, winning their sympathy. He came and went with such ease, feeling at home inside and out of the brownstone house, that Paul labeled him the "Duke."

Before she knew it, Marietta found the school year drawing to a close and she had the whole day to herself. As long as she stayed out of Teresa's way and didn't dirty the house, she could do whatever she pleased in the confines of the apartment or within a block's range. Her favorite activity was to sit on the wrought iron fire escape landing outside the kitchen window and read. There she felt the intense heat of the sun comfortably cooled by the morning air on her shoulders while scents of roses and lilacs rose up deliciously from Teresa's garden below. If she closed her eyes, she could find herself on Nonna's street, in front of the 1,100 year-old home, Lucia's voice singing in her ear. When it was time to come back inside, the daydream ended. With nothing to offset the heat and length of summer, Marietta read voraciously. She read long books that would last until her next trip to the library. In the afternoon, when the sun lacked the cooling effects of the morning air, she opted for the shade on the front porch and read until her eyes blurred and her neck ached.

After dinner, Paul and Marietta were sent out of the kitchen while Teresa washed the dishes. Paul brought down a brown throw cushion to the front stoop and sat on it, refreshed by the cooler air. On the edge of the top landing, with his feet on the step below, he read the newspaper. Marietta sat beside him and read her novels. When it was too dark to see the printed word, she played stoopball against the concrete steps or handball against the sidewall of the public school directly across the street. On very hot days, the other tenants also joined Paul for the cooler outdoor air. They stayed out as late as ten, waiting for the temperature to drop a few degrees before retiring. Every evening the Good Humor man parked his truck in front of them and they bought ice cream. The days he didn't show, the neighborhood children walked together to the corner candy store and bought Dixie cups, Italian ices or ice cream cones. Marietta's choice never veered: a "Mello-Roll" filled with vanilla ice cream and multicolored sprinkles.

The summer gave in to fall's crisp air. Brooklyn's tree-lined streets turned to heavenly bands of magenta, yellow and brown. On her walks to school Marietta noticed the golden glow of leaves slowly turn to brown and prepare to fall. Eventually, as if giving up their spirit, they let go and fell to the ground. Time moved faster in school. Soon winter was at the door and then, in full swing, March rolled in with its unpredictable charm. Marietta remembered the Italian saying

Nonna often repeated during this time of year. *"Marzo pazzerello, esce il sole e prendi l'ombrello.* Crazy March, the sun comes out and you must take your umbrella." It didn't make sense, but it was true. Just like her coming to America didn't make sense, but it was true.

"It's time for you to become an American citizen," Paul boasted one windy March day. "As our legally adopted daughter, you can get your papers in two years instead of waiting the usual five, the way your father has to," he added. He'd gotten used to referring to Antonio as her father, but Marietta viewed him more like a visiting uncle who by now, having apparently found a job as an auto mechanic and a place to live nearby, came to dinner just on Sundays, gave her a kiss hello and a five-dollar bill before proceeding to eat and talk with the adults.

"What will I have to do?" Marietta asked, excited. Once she became an American citizen, no one could label her as the girl who came from Italy.

"Just answer a few questions about our government and the history of our country in front of the judge. Then you'll be sworn in." His eyes beamed, lighting his dark face. "You won't get bawled up like Sofia did," he laughed. "She couldn't get the presidents' names straight even though I coached her up to the moment she walked up to the judge. She said George Washington was our present president, Lincoln was the first and Roosevelt freed the slaves. Everyone laughed including the judge."

"What happened?"

"They sent her home to study."

Marietta didn't tell anyone in school about becoming a citizen. When she took the day off to stand in front of the judge, she had Paul write a note saying she wasn't feeling well. She handed the note to the teacher the next day, hoping she looked pale enough to be believed.

When the citizenship certificate arrived in the mail, Paul wanted to put it in a frame and hang it on the wall in her room. He wanted her to display it for all to see, just as he had wanted her to display the framed certificate of flight from Rome to New York that Marietta had, nonetheless, hidden in the back of her desk drawer. Both certificates had her previous surname, the one that gave her away, as well as her adopted name in large print. They reminded her of all she'd been trying to forget.

For a change, Teresa agreed with Marietta. "I don't want the walls to get full of holes and scratches," she said firmly. Paul never liked it when his wife refuted him. Marietta felt the air grow heavy with tension.

"Please, keep my citizenship certificate with the Bill of Congress and the other papers you filled out for me to come to America. That way nothing will get lost," she said, and it'd be out of sight, she thought to herself.

Chapter Eleven

On the morning of her thirteenth birthday, Marietta was surprised when her friends pinned a candy corsage on the strap of her jumper after she entered the classroom. The corsage consisted of a pink bow from which thirteen pieces of bubblegum hung on strings. A fourteenth piece of gum – for good luck – dangled an inch lower. Before the start of class, the girls lined up and took turns landing fourteen soft punches on her back. With all these good luck punches, Marietta hoped for something good, not just for the day but for the rest of her life.

"Here's the birthday girl," Paul said when she returned home. He'd come home early in honor of her birthday and handed her a check as he had done the year before. She knew he expected her to give it right back so he could deposit it in the savings account he'd opened in her name, in trust for Teresa. But this year Marietta preferred to do something different with the money. It must have shown in her face.

"Would you rather go shopping and buy clothes with the money?" he asked, realizing she couldn't remain a little girl forever. She eyed the check still in her hand, unsure how to formulate her request.

"Thank you for the money, but what I really want is a record player and some records. All my friends in school have one. I have a list of the songs I want." She hesitated, worrying about how Teresa or Paul would feel if rock and roll entered the house. They never played the radio or listened to music. The only sounds Marietta heard in the house came from them or from the TV.

"Would you go with me to buy them?" she asked, speaking low so Teresa couldn't hear and say no.

"First thing in the morning, as soon as the store opens," he said. "Let's have dinner now." With the mention of food, Teresa was distracted by the need to set the table. Marietta took the forks and knives out of the drawer and set them to the left and right of the plate. Then she folded a napkin and placed it under each fork. Paul watched in admiration. His daughter was developing into a refined young woman under his care.

"When Mommy and I grow old, you'll take care of us the way we're taking care of you," he said, as if it were the most natural thing to do. But the future was too far away for Marietta to contemplate. She thought only of the songs she'd love to have now. With each bite of food, she added up how many the money would buy – as many as ten, she concluded.

"So, you're a teenager now," Teresa said.

"Yes. Thirteen is a passage year for everyone in my class," Marietta said as if she were reporting an extraordinary phenomenon. Teresa looked confused. Marietta realized she didn't understand the meaning of the word "passage."

"It's supposed to be a big change in...," she began but stopped mid-sentence. Teresa had lost interest when she heard a chorus of "Happy Birthday," very much out of tune, come from the hallway. Marietta opened the kitchen door and spotted Sofia with a package behind her back and Sal, balancing a cake lit with candles, right behind her. He was fighting hard to keep the flames away from his shirt as he sang. The verse ended just as the two reached the door, Sofia's heavy English contrasting sharply with Sal's Brooklyn accent.

"Thank you, Aunt Sofia and Uncle Sal. It's a beautiful cake." At that moment, the doorbell rang.

"It's the Duke," Paul announced with mischievous eyes, guessing the shadowy figure in the vestibule. When Antonio came through the door, he kissed Marietta on both cheeks.

"Buon Compleanno. Happy Birthday!" he said. He dug into his pants pocket and produced twenty dollars. *"Sei una signorina adesso.* You're a young lady now," he added to explain the extra cash. He was too late to eat dinner with them, but Teresa had reserved a plate for him. She took it out of the oven.

"Don't you want to see *our* present?" Sofia said, giggling like a schoolgirl. She placed the gift on Marietta's lap. She couldn't wait another moment. Marietta unwrapped the box and opened it. The gift was buried in tissue paper. Sofia and Sal leaned forward in anticipation. Marietta unfolded one side of the tissue paper and they both squealed. When she unfolded the second side, two oranges protruded out of the cups of a white bra. Everyone roared with laughter. But not Marietta. For a brief moment her mind seemed to separate from her body as if she were observing the scene from a place above. What she saw was a girl, miserably lonely, among a group of people thoroughly enjoying themselves. She wanted to join them and laugh at the silly bra filled with fruit. She wanted to be free, to let go of all she held locked inside. But her body wouldn't let her. She mustered a nervous smile, then, pulled the box shut and laid it on the table.

"That's not funny," she said, jumping up from the table. They were laughing at her expense. She wanted to get away, not from them but from herself, who was so prim and proper. Why couldn't she have loosened up and laughed along with them?

"Miss High-Hat," Teresa said. "She thinks she's better than us."

"No. It's not true!" Marietta shot back. "I just don't think it's funny," she lied, running to her room.

"There she goes, talking as if she's above us," Sofia snorted. "We're just having a good time. She can't even have a good time with us."

From that day forward, anytime Marietta disagreed with them, they called her "Miss High-Hat." If she chose not to eat the salted codfish, *baccala,* on Fridays, she was too "High-Hat" to enjoy their meal. When Marietta used vocabulary words Teresa didn't understand, she was too "High-Hat" to speak their language. When she chose to read a book rather than watch TV, she was too "High-Hat" to spend time with them. The list went on and on. Marietta went to bed envisioning a high hat on top of her head, wide-brimmed with feathers sticking up in the air. She remembered seeing a picture of the tall hat that Lincoln wore, and she mentally perched it on her head and laughed. But she laughed alone, never giving Teresa and Sofia the pleasure of knowing it.

The next two weeks were extremely busy for Marietta. Now that she was thirteen she had to attend Confirmation classes in preparation for the sacrament. Marietta was glad to be confirmed. If it weren't for God, she would have fallen apart after arriving in New York. God had been her steel, the iron rod she leaned on. He had supported her. And God was with her now. He was the protective arm around her back, the extended hand pulling her forward and the smiling face loving her unconditionally. She felt His presence strongest in church. It was natural, she thought. After all, church is God's house and a house reflects those who live in it. In Nonna's house every pot, dish and spoon spoke lovingly of her goodness and patience. Nonna's house was too far away to reach now but God's house, on the other hand, was everywhere and always available.

In Italy, she used to be in God's house regularly especially since Lucia's mother had been the church sacristan. She often allowed Lucia and Marietta to climb the circular stairway that led 102 feet up to the church tower where the bell hung. The steps were steep and made of stone. There were no handrails. A quick misstep or playful push, the two girls could fall hard to the ground and perish. They were

126

aware of the danger and feared for their lives, but it didn't stop them. They trusted God to keep them safe.

Teresa and Paul had no such connections with the local church or with God. Though they sent Marietta to Catholic school and encouraged her to receive the Sacraments, they didn't attend Mass. The one exception was October 18th, the feast of the twin brothers, San Demetrio and San Cosmo, the patron saints of Teresa and Sofia's hometown. Not much was known about the two brothers but legend told that they lived and died together. How lucky they were, thought Marietta, never to be separated from each other. Every year, on the two saints' feast day, Paul drove Teresa and Sofia to a church bearing the saints' names where they celebrated Mass. It was full of pageantry in contrast to the martyrs' simple lives. At the Offertory, four altar boys fastened the life-size statues of the Saints on a flat stand with four beams of wood protruding at each corner. Then each boy manned a beam and in unison elevated the statues of the two brothers. Halos lit the Saints' angelic faces and colorful robes draped their porcelain bodies. The congregation recited a litany of petitions: "San Demetrio, patron of our town, protect us … San Cosmo, keeper of the peace, send us peace…" At the end of Mass, the four lads descended from the altar and processed down the center aisle, the four beams that held the statues on their shoulders. People hampered their progress by leaning over from their pews to touch the saints' hands and feet. They pinned one dollar bills, sometimes five dollar bills, whatever they could afford, on the Saints' gilded vestments, genuflecting as the procession passed.

Marietta never understood how Teresa, Paul and Sofia could have such devotion to the two Saints but neglect Jesus and God. Here she was, ready to receive the Holy Spirit, the sacrament of Confirmation, as they had when they were younger, yet they never attended Mass except on October 18th.

"Daddy, why don't you go to church?" Marietta asked after Mass one Sunday. He had driven her there and, with Teresa, was now picking her up to take a leisurely car ride as Teresa's favorite pastime was to look at houses in other neighborhoods.

"As long as you're a good person, that's all that matters," Paul said, keeping his eyes purposely on the road, avoiding her glance.

"But you send *me* to church and make *me* go to Catholic school," she persisted.

"Children should learn about God but as you get older, life changes. You don't need God as much," he said.

He was right about the change, thought Marietta! She only had to look at the last three years of her life to know it was true. But he was wrong about needing God. She needed Him more as she got older. She worried about Paul's soul. Would he go to hell for missing Mass?

"If you loved me, you'd go to Mass with me on Sunday," she said.

"How come you ask all this? You *no* want to go to church or Catholic school no more?" Teresa frowned.

"Would it make you happy if I went to Mass?" Paul said.

"Yes," she answered, meekly. If he refused, it would mean he didn't love her.

"In that case, next Sunday I'll come. Anything else on your mind, young lady?"

"Well, actually, there is. Tomorrow I need to declare the Confirmation name I've chosen. I was thinking of Anne." She whispered it, afraid Paul would suggest Teresa as a token of good will between the adopted daughter whom he loved and the wife to whom he owed his loyalty.

"You can't choose Anne," Paul said firmly. Marietta's face dropped. She had wanted to honor her grandmother, changing the spelling of the name to disguise it so Paul and Teresa would more readily accept it.

"You must select Graziella," he said.

"Graziella," she repeated. It sounded strangely familiar. Ah, one of Nonna's daughters, the one who died from a fall, she recalled.

None of her classmates had chosen such an ethnic name. There was Ellen, a Mary, Rose, Anne, Helen, Elizabeth, Catherine, but not one Graziella. She bit her lip. How could she take Graziella and not be branded as coming from the olive farms of Italy?

"It was my mother's name," Paul explained. "I loved saying it."

"You called your mother Graziella?"

He laughed. "I called her 'Mamma.' Everyone else called her Grace. But her given name was Graziella. You could use Grace, if you prefer."

Grace? Marietta murmured the name quietly to herself. It sounded soft, smooth and comforting, like the satin edge of a baby's blanket. Grace meant gift from God. And it was Nonna's daughter's name as well. If she took it, it would make her Nonna's daughter, too.

"I'll tell Sister I'm choosing Grace."

Teresa touched her on the arm. "I have *una soppresa* – a surprise for you," she said. Marietta flinched. She didn't like surprises.

Paul gave his wife an icy look. "Not now, Teresa. Wait until we get home, for God's sake."

"*Tua madre*, your mother, she's *a* coming to New York." Teresa said, ignoring him.

What? Did Teresa say that Stella was coming to America? Marietta shut down from the impact. If only she'd been born an orphan, she thought. If only her parents had died when she was young, then there would be no dilemma, no double mothers or fathers. Only adopted parents. And if no one came to adopt her, it might turn out better. She wouldn't have to try to figure out whose daughter she was. Today, Stella's; tomorrow, Teresa's. The next day, Stella's and the next...Yes, to be an orphan would be better than this double identity, this yo-yo role she was forced to live in.

"Your Papà sent for her," Teresa continued, unaware of Marietta's inner turmoil.

"You *sent* for her?" Marietta said looking at Paul. When he shook his head no, Marietta realized her mistake. Teresa was talking about Antonio.

Paul glared at his wife but she looked at the road ahead. His hands gripped the wheel. She knew he couldn't stop her.

"*Arriverà* with your *piccola sorella a Settembre*. Oh how I pray to *San Demetrio per* this *giornata*." She raised her head and rolled her eyes. With her hand, she sent a loud kiss across the empty air. "*San Demetrio*, you helped me *finalmente*."

Marietta didn't know whether to believe Teresa. If what she said was true, what would happen? Would Teresa force Paul to give his daughter back to Stella? Would Stella come to claim her as soon as she set foot on American soil as she had assured Marietta she would? Or would she wait for a later time, the right moment to take her away from Paul and Teresa? What about school? Would Marietta have to switch to public school? What would her friends and teachers think when she no longer came to class? Stella had no money for private school. And what if Stella refused to take her back, if she rejected her once more? Despite the pronouncements of love Stella sent in her last letter some months before, Marietta no longer trusted her. She didn't trust anyone. She wasn't strong enough to endure rejection a second time. Her heart pounded as a conversation among her various relatives developed in her mind.

I never wanted you! You're going back to your mother.

No, she stays here! I've always wanted a daughter. She's our ticket to America.

Mamma, am I next? Will you give me away, too?

Call me once the decisions are made. I'll be at the bar down the street.

The words came in rapid succession like the lines in a play. Marietta covered her ears. Why were these voices shouting? Where was her voice? How could she remain silent, a puppet in others' hands?

When they arrived home Marietta went straight to her room. She wanted to be away from anything that moved or breathed. She went to shut the door and realized that there wasn't one. It had never been an issue before but now the open doorway made her feel vulnerable as if she were in an vast field with no place to take shelter. She dashed into the bathroom and locked the door. She turned on the faucet to muffle the sobs that rose inside her. With head bowed and hands on both sides of the sink, her warm tears blended with the water's flow down the drain. She had to get her thoughts in order. Variations of the same questions bombarded her. Was Teresa really trying to get rid of her? Was her mother, the first one, the real one, coming to take her back? The thought of being united with her mother and sister had seemed beyond her reach. Could she live with two sets of parents? Could they both claim her? She needed Solomon's wisdom to make sense of the situation. She felt as though she were cut in two. The pain in Marietta's body grew. It had now traveled down into her gut, past her abdomen and, it seemed to her, down her legs.

"Marietta, what are you doing in there so long?" Paul said knocking on the bathroom door. She hoped he wouldn't turn the handle. He hated the bathroom door locked. If she fainted or hit her head, it'd take longer for him to get help. Until now, Marietta had always heeded his advice.

"Are you all right?" He yelled. She didn't answer. She was afraid her voice would divulge the desperation and shame she felt. "Do you need help?" he demanded, this time with the authority of a policeman. The door handle turned and clicked without release. Marietta cringed.

"I'm fine. I'll be out soon." She was shocked at the strength of her speech, especially since she felt she had lost all sense of control.

"You're not smoking in there, are you?"

Marietta almost laughed. It had never occurred to her to smoke, especially at home where her father could detect it. She hated the smell of cigarettes when he lit up. And girls, good girls that is, didn't smoke, drink, or engage in sex before marriage. How often had she heard that both in school and at home? Paul and Teresa would disown her if she broke only one of these rules. If she broke all three, she shuddered at what might happen.

Marietta's abdomen continued to writhe with pain. She felt her thighs grow warm and wet. She lifted her skirt to see if her internal organs were falling out and found her legs colored red. Frightened, she took the washcloth hanging on the towel rack and wiped away the blood. Examining her thighs more carefully, she traced its origin and smiled.

Marietta had been expecting her period for the last year. A few of her friends had already gotten it. She would tell them hers had come too. They'd huddle around her and announce she was a woman. But that was tomorrow. Today she had to answer to Paul who was ready to break the door down if she kept quiet much longer.

"I'm not smoking, Daddy," she called out. But in her mind, she said, *I'm fine. I'm really fine. I'm a woman. I no longer need a mother. I can be a mother myself.*

"I'm counting to three. If you don't unlock that door, I'm busting it open."

Marietta immediately stuffed the soiled washcloth in her panties and unlatched the door.

"I'm bleeding," she whispered. Paul melted, all sympathetic. She knew just how to disarm him. His eyes roved down Marietta's body like a spotlight searching for clues. "Down there." She pointed between her legs, pretending she didn't know what was happening.

"*Mamma mia.*" He slapped his forehead. "Teresa, Teresa, come."

"What is it, Paul? What happened?" She was out of breath.

"Woman stuff," he said with a wave of his hand. "Talk to her." He removed himself quickly and went to sit in his easy chair to read the paper, which he had kept folded under his arm the whole time he had stood by the bathroom door. Teresa turned to Marietta with a puzzled look.

"I'm bleeding down there," Marietta said again, pointing with her hand.

When Teresa saw the blood run down Marietta's legs, she covered her mouth and ran to the hallway. "Sofia, Sofia," she shouted, her voice trailing down the stairs. Within seconds both sisters were in the bathroom with Marietta. Sofia wet a clean washcloth and handed it to her.

"Sponge the area with this," she said. Then her hand disappeared inside a box of Kotex. She pulled out a pad and a triangular belt.

"Here's how you put it on." She demonstrated on her own body.

"Go get her some clean panties," she told Teresa, who was glad to leave and no longer witness the bloody sight.

"You're the lucky one getting it at thirteen," Sofia whispered once Teresa was out of sight. "I got mine when I was ten. I still played with dolls and was so short I looked like

I was six. And then, this." She pointed below her abdomen. She adjusted the loops that fell down from the belt around Marietta's hips. "See, you put the pad in here, in the crotch," she continued. "You have to place it right in the middle, or you get blood all over your clothes. Teresa will kill you if you leak on the rug or stain the couch. *Questa maledizione*, this curse, comes not just once but every month. Twenty-eight days on the nose for me," she said.

Then she stuck her head out the bathroom door to check that Teresa was not near. "Did you know I got it before my sister even though she's five years older?" When Teresa returned with the clean underwear, she handed them to Sofia. But her eyes were fixed on the floor tiles, which were splattered with Marietta's blood. "I'll take care of the floor once we're done," Sofia said, noticing Teresa's discomfort. Teresa fled like the wind. "Poor Teresa," she continued. "I had my period a full year before hers finally came. She kept getting pains, but nothing, not even a drop, came out. I wanted her to see the doctor but mamma said, '*Dottore? Eh, che dottore?* Doctor? What doctor? It'll come naturally. Give her time. Time and nature, they take care of everything.' She was fifteen and still no period. Then one day Teresa couldn't stand the pain any longer. We thought somebody gave her the 'horns.' You know... the curse." Sofia rolled her eyes. "We couldn't figure out who might want to do such a thing to a young girl. Mamma rushed for the doctor then. When he came he didn't even examine her. He told us to soak her in hot water. We got the large tub from the cellar, the one we kept for the olives after we picked them, and put it in the middle of the kitchen. We heated water and poured it in. Everyone did, your father, me, mamma, even our cousins up the mountain. A parade of people came by to watch. My sister climbed in the tub and everyone waited, praying, hoping for a miracle. When the water turned pink, we all shouted for joy."

Fifteen minutes later Teresa returned to check on the bathroom. She smiled at the glistening white shine that reflected in her face.

"Thank you," Marietta said to both of them.

"No thank me," Teresa said. "Your *guai*, your worries, they just begin."

"Now you have to tell her about the birds and the bees, Teresa. You're the mother. I've taken enough time away from Sal," Sofia said, exhausted.

Reluctantly, Teresa led Marietta into the kitchen.

"You know what the blood means?" Teresa's eyes were downcast in shame.

"You don't have to tell me. I already know," Marietta told her. She didn't want Teresa to explain motherhood to her. Stella should be the one standing here, telling her what was happening. The same mother who gave her life should be telling her how life is made.

"How you know?" she asked.

"My mother told me before I left Italy," Marietta lied. What she knew she'd read in a science book.

"Good." Teresa sighed as if a weight were lifted.

Marietta walked out of the kitchen, past Paul in the living room, and plopped her body on her desk chair. She opened her History book to the geography of New York State and began to read about New York Harbor, wondering how the landscape would be affected when Stella came across its shore.

Chapter Twelve

Almost immediately the two sisters embarked on "fixing a place" for Stella and Antonio. Though busy with their own homes, they found time to sew curtains, sort through pots and pans they hardly used and sheets and towels they could spare. They soon built up an arsenal of furniture and house supplies. Teresa put cleaning supplies under the kitchen and bathroom sinks including a gallon of *chavelle*, a type of strong bleach, and several blue sticks, which served as whitening agents. Stella would need them to brighten Antonio's shirts when she scrubbed them against the washboard. They checked that the broom and mop rested neatly out of sight in the hollow between the refrigerator and the wall. When they were finished, they both stepped to the center of the room and looked around. Not bad, they thought. Antonio and Stella should be grateful for all they'd done.

From the beginning Teresa wanted Marietta to help. "She's got hands," she argued. "She can carry." But Paul intervened.

"Leave the kid alone for Christ's sake. We have to protect those hands. She's going to be a doctor someday and take care of all of us when we're old. Isn't that enough?"

By the time Stella and little Pia were to finally set foot on American soil, it was the eighth of December, the feast of the Immaculate Conception. A holy day of obligation in more ways than one for Marietta. School was closed, but Marietta had to attend Mass and then go meet her mother when she arrived by boat.

The air was cold and damp when she exited the marble Church with Paul beside her. Above them dark patches of clouds formed. Stoked by the wind, they swirled in wild spirals.

"Hope it doesn't snow," he said. "It'll be a hard drive to the dock." Marietta, on the other hand, wanted snow. She hoped the snow blanketed the world and stalled the ship in the middle of the ocean. She wasn't ready for her mother's coming. Stella would bring a definite change and Marietta feared it.

Pia was a different story. Seeing her sister would be a welcome change. She missed her. She wondered how much Pia had grown since she left. Marietta remembered how Pia followed her every move at Nonna's house. Neither one knew how short-lived their relationship would be.

As soon as they returned from Mass, they found Teresa and Antonio waiting by the front door, their coats on, anxious to leave to go pick up Stella. It seemed only seconds to Marietta when Paul's car pulled up to the harbor. "There's the boat nearing port," Paul pointed out. He avoided Marietta's eyes. Afraid he'd find them longing for someone other than himself, he missed the dread that lay in them.

Marietta wondered if Stella would recognize her. She'd grown several inches, no longer the little girl her mother had put on the plane three years before. Her long, curly hair had been cut short, just below her ears, thanks to Teresa, and a few extra pounds had settled on her chest and hips. She tried to reconstruct Stella's features. Black hair, red lips, light complexion. But the image came distorted. Could she have forgotten her mother's face? She wondered what she would say when she first saw her.

She wondered, too, what Antonio was thinking. Would he warmly welcome the dark-haired beauty he had pursued and won from so many suitors? Would he be more faithful to her in America than he had been in Italy? His face was blank and Marietta couldn't decipher it.

Orange Peels and Cobblestones

As people filed out of the boat, Marietta stood on her toes to see around the taller heads in front of her. She recognized no one. Suddenly a hand pressed on her shoulder from behind. Marietta jumped. It belonged to a stooping, overweight woman with short black hair. Her skin was pale and weather beaten. Her clothes, stained, were too tight for her bulging frame.

"Marietta, tu non mi cognosci piu? Mi hai dimenticato? You no longer recognize me? You have forgotten me?"

"Mammina?" She had used the diminutive form of "Mamma," the one from when she was a toddler. *Can it be you? Tell me it isn't you. You used to be young and pretty, slim and elegantly dressed.*

"Si, sono io. Yes, it's me," Stella said. *"Ho tagliato i miei capelli. Non ti piace?* I cut my hair. Don't you like it?"

Marietta stood in disbelief. She had loved her mother's long black hair as she had loved her own when she c came from Italy. But Teresa and Sofia, claiming it carried lice, made her cut it short against her head. And now Stella had done the same. Would nothing be left of her past?

"Dove sono it miei fiori? Non mi hai portato neanche una rosa? Where are my flowers? You didn't bring me even one rose?"* No one had mentioned flowers. Marietta didn't know she had to bring a gift.

"Let's get your bags," Paul interjected. "Customs will take a long time and I don't want to get stuck in snow driving home." Teresa immediately flanked Stella. The two women talked at once, Stella about the hardship of the voyage, Teresa about the hardship of setting up her new apartment. It was then that Marietta noticed the small, thin girl with her hair in a bun emerge from behind Stella. Pia was seven years old now but she was short and delicate. Her round eyes were sunken, questioning Marietta, as if she were a stranger. Marietta wanted to touch Pia, to see if she were real. She wanted to tell her how much she loved her and that she wanted to share a bedroom with her and fight over toys and clothes and talk into the night like all sisters do. She kept her eyes glued on Pia, refusing to blink in case her sister found a thread of recognition. But the closer Marietta drew, the more Pia recoiled into Stella's skirt.

"*Andiamo a casa.* Let's go home," Teresa said, meaning Stella's apartment. When Marietta was told to sit in the front seat of the car between Paul and Teresa while Stella and Pia were shown the back next to Antonio, the lines of division between the two families were clearly drawn.

"*Ecco*, here it is," Teresa pointed to the apartment. Sofia met them at the door and everyone could smell the ragu that was simmering on the stove. Marietta followed her mother's eyes as she examined her surroundings. The dwelling was really one large room divided in two by a heavy brown curtain across the center. A small kitchen table stood in the middle. The stove, refrigerator and sink ran along one wall with cabinets for the dishes and glasses. Next to the front door stood a small, white, portable metal cabinet that Marietta recognized from Teresa's cellar. The curtain had been left open just enough to spot a double bed on one side and a single bed on the other with a bureau in between. Stella tried to drink it all in. Marietta couldn't tell if Stella was affected more by what was present in the apartment or what was missing. Then, as if she, and not Stella, were the lady of the house, Teresa opened the refrigerator door and pulled out a white bakery box filled with jelly doughnuts and cream puffs. She marched over to the portable cabinet, opened the door and took out a can of Medaglia D'oro coffee and proceeded to brew espresso. Antonio emerged from behind. He took out a brown bag from his pocket and produced a small bottle of anisette liqueur. He leaned over and placed it on the table.

"*Per il caffè.* For the coffee," he said.

Orange Peels and Cobblestones

"Sit, eat, drink," Teresa said as soon as the coffee had finished percolating and the liquid was black as night. Antonio pulled out a chair for his wife and Stella smiled for the first time. He sat beside her as she took a bite of the doughnut.

"*Buono*," she said, wiping the powdered sugar from her mouth with the paper napkin.

"*Il nostro desidero è che tu e Antonio state contenti in America.* Our hope is that you and Antonio are happy in America," Paul said.

"*Con la grazia di Dio.* With the grace of God," Stella said. She turned to Pia. "*Pia, perchè non mangi?* Why aren't you eating?"

"*Non ho fame.* I'm not hungry," Pia said in a voice so low that it sounded as if she hadn't spoken in days.

"*Quella-là non mangia mai.* That one never eats,*"* Stella sighed.

"*Sono stanco.* I'm tired,*"* Pia said in self-defense.

"*Fa'la dormire.* Let her sleep," Paul advised. Marietta gazed in admiration at his comment. Paul was an androgynous mixture of father and mother, protector and nurturer rolled into one. She knew he loved her but now, watching him interact with her sister, she was sure he loved all children. Perhaps he'd adopt Pia too. Then she'd have her sister again. She wouldn't be alone. But would Stella let her go? The bigger question was: would Teresa want another child that was not her own? Marietta thought of the benefits of such a union even for Stella. She could go to Hollywood and pursue her acting career. No doubt, she'd come back to New York from time to time to visit and the children could fly to Los Angeles and watch her shoot a movie during school vacations.

"Marietta," Paul's voice rang from far away. Her face reddened as if she were caught doing something wrong. He

140

sounded urgent. She hurried to his side. "Help your sister get into bed. She's tired," he said.

Pia saw Marietta's extended hand but didn't take it. She had yet to speak a direct word to her sister while Marietta had so much to say. She wanted Pia to know how much she wanted a sister. Not just any sister. She wanted Pia, her flesh and blood.

"Come. *Vieni qui,*" she corrected. She had to remind herself that Pia knew not a word of English. She touched her little shoulder delicately, caressed it as if Pia might implode from the pressure. Then she tried to undress her, to show that, like Nonna, she would always help.

"*Lo faccio io.* I can do it myself," Pia said, putting her hand forward to stop her. Marietta watched as she unbuttoned her own dress and lifted it over her head. Once in her slip, she climbed into bed and pulled the covers up to her waist. Clearly, Pia had been used to doing things on her own. Marietta was left to sit on the side of the bed and stare at the innocent face in repose, so still and poised. How beautiful it was, she thought. The bun on the back of Pia's head was strangely familiar. Nonna wore her hair the same way. Her sister's eyes seemed unusually large for such a small face and frame. Housed deep in their sockets, they seemed to retreat to a private place where no one could enter. She closed them without making another sound as if she were alone in the room.

Marietta envisioned her sister's closed eyes as buckets going deep into the well of her soul. She spoke to that well as if she could see in, as if its core had been pulled up with ropes and now lay exposed. Pia's soul would see how much Marietta loved her. Watching the blanket gently rise up and down with Pia's breath, she wanted her younger sister never to feel cold as she sometimes felt when her feelings numbed. Like a mother, she instinctively pulled the covers up toward the shoulders, covering every inch of Pia's chest. Pia stirred and lowered the covers down to her waist. Marietta brought them up again. They played this game, covering and uncovering, until finally Pia touched Marietta's hand. Marietta could stop trying to convince her. She knew how much her older sister loved her.

Routines shifted to accommodate the new arrivals. On Sunday, Stella, Antonio and Pia came to dinner at Paul and Teresa's house. After dinner Marietta led Pia, who now easily followed, to her room and to the stacks of books that lay in the built-in bookshelf on the side of her desk. She picked up her blue, clothbound Italian-American dictionary that she'd received from Sister John Francis a few years before. She coached Pia on how to pronounce many English words. She modeled how to shape her lips for "w" and where to put her tongue between her teeth when making the "th" sound, which were foreign to the Italian language. They practiced for two, sometimes three hours, however long the adults talked in the kitchen.

Pia was an avid learner. It was hard to tell who persevered longer, Pia who wanted to learn English as quickly as she could or Marietta who treasured every moment they spent together. One afternoon, as the two girls were conquering the letter "y" with all its peculiar sounds and uses, Marietta decided to give Pia the dictionary. "Dear Pia," she inscribed inside the front cover. "I am giving you this book so that you can study when we're not together. Let this book and each of the words in it remind you of me and of the moments we've spent together, but most of all, let it remind you of how much I love you." She went over the words with Pia to make sure she understood them.

The following Saturday, as Marietta thumbed through books that she and Pia would study the next day, she heard Teresa and Paul shout to one another, their words volleying back and forth like tennis balls. At first, she dismissed it. She was used to hearing them talk loudly. But something in their tone disturbed her. She got up from her desk and tiptoed closer, hiding behind the kitchen door. There was a familiar ring to the Italian curses and obscene hand gestures they hurled at one another. For an instant, she thought she was back in Italy witnessing the fights between Antonio and Stella. Images of knives directed threateningly at the other resurfaced. She closed her eyes in terror. But it was more terrifying not to know what was going on. She opened her eyes and saw something fly through the air. It made a hissing sound. She looked up and recognized Teresa's meat cleaver as it wedged into the wooden doorjamb, inches from where Marietta stood. It had been intended for Paul. The moment he spotted Teresa opening the drawer to snatch the cleaver, he lunged at her like a seagull. It deflected her aim. Afraid he'd use the knife on her, she hurled the blade through the air.

"*Puttana.* Bitch," he said. Marietta had never seen Paul so angry. "Bitch," he repeated. He turned toward the door, past the knife, where Marietta stood. Not at all surprised to find her so near, he said, "Get your coat. You're going to your mother's."

Why were Paul and Teresa so angry with each other? Many thoughts crossed Marietta's mind. Had Teresa finally gotten her wish to give Marietta back and Paul refused? Did he finally give in to his wife's demands? Were they now trading her for Pia? In the car Marietta wanted desperately to ask these questions, but Paul's face scared her. They drove in silence. When they reached Stella's apartment, he kissed her goodbye.

"I'll come back later," he said and Marietta was left to guess whether he'd return with her belongings or come to take her back home.

Inside the apartment, Stella had prepared a regal lunch. No ham or salami sandwiches on white bread as Teresa put together. The table was white with flour, and hundreds of *orecchiette*, ear-shaped pasta, laced the tablecloth. Red sauce with the scent of fresh basil and cloves of garlic simmered on the stove. Marietta sniffed it. It smelled like Nonna's kitchen. *"Il cibo tuo, quello piu favorito.* Your favorite foods," Stella said pointing to the table. Marietta smiled at the familiar spread, colorful and artfully arranged. The plate of fried dough that ballooned out in different shapes and sizes reminded her of the animal guessing game she would play with Nonna as she dropped spoonfuls of dough into the hot oil. This one looks like a pig. This one has the nose of an elephant or the tail of a cat or the body of a chicken or the ears of a rabbit.

The meatballs were perfectly round. They were red and green, because they were drenched in sauce and had fresh parsley sticking out all around them. The chicken soup had miniature meatballs sailing in it like tugboats. The lasagna was generously filled with ricotta and sauce and Parmesan cheese. Breaded slices of succulently round fried zucchini stood near a tomato salad with olive oil and herbs. Cookies rounded out the sumptuous fare. Some were deep yellow in color because of all the eggs Stella had used to make them; others like biscotti were laden with nuts or dried fruit and washed with white icing. A few had indentations in the center, filled with apricot jam. Some smelled of rum. Last were the amaretto cookies, dull gray in color, bittersweet in taste that melted in the mouth. Marietta was ecstatic when she saw the cartellate, a special dessert from her hometown, drenched in honey and shaped like pinwheels. Nonna used to make them at Christmastime. Stella must have worked for days to prepare all this.

They ate in silence, Stella, Pia and Marietta, as if under a spell. The familiar food had transported them to another place, another time when they used to be a family. The revelry suspended everyone into a hypnotic state of euphoria, until Marietta realized someone was missing. Antonio. Why was he not eating with them? But the thought was short-lived.

The big smiles on their faces as they chewed revealed only their bounty and not their lack. Marietta felt like a little girl again as she relished the food of her ancestors, the food of her roots.

At the end of the day, Paul pulled up in his car and rang the doorbell. When Stella opened the door, Marietta couldn't see past her mother's frame if Paul had luggage and books with him. Stella shifted her weight from one foot to the other, allowing Paul a glimpse of both girls playing with dolls in the corner next to the bed. It brought tears to his eyes.

"I've come to take you home," he said. Marietta wasn't sure whether Paul was addressing her or Pia.

"Ritorna la settimana prossima? She'll come back next week?" Stella asked, kissing and wetting Marietta's cheeks with her tears. Marietta looked at Paul for confirmation. He gave none.

Chapter Thirteen

For the next three months, Paul drove Marietta to Stella's apartment every Saturday and dropped her off without getting out of the car. In the evening he was back, waiting behind the wheel with the motor running until she got in. Stella never came to the door. Mother and daughter kissed hello and goodbye inside the kitchen. But instead of feeling enriched by two families, Marietta became increasingly confused. Could she be a daughter to both sets of parents? Why wasn't Antonio home when she visited? And why were Stella and Pia no longer present for Sunday dinner at Paul and Teresa's house while Antonio continued to come? The distance between the two families thickened and Marietta was afraid to be the solitary bridge between them.

She felt torn. When she was home with Teresa and Paul, she thought she ought to be with Pia and Stella. When she visited Pia and Stella, she wondered about Paul and Teresa. Her body in one place and her mind in another made her listless. When someone spoke to her, she jumped; it took her twice as long to do homework and she daydreamed more.

"Marietta, are you all right?" Stella asked one Saturday afternoon. The child could barely answer. The question froze in her brain with nowhere to go like puzzle pieces that don't fit. On the outside, the adults acted civilly. On the inside, they seemed to seethe with a deadly rage. Marietta knew the whip of their anger, the slash of their tongue, the punishment they could brand on one another.

"Ma che cosa c' è? What's the matter?" Stella repeated when Marietta had turned as white as the wall. In contrast, Stella's cheeks were pink from kneading bread. She was explaining how Nonna had taught her to knead. *Make a*

tight fist with both hands and, like a dance, rhythmically plunge the fists into the dough one after the other in an artful but strong twist. Fold the dough and punch it down repeatedly until it pulls away like elastic and feels like silk. Listen to it crackle as if it's tickled by your touch. Little Pia kneaded far better, Marietta observed. She could cook too, though in front of her older sister, she pretended to learn when Stella modeled how to chop garlic and parsley, wielding the knife in an up and down motion, creating the rat-tat-tat sound that cuts each ingredient really fine.

When Marietta moved from one house to another, she felt as though she left one world and entered another. Pia's bread was made by hand and her clothes were sewn at home. In contrast, Marietta's bread was bought at Gino's Bakery and her clothes came from a department store. While the two families lived only blocks away, to Marietta they were thousands of miles apart.

The adults had no problem living in both worlds. During the day Teresa and Sofia could scrub floors on their hands and knees using a pail and old towel like they did in Italy, and at night they could don long, flowing gowns to attend the Policemen's Annual Christmas Ball. Paul was no different. He, too, traveled in and out of both worlds as freely as going from one room to another. When he worked his beat, he patrolled streets full of Italian men and women who went from store to store getting their daily supply of food from local vendors. Pinuccio unlocked his door first. He needed time to set up his colorful displays of fruits and vegetables on sloping stands outside his doors. Giuseppe ran the pork store that featured the best provolone, mozzarella and soppresata as well as the leanest cuts of meat – beef, veal, pork – but not chickens. Those you had to buy live at the farm four blocks away. You could follow Alfredo to the back of the store and watch him wring the chickens' necks. Gino's bakery made the crustiest bread and his wife, the best pastries. From one street to another, people greeted one another with a hearty *buon giorno.* They waved their hands. *"La famiglia, come sta?* How's the family?"* they shouted. *"Bene, bene,* Good, good," came the quick response, a mixture of dialects blending. The elevated train above screeched to a stop and car horns blew in frustration as old ladies, in complete disregard of oncoming traffic, crossed against the light. Paul acknowledged everyone. They were part of his daily landscape. He knew their habits and their language.

But when Paul reported back to his precinct, his tongue easily switched to English   He joked with cronies. He dreamed of a promotion that would, someday, seat him in the captain's chair and get him off the street. If only he could pass the test. For now, though, he was happy to be a patrolman. His fellow officers respected him. Most were Irish and weren't familiar with the Italian culture. So they relied on Paul to understand and control the neighborhood. And when he came home, he turned into a chameleon. If Teresa met him at the door, he greeted her in Italian. If Marietta stood there, he spoke in English.

One afternoon, much to her surprise, Marietta found Stella sitting in the kitchen with Teresa. She brightened. Perhaps they'd settle their differences and get along.

"Is Pia here?" she asked. No, Stella had left her with a neighbor. Partly out of habit but also out of desire not to interfere with the reconciliation that was most likely taking place, she headed straight to her room to start her homework. Her eyes rested on the math problems she had to solve, but her ears and mind were wired to the kitchen.

"Your brother and I, well…we couldn't live together in Italy and we can't live together here," Stella said with an even voice. They sipped espresso ceremoniously. *"Devo fare altre cose, cara cognata.* I have to make other plans, dear sister-in-law."

148

"*Che peccato!* What a shame," Teresa said, but inwardly she gloated. Stella had yet to show appreciation for all she had done to prepare her apartment with Antonio. As far as Teresa was concerned, the sooner Stella was gone, the better. She waited for the words she longed to hear, that Stella was returning to Italy and that she'd take Marietta with her. If the words came from Stella, Paul couldn't blame her.

The stairs creaked and, from the hour on her wristwatch, Marietta knew Paul was climbing them on his way back from work. She felt a certain dread come over her, as though he were bringing bad news, the way he sometimes did when he notified the families of crime victims. Teresa poured a second cup of coffee. The spoons clinked against the cups. Fearing trouble, Marietta dropped her book and ran into the kitchen hoping her presence would temper whatever storm arose. When Paul entered everyone looked up. He seemed surprised to find Stella there.

"What brings you here?" he asked, harshly.

"I've come to tell you I can't stay with Antonio. He's hardly home and when he is…" she paused. She wanted him to believe her. Reaching behind her, she pulled her blouse loose out of the skirt and lifted it up to her shoulders. Stella's back was a canvas of black and blue welts. Marietta gasped in horror. Even Teresa put her hand to her mouth in shock. Paul didn't flinch one bit. He was used to domestic battles. He couldn't trust the scars. He never knew which spouse had provoked the other. Victims were often more loyal to their spouse than their injuries and, sometimes, turned on the policeman who made the mistake of defending them. The department's unwritten rule with domestic cases was documentation followed by non-interference.

"So," he said matter-of-factly. "I suppose you'll go back to Italy." Precisely the words Teresa wanted to hear!

"*No. Non posso.* I can't. My brothers and sisters, everyone in town, they'd laugh at me, call me a failure." She stood up. *"Vado a California e voglio prendere Marietta con me.* I'm going to California and I want to take Marietta with me." Teresa smiled in triumph but Paul's chest swelled with anger. The buttons on his blue shirt strained ready to burst. Marietta was concerned they'd go flying through the air. She'd be on her hands and knees trying to pick them up so Teresa could sew them back on.

"She's our daughter now," he said, his voice hard and possessive. Then, as though remembering the rule he'd learned at the police academy, he took a deep breath. "I have your signature," he said more calmly.

"Lei era mia figlia prima. Io diedi la sua vita. She was my daughter first. I gave her life," Stella screamed, raising her fists in his direction. Paul thrust his right arm in self-defense and blocked their oncoming path. Then, suddenly, he grabbed her arm, twisted it behind her back and shoved her out the door.

"Vai via e non ritorni mai. Go away and never come back," he shouted.

"No," Marietta shouted back, as if she'd been the one pushed.

"Vedi," Stella boasted. *"Conosce la mamma. Io sono la mamma.* See, she knows her mother. I am her mother." She banged on her own chest. *"Non vado senza mia figlia.* I won't go without my daughter. *Mi devi méttere fuori tu perchè non lascio senza Marietta.* You have to throw me out yourself because I won't leave without Marietta."

That's when Paul forgot his police academy training, his sense of right from wrong, and his respect for women or guests in his home and for people in general. He lunged forward and pushed Stella further out the door. She hit the top step near the landing's edge, where she lost her balance and fell, toppling down the staircase Teresa had washed and lacquered that very morning. She landed in the middle of the hallway one floor below. Stella was dazed but conscious. She touched her swollen lip and blood ran down her finger. Her back ached.

Once Marietta heard the thump-thump of Stella's flesh against the wooden steps, something snapped inside her. She felt it in her core. She ran from the kitchen as if she were on fire. If she could, she would have run out the door, gotten as far away from the lunacy that had become her life. But when her eyes beheld Stella lying on the hallway floor, her drive to leave seemed cowardly. Marietta ran to her mother's side and lifted her blood-smeared face off the floor.

"*Il sangue*. Blood," Stella murmured, managing a wry smile. She referred not to the blood that ran down her chin but the blood that tied Marietta to her. Blood was thicker than water, she explained in a show of victory.

Almost immediately Paul rushed down the stairs, taking them two at a time. He pulled Marietta away from Stella, holding the child tight in his arms. He had caused her to suffer. How could he forget she was still a child? He needed to protect her. It was his duty as a policeman. But more, that's what a loving father does. He hadn't meant to hurt anyone. He only wanted Stella to go away so he could keep the child he had worked so hard to get.

"Stop," Marietta screamed as if she were delirious. "Stop, stop." It gave her pleasure to see their shocked faces as she repeated the words. She had finally touched them as she had never touched them before. Sofia rushed out her apartment door from where she had stood watching. The other tenants peeked out from their kitchens, craning their necks to see without being seen, one down the banister, the other up it, as if a movie reeled before them. Suddenly Sofia reached out and took Marietta's hand.

"Let her come with me," she said to Paul. Without waiting for a response, she pulled the child into her apartment and closed the door. Exhausted, Paul leaned against the wall. He shook his head. How had the events deteriorated so much?

He had to repair the damage before it was too late. His duty was to uphold the law, not break it. He arrested those who broke it. He was afraid someone might come and arrest him for his behavior today. His job was in jeopardy. He was counting on enjoying his pension in a few years. Breathing more slowly, he grew calmer.

Stella stood and straightened her skirt, which had risen up to her thighs during the fall. *"Non ho finito.* I'm not through," she said, pointing an accusing finger at Paul. She went to the door and walked out.

"The courts will decide," he answered after her, glad to see her leave.

From that day forward Paul drove Marietta to school every morning. Every afternoon at three, he parked illegally in front of the school with his Police Business sticker on the windshield, his eyes glued to the school gates for sight of Stella. Marietta felt as if she were under house arrest. She didn't know what crime she'd committed. Rather than feel safe, she felt as if a bomb could hit her at any moment. The fear of someone snatching her away never lessened for her or for Paul. In class, Marietta consciously tried to direct this heightened awareness toward her lessons. If she didn't, the fear would paralyze her from learning altogether.

Several months later, the tension climbed to new heights. It happened on a beautiful day in June, about ten in the morning, while Marietta was taking an English final. She had identified all the grammar mistakes purposely placed there, defined the vocabulary, located antonyms and synonyms and had just finished writing a creative essay on "How I Will Serve Society as an Adult." She said she'd be a cardiologist and mend broken hearts. It was a wonderful composition, selfless, full of service to humanity. She wrote about physical breaks like valves that malfunctioned, cardiac tissue that had lost its resiliency and clogged arteries that could cause strokes and heart attacks, but her mind pictured hearts wrought with emotional pain begging to be healed. That's when and where she'd utilize the techniques learned in medical school. And if these methods were not yet perfected, she'd spend time to research them. Marietta was proud of the essay. It had three or more sentences in each paragraph, supporting paragraphs to prove her premise and the words of the Hippocratic Oath, which she had memorized. She hoped it merited the high mark she coveted.

The event began quietly at first in the form of a directive. "Marietta, come up to my desk," her teacher said softly. She had to repeat it as Marietta was lost re-reading her essay to make sure no word was misspelled or left out. Marietta paled when she was told to report to the principal's office.

"Why?" she whispered. There had to be some mistake.

"Go quickly and return for the math final which starts in a half hour." The nun forced a smile. "Maybe it's something good. Maybe you won an award," she said, trying to lift the fear out of Marietta's eyes.

Marietta's legs shook as she made her way to the principal's office. Only girls who smoked or swore or failed their subjects knew the interior of that room. Except for the day Paul had enrolled her in school, she had never set foot in that office again. Marietta knocked on the door and felt a heavy weight across her shoulders. When the door opened, to her surprise, she found Stella and Pia sitting on the same chairs she and Paul had sat on several years earlier, directly in front of the large desk.

Stella had changed in the time they'd been apart. She'd become slimmer, prettier. Her wide red lips accentuated her high cheek bones, reminding Marietta of how she used to look in Italy one lifetime ago, one family ago. Her black hair was long again and just as striking. Marietta was aware of a polite stiffness between them, not knowing whether they were still mother and daughter or simply two strangers who at one time were tied to one another through an umbilical cord.

"Marietta, I've met a wonderful man who can support us. I'm leaving with him for California. Sister was kind enough to let me see you before I go," she said. This is goodbye, Marietta thought. She'd never see her mother and sister again. She looked at Pia who sat with a helpless expression. Her heart fell.

"I'd like you to come with me, with your sister and me. We can be a family again," Stella added. Marietta's heart leaped. It was fitting that Marietta should be with her real mother, the way her sister was. They were rooted in one another. With Paul and Teresa she grew, but not in the same way her school friends flourished. She was like a plant pulled from the ground, uprooted from her native soil. Her adopted parents were the water she was put into so that she would not shrivel up and die. But there was no flavor or spark to her life. Her ties had always been with Stella and Pia, who joined her to Nonna. Yes, Marietta would say yes. She was set to say yes, when suddenly the word "no" came out, surprising everyone, including herself.

"It's too late," she explained. She thought of all Paul had given her: a wonderful education, a home, clothes and books. How could she leave him like a thief in the night, without notice, without saying goodbye, without his consent? She couldn't betray him the way she felt Stella had betrayed her.

No, their lives together had ended that fateful day when Marietta boarded the plane to come to America. There was no turning back, no matter how much she wished to undo the past.

"What are you afraid of?" Stella demanded. The rejection stung her deeply.

She was afraid of so much. Especially, she was afraid that Paul would find them and have Stella arrested for kidnapping. Despite everything, she didn't want her mother to go to jail. Stella got up from her chair and put her arms around her daughter. *"Cara, cara figlia. Dici si e ti porto via subito.* Dear, dear daughter. Say yes and I will take you away quickly," she said.

"If I come, I know it's wrong. If I stay, it's also wrong. How can I choose?" She wiped away a tear with the back of her hand. Why couldn't her mother see the decision was not hers to make? It had never been hers to make. Stella had made it years ago, when she signed the papers, when she sent her daughter away.

Marietta searched her sister's face for signs of anger or disappointment. There were none. Only eyes that glowed with energy, assuring Marietta their bond was secure.

The principal could no longer remain silent. "You said you wanted to see your daughter one last time to say goodbye. I cannot dismiss Marietta in your custody even if she chooses to go with you. Legally she is not your daughter anymore."

Stella stiffened. "I claim my child because I am her mother. If Marietta agrees to come with me, you cannot hold her back."

"Don't force me to call the police. Kiss your daughter goodbye and trust in God to guide the course of the rest of your lives."

Stella knew she was beaten. With tears running down her face, she kissed Marietta on both cheeks. Then Pia spoke for the first time. "Goodbye, Marietta. I will never forget you."

"I won't forget you either, Pia," Marietta said through tears of her own.

The principal gave out tissues to dry their eyes. She turned to Marietta. "You must put all this behind you, for now, at least. Your math exam has begun."

Closing the door, leaving her mother and sister behind, Marietta walked back to the classroom. She hoped her eyes were not too red from crying and that the image of Stella's and Pia's faces would clear from her mind so she could focus on the numbers of her math test.

Chapter Fourteen
Eight Years Later

In order to ease the tension that developed with Paul and Teresa, Marietta and John made every effort to attend movies that began no later than eight so that they could return home early from their dates. One Thursday evening, however, John called all excited. "I have two tickets to the Hospital Benefit Ball at the Pierre Hotel in New York City for this Saturday. It's a pretty big event. All the bigwigs will be there. Not too late to ask you?" he teased, remembering her "calling no later than Wednesday for a date on Saturday" rule.

"No," she laughed. "But will it end late?"

"We can leave any time you want. It's no problem," he assured her.

"Will I know anyone at the dance?"

"You'll know me," he said without conceit. "And I'll know you. I'll introduce you to some of my colleagues."

The lobby of the Hotel Pierre had high ceilings with plush, thick carpeting, royal blue velvet couches and Queen Anne chairs. Sprays of multicolored carnations filled a gigantic vase in the center of a round mahogany table. Marietta wore a long, white form-fitting gown with spaghetti straps. John had on a white tuxedo. They made a lovely couple together as they waltzed across the dance floor. Marietta couldn't help thinking how much Stella would love this place. Normally, Marietta would reject such a showy display, but tonight she found herself liking it. She was with John. He made all the difference.

It was June. Soon he'd be graduating from medical school and in September he'd be starting his residency at Kings County Hospital. Marietta had one more year of college. Medical school applications were very much on her mind.

"You look and sound lovely," he whispered in her ear as they danced to Johnny Mathis' 'Chances Are.'" She looked up, confused.

"You're singing along with Johnny," he explained.

"Am I?" She wasn't aware of it. She was aware only that she was in love with him and, chances were, that he loved her, too. But he didn't know it or wouldn't admit it. And she wanted him to see it very much. She was grateful their heads faced in opposite directions so he wouldn't see the tears forming in her eyes. As they moved across the dance floor, she concentrated on the strength of his arm across her back and the warmth of his hands. When the song ended, John finally noticed her wet eyes.

"What's wrong? I didn't step on your foot, did I?"

"It's nothing. Forget it," she said, annoyed. It irritated her how he always joked when he didn't know what to make of a situation. On their way back to their seats, they bumped into his friend Eric and his date, Damaris, who was heading toward the ladies' room. Marietta joined her. John and Eric walked over to their table where their unfinished drinks lay.

"I'm so glad you came, John. Are you having a good time?" Eric said.

"Very much, except for one thing. She cried while we were dancing. What do you think it means?"

"You're in trouble, man. When a girl cries, it's never a good thing." The girls returned and the men's conversation turned to sports.

"Look," Marietta pointed, "a balcony. It must have a view of the city. Let's go see." John took her hand and led her out. The air was balmy and the New York skyline was aglow with lights. A hint of stars twinkled above them. The moon was cut in half. John pulled Marietta away from the edge, closer to him, as if she might fall and then he kissed her tenderly on the lips.

"Why did you cry on the dance floor?" he asked.

Marietta sighed. She could feel the tears returning. "I'm afraid you will leave," she said.

"Leave you? Why are you so worried about that? Help me to understand you."

"I'm afraid that once you find out what love is you will tell me you don't love me. Or that you'll never find out you love me or feel comfortable saying it. I…I can't risk that."

"I know it's disappointed you that I haven't said I loved you. It's just that I have to be absolutely sure. What I have to say is hard." Marietta closed her eyes and took a deep breath. She needed all the oxygen she could muster to face his parting words.

"Here's the first part. I've come to realize that if what I feel isn't love, nothing is. "I love you. There, I've said it. I love you. I think I have always loved you but didn't know it." Marietta smiled as much out of relief than out of happiness.

"And the second part?" she said, her head whirling, wondering if she had really heard the words she had wanted to hear for months.

"Will you marry me?"

"Yes, oh yes," Marietta whispered.

"The third part is…"

"There's more?"

"Well, I've been thinking. If you go to medical school, it will take us at least four more years to start a family. I'd like to get married. I'd like us to have children… I know you want a family, but the wait… Can we manage it?"

"Well," Marietta said. "I want to marry soon, too. Perhaps, next year. After I graduate. I need to get out of the house, be my own person as soon as I can. I'm not marrying you for that, mind you. I'm marrying you because I love you." She looked into his face. Once she was satisfied that he had understood, she continued. "Perhaps I can post-pone medical school. For a time, at least."

"Whatever you want to do is fine with me, as long as you love me."

"John, I think I have loved you from the moment I first saw you, when you first tapped my shoulder and asked me to dance."

She wondered how they would break the news to Paul and Teresa. No medical degree in the near future and a husband who wasn't Italian. A tall order for them to accept. They decided to tell John's parents first, over dinner at his house. His mother had roasted a huge chicken. John's father sliced the bird in thin pieces and placed it in the center of the table alongside four of the biggest baked potatoes Marietta had ever seen. Creamed corn and canned string beans completed the side dishes. There was no bread or salad the way Marietta was used to at home but the smell of cinnamon from the apple pie just out of the oven intoxicated her. After John's mother cut the apple pie in four and topped each piece with two scoops of vanilla ice cream, John cleared his throat to speak.

"Mom, Dad, we have an announcement to make. We're engaged."

"Oh, that's wonderful," his mother said. Forgetting all about her apple pie and melting ice cream, she rose and hugged her son, then Marietta.

"Congratulations," his dad said, shaking John's hand and kissing Marietta on the cheek.

"I knew from the moment you first brought Marietta into the house that she was the one for you," John's mother confessed.

"You did?" John said, surprised.

"I could tell from the way you introduced her. It was written all over you, John." Then turning to Marietta, "And I can see in your face that you love our son."

160

"Very much," Marietta replied, her eyes resting on her new family. She never felt so wanted and appreciated. John's mother reminded her of Nonna. Nonna would be happy for Marietta today as John's mother was.

"Have you told Marietta's parents yet?" they asked.

"We'll tell them later," John said. "I'll ask for their blessing. They'll like that."

"You can't," Marietta said adamantly. "They'll say no."

John gave her a gentle squeeze. "Don't worry so much, darling. Trust me. I'll win your parents over." But Marietta was not assured. How could he understand? He wasn't Italian.

The following day they stood in front of Paul and Teresa. "Mr. and Mrs. Marino," John began. "I'd like to speak to you about an important matter."

"Shoot," Paul said. Marietta pictured John's words coiling into a bullet and hitting Paul directly in his gut.

"Your daughter and I love each other very much. We plan on getting married. We would both like the honor of your blessing on our marriage."

For a few minutes Paul and Teresa stared through him, as though he were transparent. John had spoken so softly and with such facility that Marietta feared they hadn't heard a word he'd said. When no one broke the silence, Marietta waited for the loud thunderbolt to crash on John.

"Huh, um," Paul grumbled, finally. "Let me see if I got it straight. You want to marry our daughter and you want our blessing. Is that right?" He smacked his lips, as if they were searching for something. Rubbing his chin with his left hand, he folded the sagging skin below into a pleat and thought some more. He bobbed his head from side to side and finally let go of his chin. He pointed his forefinger at John, almost touching his white starched shirt, as if John were in a police lineup.

"How do you propose to support my daughter? How much money do you make?"

"I'll be starting my residency at the hospital soon. The first few years won't be easy. I have loans to pay off. But after that, life should get better."

"With both of you as doctors, I suppose our health needs will be taken care of. Here's the deal. We buy you a house for a wedding present. Then you live upstairs. Not bad for starts, eh?"

For starts? Marietta shrank with terror. What would follow? Paul was set on controlling their lives no matter what.

John smiled. "That's very kind of you, sir, but not necessary. We're not sure where I'll have my practice. And Marietta has decided to forego, I mean, post-pone a medical career. She's chosen to teach science instead. We can have a family sooner and give you lots of grandchildren."

Teresa's jaw dropped. Children would remind her that she couldn't have them. Why should Marietta have them? She wanted Marietta to be barren just like her. Just like Sofia. She stirred, ready to speak, but Paul pulled her back.

"It sounds like you two have this all planned out whether we like it or not," he said wryly, not amused.

"We plan on getting married," John said. "But we still hope for your blessing."

Paul turned away as if he'd had enough of the conversation. Marietta gave John an "I told you so" look. Paul would never agree to the marriage now.

"Well, Teresa, it looks as if the kids leave us no choice," Paul said. "We'll show them. We'll show the Ireesh how Italians throw a party. We'll give them a wedding they'll never forget."

Teresa went white. Was her husband crazy? What about their old age? Who would take care of them? She had to take matters into her own hands for it was obvious to her that Paul had lost it.

"Where's the ring? You can't get married without a ring," she said, noting Marietta's hand was bare.

"I thought Marietta might like to pick it out," John said.

Paul took the reins again. "Pick it out this week. Next we invite your parents to Sunday dinner at our house and you give Marietta the ring then. *Capish?*" he said.

"*Capish*," John laughed.

Marietta walked over to Paul in a daze. "Thank you, Daddy. I didn't think you'd take the news so well," she told him honestly.

"You don't know your father then. And Mommy is happy for you, too. Isn't that right, Teresa?" He turned to his wife who glared and snorted. Ignoring her, he continued, "Mommy will go shopping with you for the wedding dress. You two can plan the flowers, the menu and all the things womenfolk like to do together. The hall, I will do. You're going to get married in Bay Ridge where my police partner's daughter was married. They could only afford the smaller reception room but we'll take the grand ballroom. We'll invite all the people who owe me big for every time I went to their children's affairs. It's payback time." He smiled.

"Why sure, Paul," Teresa said, brightening. She was glad to have a role in the festivities. "We'll have the shower above the Chinese Restaurant downtown. Sofia can give it with me as a surprise. We do it two months before the wedding. And for your maid of honor, you ask Concetta."

"Who?" Marietta said.

"You know, Concetta. The daughter of our *cummara,* our maid of honor, who came from San Demetrio."

"Wait a minute," Marietta cried. "Why would I ask Concetta? I've never even met her." The arrangements were moving much too fast.

"You don't know Concetta now, but we fix that," Teresa said. "We invite her and her family to dinner and you ask. She has to say yes. She can't insult."

"Even if she doesn't want to?"

"*Si,* even if she doesn't want to. It would be dishonor for her to refuse."

Marietta bit her lip. She'd always dreamed of having her sister as maid of honor.

Chapter Fifteen

The sky was a giant cloud of gray the day the Sullivans were scheduled to arrive at the Marino house for the engagement dinner. The radio had forecast a balmy 75 degrees with a falling barometer – a sure sign of an impending storm. Marietta walked into the kitchen and found Teresa bent in half, her head in the oven, her bare thighs and pink bloomers in full view. Holding a long plastic tube with a black, hollow rubber bulb at one end, she drew the fatty juices up from the roasting pan and squirted them on the skin of a small turkey. Teresa and Paul weren't fond of turkey. On Thanksgiving they cooked only a rolled breast of turkey tied with white string. No one found the dry white meat palatable and since it was served after the lasagna, meatballs and braciole, they were too full to eat anything else. Most of the turkey ended up in the garbage. But Sofia had convinced them that the Irish loved turkey and if she wanted to make a good impression on the Sullivans, that's what she should cook.

"Can I help?" Marietta said, nearly fainting from the blast of heat out of the oven.

"What and have you say you cooked the meal? Remember, I slave for you," she said. Then, to prove her point, she lifted the hot turkey pan with her bare hands and placed it on top of the stove next to the pot of boiling string beans. Her fingers turned red but she didn't flinch. The turkey skin was dark brown, burned to a crisp. Overcooked again, Marietta thought. All that work, all that basting, and the meat would end up dry. The baked potatoes wrapped in aluminum foil were at least somewhat protected as was the salad and eight ricotta-filled cannoli pastries keeping cool in the refrigerator.

Why hadn't Teresa listened to Marietta instead of Sofia and cooked her usual Sunday meal? John and his parents loved Italian food. Teresa and Paul would have enjoyed it, too, and been complimented on it.

Within a few minutes John arrived, his parents climbing up the stairs behind him. They removed their shoes before entering as John had instructed them. The shoes were paired neatly on the floor outside the door as if they'd visited many times before.

"Mr. and Mrs. Marino, my parents, Margaret and Tom Sullivan," John said.

"Glad to meet you, Mr. Marino, Mrs. Marino." John's dad extended his hand in greeting. His wife smiled and offered the apple pie she carried in her hands. It was unwrapped, still hot in the glass dish she'd used to bake it that very morning. Paul took the pie and handed it to Teresa who placed it in a corner on the stove.

"Please, none of this Mr. and Mrs. stuff. Paul and Teresa to you. Mom and dad to them, of course. With these two young ones getting married, we're now family," Paul said winking at Marietta and John. He shook Tom's hand and placed his left arm on his shoulder as if they'd been buddies for years. "Sit. Sit, Tom. Teresa has prepared a feast as usual. She cooked your kind of food to make sure you eat. Sit. Get a load off your feet."

"We want you to know how happy we are with your daughter. She's such a lovely girl. John's very lucky to get her," Tom Sullivan said.

"We're all lucky. They're young ...and we... well, the four of us are getting on in years, no? They'll take good care of us in our old age, right?" Paul winked.

Tom looked confused. "I'm not quite sure I know what you mean..."

"We talk business later. Now you eat," Teresa interrupted. She didn't want the turkey to get cold. A glance at Paul clued him to begin slicing the meat. He took a butcher knife from the silverware drawer and with a long fork for balance cut the legs and thighs whole so they fell freely in the juices of the baking pan. Then, because he was not used to carving anything but a roast beef, he studied the body of the bird as if he expected imaginary lines to show him where to place the knife. When none appeared, he cut the bird in four. With the legs and thighs, he knew it made six pieces, perfect for the six of them.

Marietta heard John's father gasp. She'd eaten turkey at their house once and watched with awe how meticulously thin he had cut the meat. Flawless slices gently fell into the oval serving dish his wife provided, picture-perfect, as if it were a photo in a magazine. When she took a slice, the white meat tasted tender, moist and full of flavor.

"Eat. Eat. Don't be shy," Teresa shouted. John's parents didn't know where to begin. The salad, which was their usual starting point, was missing. John had prepped them that Italians eat their salad after the meal. "We don't fill up on weeds," John had quoted Paul to them. "After dinner the weeds help digest." But in the confusion of the meal, they had forgotten.

"This piece is too big for me. I'll never fit in my clothes if I eat all of it," Marietta said, trying to remedy the situation.

"I'll share it with you," John said, coming to the rescue. He took a leg and thigh, cut it at the joint and gave the thigh to Marietta.

"That's a great idea," Tom said. He lifted his fork and took a chunk of white meat and placed it on his plate. For a brief moment he was tempted to carve it into thin slices but he didn't want to offend his host. He also didn't have the proper knife. Splitting the piece not quite evenly, he gave his wife the lesser portion. Paul and Teresa each took a full piece, nibbled at it and left most of it on their plate. No one spoke, only the forks and knives clinking in the silence.

"John tells me you're a policeman," Tom said, finally breaking the silence, glad to rest his jaws from chewing on the dry meat.

"I could tell you stories that would make your blood curl, but," he glanced around the table, "this is not the place to bring them up. And you? How do you make a living?"

"I'm in the insurance business. I, too, have gruesome tales. Men die and leave their wives and children destitute. But, as you say, now is not the time or place."

"I don't believe in insurance," Paul said. "It's a waste of money. Better to put the money in the bank and then it's yours when you need it."

Marietta tensed. She grabbed John's hand. She hoped Paul had not offended John's dad. She didn't want a confrontation their first meeting.

"Good point. But not everyone is disciplined enough to save, and if you die young, where does that leave the wife and kids? In the street," Tom said, impressing Marietta with his diplomacy.

"Italians believe in *la famiglia*. The parents take care of the children when the children are young. Then the children take care of the parents when the parents get old.

"So where's the ring?" Teresa blurted out. "You gotta have a ring to be engaged, no?"

John put his hand in his pocket and produced a blue velvet box. Opening the box, he turned and gave it to Marietta. "Marietta, will you marry me?" he said, more for their parents' ears than their own.

"Yes," she said, smiling. John took the ring out of its depression and slipped it on her finger. A solitaire diamond on a Tiffany setting cast in white gold. Aglow with happiness, Margaret and Tom clapped. Teresa and Paul stared at the ring.

"Too small," Teresa said.

"It's what I picked out," Marietta said defiantly.

"Shame ... so small," Teresa went on. She eyed John's mother's ring. It was larger than Marietta's but still half the size of her own.

"I'm the only one who has to like it. The jeweler said its clarity makes it higher in quality than a larger sized stone," Marietta explained. She wanted to erase the smug look on Teresa's face.

"No matter. Someday you wear mine," Teresa said, satisfied she'd solved the problem.

"I don't want to wear your ring. Daddy gave you that ring. It's for you to wear. I want to wear my own, the one John gave me." John's parents began to squirm in their seats. "What I mean," Marietta added, "is that you'd be insulting Daddy if you gave away your ring to me. I'm perfectly happy with mine. What's important is not the size of the ring but what it signifies."

"Well, now that we have that out of the way, how about some espresso with dessert," Paul urged.

"The espresso is good. But if you'd rather have American coffee, I'd be happy to make it for you," Marietta offered.

"We've never had espresso. I hear it's quite strong but today, we'll try anything Italian," Margaret said laughing, relieving any lingering concerns in Marietta.

As they bade each other goodbye, Paul said, "Remember we're family now." He kissed them and sent them home with the leftover turkey Teresa had packed in aluminum foil.

The next day John phoned to thank Paul and Teresa for their wonderful hospitality but neither was available. Paul had driven to the store to buy a carton of cigarettes and Teresa was downstairs talking to Sofia, telling her all about the Sullivans, how different they were from people they knew.

Feeling safely alone, Marietta sighed into the black mouthpiece. "Last night I had a horrible dream," she told John. "I dreamt that I was at the back of the church all dressed in white ready to come down the aisle. I could see you waiting for me at the altar with the priest. Then I heard a noise, turned and spotted my mother huddled in a corner with a large kerchief on her head. She was dressed in black, as if I had died, and she was crying. Instead of 'Here Comes the Bride,' the organist played 'The Lord Is My Shepherd.' John, I'd love to have my mother and sister at our wedding, at least at the church. I want Pia to be my maid of honor, not Concetta."

"It's our wedding," he stressed. "Why can't we invite them? You still have that P.O. Box address, don't you?"

"Yes, but even if it's active and I'm able to contact them, my parents will never allow my mother to come. Pia... maybe, but never my mother. They'd crucify her with insults. I couldn't bear to see my mother hurt, no matter how angry and disappointed I am that she sent me away. And maybe I'm being selfish, but I don't want anything to ruin our wedding."

"Nothing can spoil our wedding. And I'm not disappointed your mother sent you away. I would have never met you. Aren't you glad we met?"

"Meeting you is the best thing that's happened to me," she said. But the price was steep, she thought. She wished she could have met John without losing everyone she loved.

"Let's see if your parents would accept your sister. How can they object to a sixteen-year-old?"

"You don't know them."

"They might surprise you. Look what happened when we told them we wanted to get married." Marietta agreed that had worked out better than expected. Still, she became anxious. She hadn't seen Stella or Pia in such a long time, since she saw them in the principal's office. She had no news of them except overhearing Teresa tell Sofia once, *"La puttana è risposata* – the bitch is remarried. *Che vergogna!* What a disgrace!" Marietta swallowed hard at the memory. Stella would have a different last name now. How would she find her?

There was another issue to contend with. What if Stella no longer wanted her? It was Marietta who had stopped writing. How would Stella and Pia know that she was forbidden to write and not that she quit on her own? Oh, why couldn't she just have been raised in a normal family where she and her sister would have grown up together? They could have come to America as one family, all four of them intact, instead of one by one, broken and apart.

"Why do you want to marry me?" she asked John. Did he know what he was getting into?

"Because I'm happiest when I'm with you," he smiled. "You make me feel alive."

"But I come with such baggage. Sometimes I think I'm still ten, sitting on an airplane, stunned with what was happening. I didn't feel loved for a long time, John, until I met you. I don't know what I would have done if you didn't love me."

"You would have moved on. You're a survivor."

Armed with John's love, that evening Marietta gathered the confidence to ask Paul if Pia could attend the wedding.

"Do you know what would really make me happy at my wedding?" she said.

"What, we're not doing enough for you and your Irish boyfriend? Is his side complaining?" Paul countered.

"Oh, you're doing more than I expected." Marietta said. Paul had put a hefty deposit on a beautiful reception hall. He'd ordered the limousine to take them to the church. A photographer had come to the house and shown them albums highlighting his work. Nothing was too good for her and John. "But I've always dreamed that my sister would be my maid of honor at my wedding and I would be hers when she got married."

"I see," he said, pensively moving his jowls. "Maybe we can send for her."

"What you say? I no hear." Teresa stormed into the room.

"I was hoping Pia could be my maid of honor," Marietta repeated. All my friends who are getting married are having their sisters in the wedding party, either as a maid of honor or a bridesmaid." She swallowed. "I'd like to contact Pia and see if she'll come."

"She come, she stay here with us," Teresa answered. Precisely, Marietta thought. They'd sleep together in her room. They'd catch up with their lost years. Not enough time for everything but it'd be a start.

"We talk to her. She won't want to go back. She'll be our daughter next. If Marietta and her new Ireesh husband no help us when we old, Pia do it."

"Teresa, what are you saying?" Paul interjected. They were getting too old to raise another child.

"No," Marietta screamed. "You're not going to imprison her here once she arrives. She's not coming for you. She's coming for me, just for a couple of days, for the wedding. She's not personal property. I'm not going to let you steal her from me, the only person I have left from my past who could love me."

"Then we no want her," Teresa said, sliding the palm of one hand against the other with finality. "Concetta be your maid of honor, and that's that!"

"Fine," Marietta puffed. "Have it your way." She yanked her jacket out of the closet and walked out the door. Outside she welcomed the cold wind biting her skin. She walked past storefronts, admiring the ease with which their doors let people in and out like air in one's lungs, past brownstone houses flanked by trees and garbage cans, and around schools and playgrounds. After two hours, she grew tired and slowed her pace. She stopped in front of the church she attended every Sunday. The street was dark. Climbing up the outside steps, she pushed the heavy door in. It opened into a greater darkness. Exhausted physically and mentally, she took a seat in the last row. Soon her eyes adjusted and she began to see the marble altar, the crucified Christ above it, a statue of the Virgin Mary on one side and St. Joseph with his staff on the other. A feeling of déjà vu enveloped her. She'd been to church like this before. In Castellaneta many years ago, on the eve of her departure to America. She remembered praying with the same fervor, the same longing not to be separated from her family. A shiver ran down her spine. She placed her hands in her jacket pockets for warmth and found two quarters. Walking up to the altar, she lit a votive candle in front of a statue of the Blessed Virgin who was, perhaps, the only true mother she'd ever have. She dropped one of the coins through the metal slit and heard it clink. The sound soothed her as though it were a bell attesting to her presence. She was all set to place her last quarter through the same opening when she pulled her hand away. She'd save the coin to call John. Leaving the inner darkness for the outside, she found a candy store with a pay phone. She heard the clink of the quarter and dialed John's number.

"I told you it wouldn't work with my sister as my maid of honor."

"They said no?"

"I did."

"You mean they did."

"No, I mean I did. They said yes but they don't want Pia to come for me. They want her for themselves. They want to keep her, to imprison her the way they did me. If she comes, they'll brainwash her against my mother."

"But that doesn't seem possible. They can't hold her against her will."

Anything can happen, thought Marietta. Wasn't she forced to leave Nonna against her will?

"Darling, where are you? Are you at home?"

"I haven't been home. I'm at a candy store about fifteen blocks away. They're probably getting ready to call the police right now."

"Stay right there. I'll come and meet you. I'll take you home. You'll see your mother and sister later, after we marry. I promise. Later, when we're together and you're free."

Later... when we're together... and I'm free – that's all Marietta could think of throughout her senior year of college. When the days seemed interminably long, she'd mouth the words quietly to herself, like a mantra. She lived for the future. Everything, from washing her face in the morning to studying for exams to getting into her pajamas at night, was done for the day she'd marry John and the life she'd have with him. Even her graduation was an exercise toward that goal. As she marched into the auditorium in her cap and gown with her classmates, every step brought her closer to later when she'd be free. She'd be with John every moment of the day. Later, she'd no longer be under others' rules, but could make her own decisions, follow her own mind and heart. As John's wife, she'd finally be free and wonderfully happy. Later.

Chapter Sixteen

The glass walls in the restaurant offered views of Buzzards Bay on one side and the hotel pool on the other. Sitting opposite John at a cozy table in the dining room of the seaside resort in Cape Cod, Marietta finally felt independent. For the first time in her life she didn't need to worry about getting home on time or what Paul and Teresa would say. She saw everything from the perspective of a new wife – from the white lace toppers over the windows to the baby grand piano at the corner of the room where a tuxedoed man sat playing love songs.

"We'll never have to say goodbye again," John said munching on the last bite of a strawberry. They savored their fruit with eyes only for one another.

"We don't need to talk about later any longer. It *is* later. I thought later would never come," she said.

The wedding had gone off miraculously well and with no surprises. They'd endured the dictates imposed by Teresa and Paul and emerged unscathed. Marietta assented to the expensive bouquet sprays Teresa insisted on even though she thought them a waste of money. As lovely as the flowers were, they'd die the next day. Even if they didn't, she couldn't bring them on her honeymoon. And they wouldn't keep until she and John returned. If Teresa could enjoy them even for a few days, such extravagance could serve a purpose. But no, she'd throw them out the minute they entered the house. Flowers stink up the air, she'd say, and they'd be in the garbage can in no time.

Marietta also agreed to Teresa's idea, strongly seconded by the photographer, to purchase three wedding albums: one for the bride and groom and one for each set of parents. When Teresa complained there weren't enough photos, Marietta increased the number. The guest list was another issue of contention. It embarrassed Paul and Teresa to have fewer people on the bride's side of the family, so they reduced the number of invitations sent out to the Sullivan side. John's mother solved the problem by having a party at her house immediately after the reception.

Although Paul and Teresa ran the show at the reception, John and Marietta handled every detail of the Church ceremony. They chose the readings, the songs and the priest who would officiate at Mass. They felt relieved that Paul and Teresa fussed only about the party afterward, who should sit where, how many courses to serve, even predicting how much money guests would give. They made sure to include the parents and children whose weddings they had attended over the years and who would now have to pay them back.

On the morning of her wedding, Marietta had risen early, along with the summer sun. Her mood matched its radiance. She'd been really happy weeks before when she received her college diploma with John and his parents sitting in the audience next to Paul and Teresa. Yet that joy didn't compare to how she felt when she became Mrs. John Sullivan, a name no one had imposed on her, but one she'd chosen freely. Nothing hindered her happiness on her wedding day – not the guests who were complete strangers, not Concetta the imposed maid of honor, and not the photographer who interrupted the bridal couple's every move for a snapshot. Once she accepted Stella's and Pia's absence, the day became hers.

The newlyweds spent their wedding night at a New York hotel where, the next morning, John woke up starving. They ran to the nearest diner for brunch.

"There's a pay phone. Let's call your parents and thank them for everything," he said, after he'd downed his last mouthful of ham and eggs.

"Are you serious? It's your family we should thank," Marietta explained. John's parents had gone along with everything Teresa and Paul wanted, even when it inconvenienced them.

"We will but we'll thank yours first," John said.

Marietta sighed. While she trusted John in most things, his sense of "I know what's best for both us" seemed dictatorial at times and made her uncomfortable. And he wasn't always right. He didn't know the world she grew up in. It was very different from his. A feeling of helplessness returned, the fear of having to hear her parents' reaction, knowing it would be a negative one. She wanted to stop him, but John was in the phone booth before she could get up from her seat.

"Hello," John said cheerfully.

"Who's this?" Paul shouted.

"It's John."

"John who?"

John covered the mouthpiece with his hand. "He doesn't recognize me."

"I told you it was a bad idea," she whispered. Sighing, she took the phone away from him.

"It's Marietta. And John. We... well; John has something to say to you."

"Don't tell me he wants to give you back already!" Paul yelled.

Marietta didn't know whether to laugh or cry. Swallowing hard, she handed the phone back to John.

"We want to thank you for the wonderful wedding you and your wife gave us."

"What?" he shouted. Marietta could hear him even though the phone was on John's ear. John repeated his words of thanks.

"Huh? There's no accident or anything?"

"No. No. Everything is fine. We want to thank you for everything you've done." She counted three times that John had thanked Paul.

"No problem," Paul said and hung up.

With the receiver still in his hand, John cleared the dial tone and called his parents.

"It's great to hear from you, son." For ten minutes, Tom and Margaret Sullivan relayed good wishes from friends who had not attended the wedding but wanted to drop by the house and leave gifts. Then Margaret asked to speak to Marietta.

"Everyone said you looked beautiful. You're our daughter now. You'd make us proud if you called us Mom and Dad."

"Thanks …Mom and…Dad," she said, the words feeling strange but wonderful.

When Marietta and John returned from their honeymoon, they placed the key in the door of the apartment that would now be their home. Not Paul and Teresa's home but their own one-bedroom flat. Her summer job as a camp counselor wouldn't start for another week, so she decided to use her free time to decorate the apartment while John resumed his duties at the hospital.

"I'd love to sew some curtains for the windows," she said to John the first night they'd returned, "but I don't know how."

"Ask my mother," he said. "She's been sewing for years."

The next morning, Marietta phoned her new in-laws. Margaret immediately invited her to lunch. After they ate, she brought her upstairs to the empty bedroom where her sewing machine lay. "It's easy," she said. "First you learn to thread the machine. Then your hands do the rest." Marietta practiced threading the machine a few times and later sewed a straight stitch on a piece of scrap material. She loved the sound of the needle going up and down and the feel of the fabric as it passed across her fingers. "Curtains are the easiest things to make. They usually require only a straight stitch," continued Margaret. "You can use my sewing machine to sew them until you get your own."

"Thank you, Mom" Marietta said. "Would you go with me to the store to pick out the material? I don't know which kind would be best or how many yards I need."

"Let's measure the height and width of your windows first. Then we'll know how much to buy. You can start sewing them when we get back from the store. You'll have them finished in no time, before the week is over, for sure."

That evening John went directly to his parents' house. Marietta got up from the sewing machine to greet him.

"Stay for dinner," his mother coaxed. "I've got a roast in the oven that's just about ready." It was perfect. Marietta had been so preoccupied with the curtains that she hadn't thought about food. John's father walked in and the four sat down to eat.

"This is delicious," Marietta said. "How do you make it taste so good?"

"It's easy," Margaret said with the same ease as when she was showing Marietta how to sew. "Just put the roast on a broiling pan, sprinkle some salt, paprika and garlic powder on top. Bake it at three hundred and twenty five degrees and let the oven do the rest. About twenty minutes to the pound depending how rare or well-done you like it." Yes, easy, Marietta thought. Just like Nonna would have done.

In no time at all it seemed, Marietta's camp counselor job began and ended. The summer now over, her thoughts turned to teaching Science at the local Junior High School.

She used Saturday morning to write lesson plans and unit outlines satisfying the curriculum. In the afternoon, she thought about the week's meals. She shopped for ingredients that John would like. She was Mrs. John Sullivan, no longer Marietta Marino or even Marietta Bollina. She'd think only of the present and the future. She wanted to leave the past behind.

But the past clung on. It crept up, surreptitiously, at unexpected moments during the day. Marietta wondered if Stella and Pia knew she was married. Did they tell Nonna? Was everyone angry at her for not going to California with Stella many years ago? Would they try to contact her at some point? How would they find out where she lived? These same thoughts invaded her sleep at night. At times, they became nightmares and woke up John. He held her tightly and she'd relax in his arms. But when he had night duty and slept at the hospital, she was left alone and defenseless.

The dreams were normally the same. A woman with flowing black hair followed Marietta's every move. She stood behind her in the classroom. She accompanied her to the supermarket. If Marietta walked with slow, even steps, the woman trailed at the same pace. When Marietta picked up the pace, so did the woman. In one dream, Marietta decided she had to shake her. She started to run fast, up the street and around the corner from her apartment. She spotted an alleyway, shot through it and hid behind an open door hoping to elude her. But no, the woman still trailed behind. Marietta then sped harder, faster, with all her might. Suddenly the ground under her feet transformed itself into a treadmill. She was running in place. And the woman was gaining on her. She got so close that Marietta could feel the heat of her breath across her neck. She woke up trembling but relieved to be finally out of the woman's clutches.

In another dream Marietta was a mother who had placed her baby in a bowl of raw, chopped beef. She stored the bowl inside the medicine cabinet overnight. It was for protection, the mother said. She padded the shelf with cotton in case the baby moved and fell down. At breakfast the next morning, the mother remembered what she had done. She was petrified that the child had died during the night. When she opened the cabinet door, she found the baby still asleep and unharmed. Trembling both in gratitude and shock, she took the baby in her arms and began to breast-feed.

"What does it mean?" she asked John over the phone the next day.

"It means you want a baby."

"I'm afraid I'll be a bad mother. I have no experience with babies, except playing with my younger cousins in Italy, which was a long time ago."

"It's like riding a bike. It all comes back. Besides, I'll help. I know a lot from being with my nieces and nephews."

Suddenly changing the subject, Marietta said, "I was going through some boxes of mine from my parents' house and I found my sister's letter."

"Really? Why don't you write her now? You've been talking about it for so long."

Yes, Marietta thought, maybe that's what her dreams are also telling her: It is time to try and find Pia and Stella, come what may. Taking a seat at the kitchen table, she picked up a pen, fidgeted in her chair, and looked up at the ceiling as if to find there the words she wanted to write.

"*Dear Pia,*" she began. Her sister's name on paper warmed her. Please be there, every ounce of her flesh screamed. She touched her chest to calm her racing heart. Taking a deep breath, she put pen to paper again.

"*I'm married and am free to write to you. The reason I haven't written in all these years is because they –Aunt Teresa and Uncle Paul– had forbidden it. There's no one to stop me now. My husband, John, and I look forward to knowing you and Mom again. I told him everything. I hope you still have the same address. If you don't, I have lost you forever. I love you and long to see you and Mom. If you feel the same way about me, write back."*

She printed her new name and signed it with love. Folding the letter, she slid it in the envelope and sealed it, double-checking that she copied the address correctly. She put her return address on the envelope in case the letter was undeliverable. Then she'd know the search for her sister and mother was futile. Not trusting anyone else to mail it, not even John, she walked directly to the post office. Before she let the envelope fall into the narrow slot, she kissed it, begging it to bring back good news.

Walking home she realized there was nothing left to do but wait. There was no sense being anxious. She had to let go and be patient. She'd learned patience from Nonna, she recalled. "Nonna's street, where I used to live," she whispered to herself. Like a flash, it struck her that the address was imbedded in her memory. Surely Stella would have kept in contact with her mother. Marietta ran home and composed another letter.

Cara Nonna,

Mi devi perdonare che non ho scritto da tanti anni. Forgive me for not writing after so many years. *I zii non mi lasciavano a scrivere a te o la mamma.* My aunt and uncle wouldn't let me write to you or my mother. *Come stai?* How are you? *Spero che tu e il Nonno state bene.* I hope that you and Nonno are well. *La mia cugina, Lucia, come sta?* How is my cousin Lucia? *Io sto bene.* I'm fine. *Mi son sposata con un uomo tanto bravo.* I'm married to a wonderful man. *Si chiama John (Giovanni, in Italiano).* His name is John. *Adesso che sono libera per scrivere vorrei sapere se avete l'indirizzo della mia mamma e sorella.* Now that I'm free to write, I'd like to know if you have my mother and sister's address. *Ho spedito una lettera a loro proprio oggi ma l'indirizzo che avevo è molto vecchio.* Just today I mailed

them a letter but the address I had is very old. *Non so se la mia lettera arrivera.* I don't know if my letter will arrive.
Ti voglio tanto bene. I love you very much. *Non mi son mai dimenticata di voi o di tutta la famiglia e spero che ci vediamo un'altra volta.* I have never forgotten you or the whole family and I hope that we will see each other again.
Baci a tutti, specialment a te e il Nonno. Kisses to everyone, especially to you and Nonno.
Baci,
Marietta
She ran back to the post office and purchased the air mail postage for Italy. She affixed it to the envelope and dropped it in the slot. She sighed. She'd done all she could. Armed with Nonna's patience, she had to simply wait it out.
A week later, a letter arrived from California. "It's got a real street name for a return address," she cried, holding the envelope under John's nose.
"Well, what does the letter say?"
"I haven't opened it. What if they don't want to hear from me, if they're hurt that I never contacted them? They might not believe I couldn't. My mother might think I loved my adopted parents instead of her."
"I'll open it," John said. He tore the edge, careful not to rip the new address. "Are you ready?"
"I'm as ready as I'll ever be." She took a deep breath, pulled out the kitchen chair and sat down. He began reading:
"Dear Marietta,
Not a day goes by that we don't think about you. Mom cries over you on a regular basis. Mom is remarried. He's nice to me and I call him 'Dad.' Here are some recent pictures of us. Please write back soon and send pictures of you and your husband. We would have loved to have seen you on your wedding day. Send us a wedding picture, too. We can't wait for your next letter. We love you.
Pia"

"They want me back?" Marietta said. "They want me to write to them?"

"Let's not write," John said.

"What?" Her mother and sister finally validated her and he wanted to give it all up?

"Let's phone them," he suggested.

"We don't know the number."

"We have the street name and town. We can call the operator and get the number."

Marietta was numb. The world had turned upside down again. One minute she was the adult married to John, the next she was ten, standing on the cobblestone street below Nonna's eleven hundred year-old-house playing hopscotch with Lucia, the orange peel fragrant in her pocket.

"I got it," John said, handing her the piece of paper on which he'd jotted the area code and seven-digit number that the operator had given him. "Let's call and talk to them now."

"Right now? I'd hear their voice and they'd hear mine?" From the corner of her eye, she could see the ten-year-old she used to be, frozen like a statue. "What do I say?"

"This is what you've wanted your whole life, what you've been waiting for all these years," John said. "You'll know what to say."

Marietta heard John dial the numbers. She felt the softness of the chair on which she sat. Yet, she couldn't process what she'd say. Despite Pia's warm letter, they could reject her on the phone. She'd find out they didn't love her after all.

"Hang up! I'm not ready."

"All right," John said. "But why?"

"I don't know what this will do to me."

"You've been talking about your mother and sister from the moment I met you. No matter what happens, we have each other. We don't need anyone else to be happy." He

184

wrapped his arms around her and kissed her forehead tenderly as if she were a fragile piece of glass. Then he added, "I know how much your childhood scarred you. The hard part is over. You survived. This is the reward you've been waiting for."

"You're right," Marietta sniffled on his shoulder. His confidence energized her. "Waiting won't make me any less scared. Let's get it over with."

John redialed and handed her the phone. Marietta counted the rings. Two, three, four...they're not home, she thought. Or maybe they had the wrong number.

"Halloh," a voice finally said. Marietta recognized the timbre immediately. Unmistakably Stella's.

"It's Marietta." The words choked in her throat.

"*O caro Gesù, sei veramente tu?* Oh, dear Jesus, is it really you?" Stella sobbed. "Pia. Pia, come. Marietta is on the phone. *Non posso parlare.* I can't speak. God finally granted us the miracle." The crying got louder. To Marietta, it felt like Stella's tears were hitting her face right through the phone wires, until she realized the water came from her own eyes. Marietta couldn't talk either. She thrust the phone back to John.

When John took the receiver, Pia was on the other end. "Yes, we were married about four months ago.... I'm a doctor. Marietta teaches junior high school students... science... She's told me so much about you and your mother. She's always wanted to get back in touch with you... She wasn't allowed... Your aunt and uncle were very strict... We'd love to see you too... Soon, yes. Take our phone number...Yes... Yes... She loves you too...She would tell you herself if she could...It's overwhelming for her now...for your mother, too...Yes...Yes...Talk to you soon...Goodbye."

With the call over, Marietta was worn. She went to the bathroom and splashed cool water on her face. For the next week her emotions whirled like a coin tossed into the air. One side was Marietta's joy for finally reestablishing contact with her family; the other, resentment for all the years they were apart. It threw her back into childhood. Into the panic she used to feel when her mother talked about America. Into the confusion she experienced when Stella forged Marietta's name in letters she sent to Paul addressing him as "*Papà*." Into her desire to be Nonna's daughter so that she could stay in Castellaneta forever. She'd caught up with the past but the darkness came with it, more entrenched and powerful than before.

A week later the phone rang. Marietta assumed it was John's mother who often called to invite them to dinner. That would be nice. A home-cooked meal, four people around the table, a real family. She'd say yes.

"It's Pia."

Marietta's heart stopped. "It's good to hear your voice, Pia," she said finally.

"I'm sorry we couldn't talk the other day when you called."

"I'm sorry, too. I wanted to talk to both you and Mom. I don't know what came over me. I guess I couldn't believe it was really happening."

"I have a message from Mom. She would love to have you come spend Christmas with us. She's already mailed you and John plane tickets. Please say you'll come."

Christmas was more than a month away. Her school would be on Christmas break, but she doubted John could spare the time off. She cupped the phone and asked him.

"I'll work out my schedule to be free. Tell her yes," he shouted, surprising her.

"Mom will be thrilled," Pia said, overhearing. "She's here if you want to speak to her. She's dreamed of this day for a long time. She cries every time she thinks about it." Marietta certainly recognized the emotion. Breathless she waited for the mother she'd longed for all these years to come on the phone.

"*Cara figlia!* Dear daughter!" Marietta's heart stopped again. She smiled into the phone at Stella's use of the words *figlia* and daughter. Stella's English had improved, but the Italian still remained in the combination of words she used and in her accent. "Jesus answered my prayer. You and John are the best Christmas present *nel mondo* – in the world."

"Thank you, Mom. You and Pia are the best Christmas present I can have, too."

"I sent you the tickets, *cara figlia*. You come. I will see you soon. *Ciao. Fin'a Natale. Ciao...*Bye. Until Christmas. Bye."

"Ciao," the Italian echoing in Marietta's head long after she hung up.

Orange Peels and Cobblestones

Chapter Seventeen

Several days later, Stella's plane tickets arrived in the mail, along with a stack of Christmas cards, all glittery and colorful. It all seemed to Marietta like some festive chorus heralding this year's season of joy as particularly special for her. As she carried the mail up the stairs to the apartment, suddenly a blue airmail envelope slipped out from between the pile and fell to the floor. Marietta gasped at the envelope as if witnessing an epiphany: A picture of the Madonna on the stamp. *Italia* on the postmark.

"*Sei ritornata da noi.* You've returned to us," Marietta read the letter with misty eyes. "*Non abbiamo mai perduto speranza.* We never lost hope. *Il Dio ha risposto la nostra preghiera.* God answered our prayer. *Ti vogliamo molto bene. Adesso possiamo morire con pace.* We love you very much. Now we can die in peace. *Baci, baci, baci, i tuoi cari Nonni.* Kisses, kisses, your dear Grandparents."

Just below the signature was an arrow. Marietta turned the page to the other side and found another letter. "*Cara Marietta,*" she read. "*Sono Zio Umberto.* This is Uncle Bert. *I Nonni non stanno tanto bene.* Your grandparents aren't in good health. *Ma dopo che ho letto la tua lettera, erano cosi contenti che le sue faccie mi sempravano piu giovane.* But after I read them your letter, they were so happy that their faces seemed younger to me. *Scrivi, scrivi spesso e mandi fotografie di te e tuo marito.* Write, write often and send pictures of you and your husband. *Ti vogliono vedere cosi tanto.* They want to see you so much. *Baci, il tuo Zio Umberto.* Below his name was Stella's address. It matched the one Pia had sent.

188

Marietta was so happy that she sat down and wrote to Nonna immediately, telling her of the coming reunion with Stella and Pia in California. As she enclosed a wedding photo of her and John, she heard singing outside on the street. Looking out the window, she saw a group of children about the same age she had been when she had last seen Nonna. She found herself humming along with their tune: *Jingle bells jingle bells, jingle all the way. Oh what fun it is to ride in a one-horse open sleigh.* It brought to mind another song, one she and Lucia used to sing years ago at this time of year. It was called *Tu Scendi dalle Stelle* You Descend from the Stars. The words of the old song came back as if she were singing them with her cousin that very moment.

Tu scendi dalle stelle You come down from the stars
O Re del Cielo, Oh King of the sky
E vieni in una grotta And you come in a grotto
Al freddo al gelo In cold and ice
O bambino, mio Divino Oh Divine Baby
Io ti vedo qui a tremar I see you trembling here
O Dio Beato Oh Blessed God

With her letter to Nonna in hand, the tickets to California safely tucked away in her desk for the forthcoming trip, and the image of herself and Lucia singing their favorite Christmas song, Marietta was for a moment filled with a joy she hadn't thought possible with her family again.

The days before Christmas flew for both John and Marietta. Faster than they thought possible, they found themselves in the air flying to see Stella and Pia for the first time after the long absence. Marietta couldn't describe her feelings now, only a numbness that prevented her from feeling. Yet, when the plane touched ground in Los Angeles at midnight, Marietta was as bright-eyed as a child on Christmas morning. She remembered her first Christmas in America. Santa had brought her a bicycle, an English Racer, which she loved. In Castellaneta she found only fruit and candy in her stocking. The gifts there didn't come from Santa but from *la beffana*, a good old witch, and they didn't come on Christmas morning but in January on the feast of the Magi or the Epiphany. Yet, she had loved the presents just as much.

Thousands of miles away now from both places, Marietta walked down the ramp searching for the two familiar faces that for the last decade had lived only in her heart. She heard someone call her name. Stella suddenly approached and scooped her in her arms. When she let go, Marietta was free to hug Pia. The first thing Marietta noticed was how well-dressed they were. Pia had on a tweed skirt and a matching sweater that accentuated her breasts. Stella wore a classic black dress and pearls. Both looked like they'd stepped off the pages of a fashion magazine. Looking down at the inexpensive purple skirt and top she wore, Marietta suddenly felt inferior.

A man stood slightly apart behind Stella. "This is my husband, Carl," she said. Short, gray-haired and wearing a pair of wrinkled tan slacks and plaid flannel shirt rolled up to the elbows, Carl contrasted sharply with Stella's youthful and rich appearance. He was much older than Antonio and not nearly as handsome.

"I'm John, the other husband," John said, extending his hand. Carl led them to the parking lot toward the car. Stella never let go of Marietta's hand. When she turned to sit in the back of the car with John and Pia, Stella pulled her forward.

"No, come up front with me and Carl. I don't want you far away any more. I have a surprise for you," she said in girlish voice full of excitement. "I invited all our friends to celebrate your return. They're at our house right now waiting for us."

"Will they still be there when we arrive?" Marietta asked, not sure how long it would take to drive to Stella's home in Santa Barbara.

"We didn't expect the plane to be delayed as much as it was, *ma loro aspettano* - but they'll wait," Stella said.

"It's late," Carl said, giving her a look that perhaps they might have gone home.

"They're my friends," Stella countered, her voice determined. "They know how much I've suffered all these years. The pain of losing a daughter nearly broke my heart. I cried myself to sleep every night. Sometimes, I'd pull my hair out, slap my chest a hundred times, knowing you were with those animals, hoping you'd come back. I worried how you were growing up. Were you dressed properly? Did they feed you? Did they hit you?" Stella never paused for a reply. Once Marietta realized the questions were rhetorical, she leaned back against her seat and concentrated on John's deep voice and Pia's soft murmur behind her. She strained to hear their conversation, but with Stella's constant chatter, she couldn't piece their words together.

When the car finally pulled into the driveway, Marietta drank in her surroundings. Every window blazed with light, singling out the sprawling ranch house like a beacon in the dark sky. Light sprang from two long sections of rose bushes that lined the walkway. The green grass was manicured to perfection. Marietta had left a cold, stark winter in New York, where the trees were barren, no flowers bloomed, the grass was brown and the icy air stung her face. But here the scent of flowers intoxicated the air. Marietta turned to make sure she wasn't dreaming. But no, John was right there, talking with Pia as if her worlds had come together. She moved back hoping to join them, to reclaim her husband and sister, when suddenly Stella grabbed her arm again, pulling her in through the front door into the foyer. A silver chandelier with six cherubs each holding a light bulb hung from the ceiling.

"We're back," Stella shouted in the hallway to cue her guests. "They must be getting ready to yell 'surprise,'" Stella whispered in Marietta's ear. But when they entered, the only things that greeted them were the pink crepe paper that lined the walls with "Welcome Home Marietta" and a dozen white wedding bells made of paper lace hanging in a row. The room was empty. Stella's face dropped. "They didn't stay," she said.

"It's one o'clock in the morning. How long did you expect them to wait?" Carl said, pointing to his watch.

"They ate and left. They could have stayed, at least until we arrived," she said scornfully. "Well, it doesn't matter now," she brightened. "What matters is that you are here. Are you hungry? I can make pizza. Do you want something to drink?" She pointed to the table set with tall, imposing stemware and opened bottles of champagne and aged scotch.

"Mom, Marietta and John must be tired from their long trip," Pia interjected. "Maybe they want to go to bed."

At the mention of bed, Marietta realized how exhausted she was. She wanted to change out of her clothes. Before she had left for JFK Airport earlier that day, they'd felt fresh and clean in the classroom where they were protected in part by her white lab coat, but now they stuck to her skin. She glanced at John. Lines creased his brow, a sure sign he, too, was spent.

"Cold water would be fine. We're not hungry, just tired. We'll eat in the morning," Marietta said. John nodded.

"Well, all right," Stella said, obviously disappointed. Pia reached for two goblets from the table. She walked into the kitchen to fill them.

"Tomorrow we feast," Stella said jubilantly. She leaned forward, took Marietta's hands in hers and kissed them. Embracing her, she kissed both sides of her face. She kissed John the same way.

"Pia will show you your room," Stella said. "Good night then. Until tomorrow." She walked down a long hallway to her bedroom and closed the door.

Waking up the next morning, Marietta almost forgot where she was. Then she remembered the plane ride and meeting her mother and sister. Her body bolted up to a sitting position. The thought of getting to know Stella and Pia, of fusing her early years with the present, of filling the fissure that separated the child she once was from the adult she had become was daunting. She ran to the window and looked out. She couldn't believe the difference between New York and Santa Barbara. The sun was high in the sky and filtered through in strong, inviting rays full of promise and warmth. The temperature was 50 degrees warmer than at home. This was winter? It felt like a beautiful summer day. Being in the same house with Stella and Pia charged her. She planted a firm kiss on John's lips and he awoke.

"I'm famished," he said with squinting eyes.

"If my mother still cooks the way I remember, you'll get more than you bargained for."

"You didn't tell me she was rich," he said.

"I didn't know. Did you see the white French provincial furniture in the living room, the gold trim on the mantelpiece and the carpet so thick under our feet?" Before he could respond, they heard a knock at the door.

"It's me, Pia."

"Come in," Marietta said, glad to finally say a few words to her sister.

"I don't mean to intrude. Mom heard voices and she insisted I come and ask you what you want for breakfast. I told her the blueberry pancakes, omelets and anisette cookies were enough but she insisted I ask you what you normally eat." Her eyes were down, apologetically, in case they were embarrassed to be seen in bed.

"It's okay," Marietta said. After years of growing up without her, Pia could intrude all she liked.

"Just cereal for me," said John.

"All I eat is toast," Marietta added." Pia turned to go.

"Wait, I'll go with you," she added. Then she remembered John.

"Go. I'll shower first and see you in about five minutes," he told her.

In the kitchen, Marietta found more surprises. The room was larger than her whole apartment. It led into a den with several couches, chairs and a television set. Oak closets lined the length of two walls. Tiled counters stretched below them. An island housed the stove and sink and cabinets underneath, separating the kitchen from the family room. Copper-bottomed saucepots and fry pans of various sizes hung from the ceiling directly above the stove. The counters were a display of all the food Stella had prepared – pancakes, ham, eggs, and biscuits, trays of strawberries, blueberries and apricots – as if the room were a gourmet shop. Carl was sitting at the head of the long kitchen table quietly finishing up his breakfast of ham and eggs. On the stove a four-quart pot half full of oil began a rolling boil. Stella haphazardly pulled small pieces of dough from a round bowl under a kitchen towel and threw them in the hot oil. In minutes, they sizzled and browned. She scooped them up with a slotted spoon and dropped them on paper toweling to absorb the oil. She sprinkled powdered sugar on top of them and offered one to Marietta.

"You remember *pettole*? Some people call these *sfingi* or *fritelle,* but, in our town, we called them *pettole*. You used to love them. Nonna and I made them for you all the time."

"Umm...it brings back so many memories," Marietta said as one of the *pettole* melted in her mouth. The purposely misshapen pieces of dough reminded her of the animals she used to identify years ago with the shapes the *pettole* made. With or without powdered sugar, they had the flavor of her youth. The last time she ate one was at the San Gennaro Festival held in Manhattan every September. Teresa and Paul had brought her there a few times when she was a teenager.

In Stella's kitchen, Marietta felt as if she were watching a movie of her past. Nonna's 1100 year-old house clicked in front of her. At the bottom of the white stone steps she found the ten year-old she used to be with her honey-colored hair in braids, jumping hopscotch squares while dark-haired Lucia waited for her turn. With the sun shining warmly on her back and the scent of oranges pervading the air, she was totally unaware of the change that would soon beset her. The adult Marietta wanted to warn the younger one. *Dash into the house and hug Nonna once more. You don't know it now but soon you'll be leaving her forever.* There was no way to communicate through the barrier of time and space, and the child was aware only of Lucia and the orange peel in her hand.

John walked in and sat near Carl. "I followed the wonderful smells," he said. "I think I'll skip the cereal." Everyone laughed. John could make a rock laugh, Marietta thought, feeling quite contented. And she was eating *pettole* with her mother, though not with Lucia or Nonna, and not in Italy. Not even in New York. She ate them in this strange land called California with its green hills and valleys, where leaves still clung to trees in winter and warmth permeated the air all year long. It didn't make sense. But then nothing in her life had made sense. There was no sense in coming to America, no sense in calling Teresa and Paul Mommy and Daddy, no sense in leaving Nonna and the family so rich in love. Only one thing had made sense: John. Without him, she was afraid of what might have been.

Stella placed the plate of *pettole* on the table between Carl and John. "*Mangia, mangia,* eat, eat," she said. She put some in each of their dishes. Then she turned to John and said, "You like?"

"I've never had ... pet...pet...toolay? Am I saying it correctly? They're different but good. Yes, I like," he laughed that infectious laugh again.

Orange Peels and Cobblestones

They spent most of the day eating as Stella cooked and recounted stories of Italy. The recipes had been handed down by mouth from mother to child for generations, she said. Stella never measured the ingredients. She used eggshells, scooped hands and her eyes to ascertain the right amounts. Marietta noted every detail of the recipes and wrote them down. A pinch of salt equaled about ¼ of a teaspoon; three fingers of sugar, perhaps ½ cup; half an eggshell of oil, about ¼ cup; a handful of flour was ½ cup.

For the *pettole,* Marietta wrote:
1. Four or five handfuls of flour (About 2-3 cups)
2. Three or four pinches of salt (About 1 tsp.)
3. Same amount of yeast as salt
4. Two half eggshells of lukewarm water (About 1 cup)
5. A glass of muscatel (About ½ cup of the sweet wine)
6. Enough cinnamon (About two teaspoons)

"Put the yeast in water to come alive," Stella said. "Make a well in the flour. Add the yeast mixture *e mescoli con le mane* – and blend with your hands. *Aggiungi l'altre cose ma no il zucchero* – add the other ingredients but not the sugar. Mix into the consistency of pancakes and let rise for one or two hours. Heat the vegetable oil in a deep pot. When the oil jumps (she meant when it comes to a rolling boil), put your whole hand in the batter and pull up the dough. *Fai cadere con i diti* – let the batter drip from your fingers, like raindrops, into the hot oil. Within seconds, the dough will rise to the top and turn golden brown in many different shapes. Scoop out each pettola with a slotted spoon and place it in a dish covered with paper toweling. Sprinkle with powdered sugar. Eat warm for better taste."

Marietta had to go back to the list of ingredients and add vegetable oil and powdered sugar. How much oil?

"*Abbastanza* – enough, maybe fill the pot up to half," dictated Stella.

Stella also made pizza for lunch and baked bread for dinner. Marietta asked for those recipes, too.

"It's the same for both. Just make the dough for bread and then save some of it for pizza. Watch how easy," Stella said. Marietta watched with pen and paper.

1. A bagful of flour (5 lbs.)
2. Two handfuls of olive oil (1 cup)
3. Three fingered scoops of salt (3 tsps.)
4. Enough warm water to make the dough (3-4 cups of tepid water)
5. One finger length of yeast (3 one ounce packages, cubes or granular tablespoons)
6. Some buttermilk (about 1 cup)

"First add some warm water to the yeast to wake it up. In a separate bowl, mix *la farina e sale* – flour and salt and make a hole (well) in the middle. Add the oil and mix with your hands. Do the same for the buttermilk and yeast water one at a time. Continue to mix, adding warm water until the mixture looks like dough. Knead for five to ten minutes until the dough crackles and feels *come seta*, you know, the silk. Shape into a round roll, cover it with a cloth *di cottone* and put in a warm, dark place per *si crescere* – to rise," said Stella

"For how long?" Marietta asked.

"Two, three hours... how much you have time for," Stella said. "Then punch it down and knead some more. Shape into round or long loaves and put back to rise again for another hour until almost double. Bake in a hot oven until the bread is golden brown."

"How hot?"

"*Caldo*," Stella said, "Four hundred twenty-five degrees for ten minutes. Then lower the temperature to medium (about three hundred fifty *gradi)* for around a half hour until it's *oro*, you know, like gold."

Marietta felt as if she were attending culinary school. Over the next week, Stella prepared all the meals and Pia and Marietta set and cleared the table. They loaded the dishwasher together. Pia washed the pots and Marietta dried them. Then Pia put them away because she knew where they went.

"I remember when you were little," Marietta said. "You wanted to help with the dishes but you couldn't reach the sink. You were so short that Mom called you *topolina*, little mouse."

"That's a name I'd like to forget," Pia said, defensively, much to Marietta's pleasure. If they teased, they would be more like sisters who'd grown up together.

"I loved that memory, mostly because I have so few of them. I didn't mean to insult you." As much as she wanted to be "sisterly" normal with Pia, she also didn't want to endanger their relationship just as it was beginning.

"It's okay. Just keep it between us. I wouldn't want my friends to find out. They think my name is weird already."

"Do you have a lot of friends?"

"I'm on the cheerleading team. In school we usually hang out as a group."

Marietta sighed. How she wished she could have watched her sister perform. She would have cheered for Pia more than for the team. She wanted to know more of the years they'd missed together. But the vacation was ending and John was antsy to get back to the hospital. She saw his fingers tap the table, twitching and moving as if he were typing. He had checked on his patients a few times that week by phone, but now with a full stomach almost all the time from Stella's fabulous cooking, he hungered for the simplicity and routine of the hospital.

"It's been great getting to know you," Pia said to John when they were at the door ready to leave.

198

"I finally got to meet the mother and sister Marietta has talked about so much," he said. He turned to Stella who immediately planted two loud kisses on his cheeks

"You take good care of my daughter. Remember how lucky you are. Both my daughters are beautiful and you have one of them. If you're not good to her, you answer to me!" she warned.

John laughed. "Don't worry. I couldn't love her any more than I do and I promise to take good care of her."

"You come back, no?"

"Anytime Marietta wants to visit, we'll make every effort to come. Right, Marietta?" He turned and was surprised she wasn't standing next to him.

"She's probably in the bedroom packing some last minute things," Pia said, going to get her.

She came back confused. "She's not there."

"Is she in the kitchen? I left a food bag for you to take on the plane," said Stella.

"No, I have that right here. See?" John held it up as evidence. "She wouldn't be outside already, near the car?" He asked the question even though he knew it was ludicrous. Why would she be outside when she hadn't said goodbye?

"I saw her go to the bathroom. I guess she went to powder her nose," Carl said. "But that was thirty minutes ago."

"I'll go check to see if she's okay." Pia headed toward the bathroom. John followed. She knocked gently on the door. Three short taps.

"Marietta? Are you there?"

"Yes," she said in a weepy voice.

"Are you all right?" John said.

"I'm fine. I'll be right out," Marietta said wiping her eyes with toilet tissue. She had planned to come out as soon as she stopped crying. But every time she washed her face with cold water and dried it with the towel, new tears took the place of the old ones. Minutes passed but the door remained shut. Pia put her ear against the door. She heard muffled cries.

"Are you sure you're okay? Can I come in?" she asked concerned.

Finally John spoke. "Marietta, let me in. Let me help you." She unlatched the door and stood behind it so no one could see her red cheeks and puffy eyes. Seeing her so distraught, John took her into his arms. He held her tight. Every muscle in Marietta's body collapsed.

"What's wrong?" he asked.

"I don't know. I just can't stop crying."

"I can see that but we have to leave. You have to say goodbye."

Marietta's sobs grew.

"It's not Italy you're leaving. It's California. We'll come back. Your mother and sister can visit us. You're not ten anymore and you're not alone. You have me." He doused her wet face with kisses.

"Every time I think about saying goodbye, I cry."

"It's okay. I'll hold your hand. You'll stop crying. Did I tell you that you look beautiful with red eyes?"

"You're ridiculous," Marietta said, managing a laugh. It was small but enough to give her the courage to walk out of the bathroom holding on to John's hand. She faced her mother but couldn't hold back her tears.

"Goodbye dear daughter," said Stella, now crying as hard as Marietta. This is what Marietta didn't want to happen. How could she leave if they both cried for each other? Then Stella kissed her daughter's cheeks and held her in her arms so long that Marietta thought they'd never separate. Finally, John touched her and the two let go.

"Goodbye," said Pia. "We'll see each other soon," she added. Her eyes brimmed with tears but she was able to keep them from spilling. Marietta wished she had her control.

They all got in the car for the ride to the airport and the goodbyes they had just made now would have to be repeated. John tried to keep the conversation light. He talked about Stella's wonderful cooking, which cheered her enough to want to give more recipes. Marietta got out paper and pen again and wrote them down. It kept her tears at bay. But on the plane, she couldn't control them. She wiped her eyes with tissue so the other passengers wouldn't notice a grown woman crying like a child. It wasn't until the plane landed and Marietta felt New York's cold air that the tears finally subsided.

Chapter Eighteen

Back in her apartment Marietta wondered if the visit with Stella and Pia had been a dream. She eyed the two suitcases near the cedar closet where John had laid them. They were still unpacked. Proof she'd been somewhere. She touched the American Airlines tag in case her eyes deceived her. Lifting one bag onto the bed, she began to empty it. She placed the clothes in neat piles. Tops on one side, pants on another, shoes on the floor. When she found the new dress her mother had given her, she sniffed it to see if it carried her mother's scent, but all that came was the smell of new cotton. She draped it in front of her and looked in the mirror. The gift could have been from anyone.

The next day she was back in class, teaching students how to use the microscope and make their own slides. She provided them with eyedroppers, clean slides and cover slips and a bucket of pond water. "It's very simple. Watch as I demonstrate," she said modeling the exercise for them. "First, I get a drop of the liquid from the bucket and place it on a clean slide. Then, very gently, I place a cover slip over it and lay the slide on the stage of the microscope. I clip it securely. Now I focus with low power and draw what I see in my notebook. Then I switch to high power for a closer look. I focus and, again, I draw what I see. Let's get started." She walked around the room and assisted those who were having difficulty. She savored their oohs and aahs once they spotted amoebas and paramecia swimming in what had seemed to the naked eye to be clear water.

Before she knew it the week was over. That Friday afternoon, Marietta spotted one or two teachers in their classrooms grading papers. She heard the faint voices of a group of students waiting for the basketball game to begin as soon as the opposing team arrived. Within minutes the building emptied and the hubbub of activity ended. She sat alone in her classroom, enjoying the quiet as she waited for Mr. Shapiro, the school principal, to come and review with her the lesson he had observed her teach the week before Christmas. Presently, she heard his footsteps in the empty hallway and watched as he squeezed into one of the student desks next to her. She felt intimidated by his body, which was twice her size.

"Motivation is the key," he said. His breath smelled of the smoked salmon he'd had for lunch. It nauseated her. She focused on the observed lesson and hoped he had noticed the boy who sat near the window staring outside at the beginning of the period and how she had walked over and casually stood near him to get back his attention. She worried that she'd mishandled the girl who had asked an unrelated question near the end of class. If Marietta answered it, she would have lost the time to sum up the lesson. "That's an excellent question," she told the girl, instead. "We'll deal with that topic another day." Did she squash the student's interest?"

She'd been confident and not at all nervous when he had interviewed her for the job just after her graduation. She remembered how his chair swiveled from left to right as he read her transcript and letters of recommendation he had spread across his clean desk. The chair made a grinding noise as if it were a wheel processing the information he needed. She was sure that if she got up and inspected his side of the desk, she'd find deep grooves on the wooden floor beneath his feet. Mr. Shapiro cleared his throat. He raised his bushy eyebrows as he scrutinized Marietta's qualifications. "I see you excelled in science and everything else besides. Tell me. Why did you choose science?"

"Well, at first I thought I'd go into medicine. Then after I met my fiancé, I decided that teaching was as noble a vocation and its hours would allow me to raise a family more easily." Instantly, Marietta was sorry. She didn't want him to think she was afraid of long hours of work or that she would leave her position immediately to go on maternity leave. But he seemed not to notice.

"Tell me a little about you," he said, looking her straight in the face. God, she thought. Where should she start? Should she go back to the beginning, when she lived in Italy, when she was someone else? Interminable minutes passed as he stared at her, waiting for a response.

"Well, I was born in Italy," she heard herself finally begin. Then she stopped. She couldn't give a blow-by-blow description of all that happened. She took a deep breath. She condensed her thoughts. "My parents didn't get along. When I was ten I came to live with an aunt and uncle in Brooklyn. I'm engaged to a wonderful person who's a doctor. We both share a love of science." The jumps in time allowed her to omit the painful parts.

"Hold it," he said. "I hadn't meant for you to get that personal. I just wanted to get to know you a little." He smiled. "You were hired before you spoke. I'll see you at the first faculty meeting." He leaned across the desk and shook her hand. The sleeve of his jacket rubbed against her wrist as a hint of Old Spice cologne reached her nose. She left his office feeling confident.

But today, as he reviewed her lesson, she wished she had some of that confidence back. Mr. Shapiro re-read the aims and objectives she'd written for her lesson. "Your delivery was good. Remember that motivation and summary are key elements to every lesson. Once you hook students, they want to know everything about the topic. They can almost teach themselves. Then be sure to leave three to five minutes to wrap up. You summarized the material well but better if the students do it themselves. Just listen, correct mistakes, assess what they learned and review it with them again the next day at the start of the lesson. And your answer to the student who asked you about a different topic..." He hesitated. Marietta's stomach tensed. "That was a teachable moment. A gift the student handed you. Always grab gifts. I know you were pressed for time, but answer the question even if it's brief. Remember that," he said, shaking his finger in front of her face, as though it were a mistake he didn't expect her to repeat. He shimmied out of the desk and headed toward the door. When he turned to say something else, he saw her face panic. "Relax," he assured her. "You have the makings of a fine teacher. What I was about to say was that you seem a little anxious this afternoon. Perhaps you're tired from the first week back. Vacations sometimes put us out of kilter. Go home and enjoy your weekend," he said and walked out.

A little anxious! He didn't know the upheaval her mind and body had gone through the past couple of weeks. Before leaving she checked the cabinet where the goggles were stored. It was locked. Good, her lab assistant had seen to that. Then she walked over to where the microscopes were stored. That cabinet was left open. She took the keys out of the pocket of her lab coat and secured those doors shut. She surveyed the black soapstone desks where her students conducted experiments, the teacher's desk set up higher for demonstrations in front of the blackboard and she smiled. John's world was the hospital, but the classroom was her world. Yet at home in their apartment, how easy their worlds meshed into one. Not so with Stella and Pia. Their world lay on the opposite coast three thousand miles away, just like it had been after Stella sent Marietta away. Stella and Pia had traveled three thousand miles from Italy to New York only to bypass her and go three thousand miles away again to California.

When Marietta arrived home that afternoon after meeting with Mr. Shapiro, the first thing she did was throw up. She had felt miserable all week. Now she felt worse. When John came through the door, he heard Marietta groan.

Without taking off his coat, he ran and found her bent over the bathroom sink. "What's wrong, sweetheart?" he asked.

"I feel absolutely awful. I guess seeing my mother and sister has set me back."

"Nonsense. That wouldn't make you vomit like this. Do you have a fever?" He put his hand on her forehead and under her armpits but found them cool. "Maybe it's a virus. Do you feel faint? Does your stomach hurt? Any bowel discomfort?" Dr. Sullivan in full form, Marietta thought.

"No, I just can't stand to look at food. It makes me nauseous and...what?" she stopped. John sported a big grin.

"Are you thinking what I'm thinking?" he said.

"What do you mean?" she said, clueless.

"A baby," he smiled.

"A baby?" she repeated. Could she be pregnant? The mother-child bond she longed for, not severed or lost, but simply moved down a generation?

They scheduled an appointment with Dr. George Kennedy, a colleague of John's.

"All indications show you're in your first trimester," said Dr. Kennedy after examining her. "I'm prescribing prenatal vitamins, which I want you to take daily, and though you may know most of the information from your science background, here's a book about the different stages of the baby's growth inside the uterus and how it may affect you as you go through them. I've included some exercises to keep fit, to support the extra weight of the baby, and a nutritional program so that you can eat healthy for one person, not two, as some allege. Too much weight hampers the ease of delivery. We don't want complications, do we? Any questions thus far?"

"None yet, George," John said. They had wanted children but, now that the reality set in, they were in shock.

"Good. Marietta, you'll come for monthly visits at first. Then for the last trimester, it will be twice a month, progressing to once a week the last month. Call the office any time should you have problems or concerns. So, if you have no further questions, let me congratulate you both on the start of your family. You beat me to it, John, you son of a gun. But it would help if I found myself a woman I liked," he chuckled.

"Or one that liked you," John teased.

"Make an appointment with the receptionist for a month from now. I'll see you then," he said to Marietta. The men shook hands, leaving Marietta to finish dressing.

On the way home, John worried. Where would they put the baby? Another person, though tiny, congested the one-bedroom apartment. With a crib, playpen, baby clothes and toys, there wouldn't be much room. Renting a larger apartment was out of the question. They'd have to make the best of a tight situation for a while.

Marietta, on the other hand, could only think of how warm the baby would feel in her arms, how wonderful new skin would smell, how needed she would be. Would she have a boy or a girl? She thought of Nonna who'd raised twelve children in two rooms. Surely their apartment was spacious enough for a start? She knew just where to put the crib – against the wall at the foot of their bed so she could hear every sound the baby made. In the morning she and John would call out "peek-a-boo" and watch for the baby's tiny eyes to spot them and smile. She couldn't wait to go home and tell John's parents.

"That's wonderful news! We're so happy for you." It was their fifth grandchild, but you'd think it was their first from the enthusiasm they exuded.

"Have you told your mom?" John's mother asked. Marietta hesitated. Which one, she wanted to ask? Stella or Teresa?

"Not yet," she said. "We came straight from the doctor's."

Marietta expected an angry Teresa when she learned of the baby. Why should Marietta conceive so early in her married life when Teresa's body couldn't conceive at any point of her marriage? Paul would be happy for her, but in deference to his wife, he couldn't show it. And Stella, how would she react? Marietta had no clue. She decided to wait a while before sharing the news further. If something went wrong and she lost the baby, she'd have to contact every person she'd told and relive her loss. She kept the pregnancy secret until she was sure it progressed in a healthy fashion, until she couldn't keep it hidden any longer. After missing her period for the fourth month, she phoned Stella.

"Hi" she said, grateful to hear Pia's voice on the other end.

"It's great to hear from you, Marietta. I was just thinking about you."

"You were?" Marietta was pleased.

"Yes. I almost called you. I wanted to know how you were and if anything was new, like if you're coming back in summer."

"Well, there is something new. I'm…actually…John and I…we're going to have a baby."

"Wow! I'm going to be an aunt. That's great news. Do you want me to tell Mom?"

"Thanks, but shouldn't I be the one to tell her?"

"Well, okay…if you want. I'll get her. Mom, it's Marietta. She has something to tell you," Pia whispered, handing Stella the receiver.

"What is the something you have, *Cara*?"

"Mom, I'm going to have a baby," Marietta said. The words suddenly sounded hollow and strange. She placed her hand over her abdomen. It was still flat though her waistline had thickened. Was the pregnancy a mirage?

"Oh I'm so happy," Stella said. "When will the baby come? Did you pick out a name yet?"

"End of July. No we don't have names yet. John is more concerned that the baby has all its parts than a name. He knows so much about diseases and birth defects."

"Tell him not to worry. Our family comes from good stock. John will get a very healthy baby from our side of the family. Did you say the baby's due in July? That's near my birthday. If it's a girl, you could call her after me. Stella Sullivan. Sounds good, no?"

Marietta felt uncomfortable with the request. "Mom, we haven't chosen the name yet," she said. "We're still getting used to the fact that I'm pregnant."

"I'll send you a book of names. It'll be the first present you get as a new mother. And I'd like to buy you your first maternity dress too. Are you showing yet?"

"No and I'm glad. I don't want my students and principal to know I'm pregnant, in case they think I'll leave before the term ends."

"Oh Marietta, you worry too much about your kids. You have to take care of yourself now. Maybe you should stop working."

"I can't stop now." Marietta voice grew defensive, almost defiant. Teaching engaged her mind. It kept her from thinking about other things, like her past.

"I'll go shopping tomorrow for the baby book and your maternity dress."

"Mom..." Marietta stammered, hoping Stella would interject and save her from what she was about to ask. She'd admired and envied the way John's mother spent time with her daughter at the hospital after she gave birth, how she talked about the newest grandchild she'd just seen through the nursery window, how she spent a week at her daughter's helping her with the baby, cooking the meals, even cleaning the house until her daughter grew stronger.

Teresa's help was out of the question. She knew nothing about babies and was too old to learn. When Marietta had first told her and Paul that she was pregnant, just the day before, Teresa removed all hope that maybe she'd be glad. The first thing she said was, "You're not going to feed the baby with your breast like an animal? I know your mother fed you that way, but you're in America now. We're civilized here. You use a bottle, no?"

"I'm going to give the baby *my* milk. It's healthier than formula," Marietta had replied emphatically. But that wasn't the only reason. Marietta needed to be close to her baby, insure that skin touched skin so they could feel one another's heartbeats. Nothing would ever come between them. No, Teresa was not the one to offer assistance with her warped notions of "civilized" bottle feeding. Teresa would also just turn the baby into another excuse to act the martyr.

Now, on the phone with Stella, Marietta hoped her mother could read her mind.

"What is it?" Stella said. Her voice sounded compassionate and inviting.

"Well...," Marietta hesitated.

"Tell me. You can tell a mother anything, you know."

"I...I...I thought, if you weren't busy that... perhaps you'd come when I gave birth... to see me in the hospital, I mean. You could stay at our apartment...if you could spare a few days...to show me what to do. I've never taken care of a baby. I'm scared I won't know what to do, that I'll make a mistake. Do you know what I'm saying?"

"*Si, si, capisco.* Yes, I know what you mean. And I would love to be there with you. But, honey, I can't. It's so far away and...well, it's not a good time for me. Carl isn't feeling that well. I don't want to leave him."

"But you wouldn't come until summer. Wouldn't he recover by then?"

"I can't come. I don't want to run into those devils that took you away from me."

Marietta's heart sank. She tried not to give in to her disappointment. Her throat went dry.

"I tell you what," Stella said. *"Ti mando tua sorella –* I'll send your sister. She baby-sits in the neighborhood and knows how to take care of a baby just as well as I do." There was a long pause. "Halloh? Halloh? You there?" Stella tapped on the phone.

"Pia?" Marietta said, stunned. She hadn't thought of her younger sister as capable of helping with babies. Pia would do just fine. And without Stella's strong presence they could get to know each other better.

"You don't want her to come?" Stella said.

"No, no. I mean, yes. I'm happy she's coming. I'm thrilled." Why hadn't she thought of it herself? Pia would teach her how to care for the baby and Marietta could play the big sister and teach Pia in other ways. They'd nurture each other. Pia would bear witness that Marietta wasn't a loose strand of hair floating in air. She belonged to somebody. They belonged to each other. And Marietta hoped to do the same for Pia, when she needed it, if she wanted it. How strange, she thought with a wry smile. The younger sister would teach the older one how to care for a baby.

In the ensuing months Marietta's purpose in life became clearer because of the life inside her. With the coming baby, a plan lay in motion. She felt she had boarded a train that would not let her off until she gave birth. Childbirth and learning how to raise a child gave her a lot to think about that was different from lesson plans, grading tests and checking homework. As her sixth month approached, her body changed dramatically. Her abdomen rounded, making her waistline virtually non-existent, and her posture tilted back to support the extra weight. At work, the lab coat no longer shielded her.

"Do you know something we don't?" a colleague teased.

"What do you mean?"

"You're pregnant, right?"

"How did you know?"

"By the way you walk. Your body sways from side to side when you pass down the hallway."

"I was trying to keep it quiet for as long as I could."

"Why? When I had my first baby, I was so happy I told everyone I knew when I was two months pregnant. Don't you want the baby?"

"Some people are downright rude," she complained to John that evening. "Imagine not wanting my child! I'd rather shoot myself than give up my baby."

"I don't think they meant it quite the way you took it. You're being very sensitive. It's normal in pregnancy for the emotions to be raw." He tried to soothe her through his doctor-speak.

"I don't think so," she snapped, her eyes brimming with tears. "I could never 'not want' my baby. I could never part from my flesh and blood. How do you give up what's a part of you?" As soon as she heard her own words, she stopped, realizing they stemmed from her own wounds.

"That will never happen to our baby," John said, taking her hand, pulling her toward him. He held her in his arms, comforting her as if she were the baby.

That night in bed, Marietta tossed and turned past midnight. When she finally dozed off, she dreamt she was back in Teresa and Paul's house, taking a dress out of the closet. Suddenly she discovered a baby on top of the large safe they kept on the floor, directly below the dresses. Marietta melted with love at the sight of the sleeping baby wrapped in its blanket. When she tried to pick it up and hold it, the baby's back stuck to the safe. It wouldn't budge. She wondered whether the baby was a boy or a girl. She gently unfolded the soft blanket and the baby stirred, raising its arms like a doll. In the baby's hand was a large key. She feared the key would hit the baby's head as its arms flung to and fro. She tried to pry it out of the tiny hand. When she loosened the tight grip, she discovered that the key, too, was stuck to the baby's skin. She tried once more to unglue the baby from the safe without hurting it but she awoke before succeeding.

Trembling, she noticed that her hands were cupped the same way they'd been when she tried to place them under the baby's back in order to lift it. She wanted to tell John about the dream but, rather than wake him, she snuggled near him. She needed to sleep to conserve her energy for teaching. She needed it even more now that the class was dissecting frogs. One girl had fainted at the sight of the dead frog and three others came in with notes from their mothers to be allowed to leave the room while the lab was in progress. They felt the activity was cruel to animals. Class participation was reluctant at best and, though they wore goggles and rubber gloves, the students complained about the gross smell and the slimy feel of mesentery tissue around the frog organs. She closed her eyes and literally willed herself to sleep. Within minutes, she awoke in a cold sweat, shaking, tugging at John's arm.

"What is it?" he asked, turning around, still drowsy.

"I dreamt I gave birth to a frog! Our baby looked like a frog! I never bought your concerns about birth defects, but do you think that could happen?"

"Honey, you just had a bad dream. You're worried about your students with the dissection and you're worried about the baby. Come into my arms. Everything will be okay. I'm sure of it." Marietta caved under the crook of his arm. Her shaking subsided and she fell asleep.

The days turned to weeks, the weeks into months and soon the school year ended. It was time for Marietta to think solely of the life inside her and of her sister's arrival.

"You're having the baby at a perfect time," Pia said on the phone. "School ended a week ago and I've always wanted to spend a summer in New York, maybe see a Broadway show, go up the Empire State Building and see the Statue of Liberty."

"We'd love to show you as much of New York City as possible. We've never visited the Statue of Liberty either." She and Pia get to spend some time alone, Marietta thought, and that was a first, too.

Chapter Nineteen

The day Pia was due to arrive was unusually hot and humid. Marietta awoke late that morning irritable and sweaty. The baby had kicked and turned, providing her no comfortable position in which to sleep. She looked at the clock on the nightstand and moaned at the late hour. Then she remembered Pia and brightened.

She inched her swollen abdomen toward the edge of the bed and planted her feet firmly on the ground. With both hands pushing down on the mattress, she propelled herself forward. Who would have thought a little person inside her would make it so difficult to maneuver her body? Ambling toward the window, she stuck her hand out to assess the weather. As Marietta felt the air, she laughed, remembering the first time John had seen her do this.

"Is your hand a thermometer?" he'd teased.

"Yes. Seventy-nine degrees with high humidity," she played along.

"No one else predicts the weather that way."

"You don't know Italians. Our hands are like weather vanes."

"The first meteorologists, I suppose," he'd said, amused.

Looking toward the sky, Marietta's smile erased as she spotted black masses of clouds speed through the air and play cat and mouse with the sun. It'd be a blessing if it rained, she thought. It'd dissipate the horrid humidity and bring in clear, fresh air. But the stray rays of sunlight weren't ready to surrender just yet. A series of thunderbolts and lightning rumbled through before the clouds finally opened and drenched the city. Lucky that Pia was to arrive later in the day.

Marietta cleaned up the breakfast dishes and surveyed the apartment. The rugs were vacuumed and the furniture dusted. Pia's bed, a cot borrowed from John's parents, was in place in the living room against the wall. The cot was covered with a thin mattress and white sheets topped with a lavender-flowered comforter and matching pillow sham. It reminded her of the cot in Nonna's house where she slept. A painting of the Atlantic Ocean hung above Pia's cot. The comforter picked up the purple hue of the water. It was a makeshift arrangement, temporary in nature, but the best they could provide. She hoped Pia would be comfortable in it.

John had already left for the hospital hours before. He promised to dash home by 5 P.M. to make it to the airport on time. When he came home at 5:30, Marietta met him at the door frantic. Why was he always late?

"I just couldn't get away," he said, wheeling the car around the slow driver in front. "We had an emergency – a massive accident on the Belt Parkway. A dozen people came in bleeding."

"It would help to say you're sorry sometimes."

"Why? It wasn't my fault," he insisted.

It's never your fault, she thought, annoyed. "Forget the hospital now. Just get there quickly and safely," she said. They reached the airport only ten minutes late. When Marietta read the arrivals board screen, she learned the plane had landed five minutes earlier than scheduled. They rushed to the baggage area and saw the carousel revolve dropping luggage while a throng of people stood around it. Pia was not among them. Marietta concentrated on the passengers streaming through the double doors but there were none she recognized. She was struck with the many human faces she saw and how the brain could distinguish that of a loved one. Soon Pia would walk through and they'd recognize each other the same way.

"There she is," John pointed. Marietta stood on her toes and followed the path of John's finger.

"Pia," she yelled, raising her arm and waving her hand in the air.

"Pia, over here," John's more powerful voice blasted. Pia saw them and walked toward them.

"Someone's come between us since I last saw you," she laughed, hugging Marietta. "How does it feel to be two?"

"Not too great. Yesterday, at the supermarket, a man had the nerve to ask me if I'd swallowed a watermelon."

"Some people have no manners. You're really not that big. I know someone who looked like you when she was only five months pregnant. I was afraid you'd give birth before I came and then I'd miss the whole thing. I'm glad you waited."

"Do I have a choice? The mothers I talk to inform me that childbirth is the most painful thing they've ever experienced. They also complain of afterbirth pains and how their breasts hurt when they fill with milk. I don't know what to believe. If I could have my way, I'd reverse the last nine months. But John's mother says not to worry. Everyone's delivery is different. And once you see the baby, there's no memory of pain."

"There must be something to what she says or women would stop having children." Pia said.

"You're right. And now that you're here, John and I want to show you as much of New York as we can before the baby comes. After that, I'll be tied down and then the summer will end and you have to return to school."

"Sounds great to me," Pia said.

"The first stop will be John's parents' house. They invited us to dinner tonight. After all the things we told them about you, they can't wait to meet you," said Marietta.

"If they're anything like John, it'll be a pleasure. The only people that invite our family to dinner, or Mom has at our house, are Italians. I'd like to see how the rest of the world lives," she said.

Pia's presence and good humor gave Marietta abundant energy. Something inside her reawakened. On John's days off they went up the Empire State Building, ate in French restaurants, saw a Broadway play, walked around Rockefeller Center and Times Square, and of course paid a visit to the Statue of Liberty. When Pia remarked she'd never been to a discothèque, they scheduled that in that evening's program.

"Are you sure? It may not be safe for you. Someone could bang into your stomach and hurt the baby," Pia cautioned.

"I'll sit out all the fast dances. John can dance the slow dances with me and the fast ones with you. It's John we have to be worried about." She turned and looked at him. "Can you handle two women?"

"Anything you two ask is my command."

"Then leave. The bathroom is our domain until we're ready," Marietta said. The two sisters took turns showering and dressing. To conserve Marietta's strength for the late evening ahead, Pia combed her sister's hair and put it up into a bun with tiny curls hanging down. Then she fixed her own hair, brushing it under into a semi pageboy. After she applied her makeup, Pia helped Marietta with hers.

"I only wear lipstick and mascara. I don't like too much paint on my face," Marietta said.

"Don't worry. I'll make it light. It'll seem as if you have no makeup at all after I finish. The natural look of beauty takes a lot of care." When they emerged two hours later, John whistled. They smiled in appreciation as he escorted them out the door.

The discotheque lounge was dark, smoky, loud and crowded. Small wrought iron tables lined the perimeter of the room, creating an open circle for dancing. John, Marietta and Pia were seated at a corner table near a window. They were pleased. If the smoke got too thick, they could let in some of the night air. They kept to their plan. John danced the slow dances with Marietta and the fast ones with Pia. As Marietta and John danced, a young man approached Pia. She got up and danced with him.

"Who was that?" Marietta asked when they sat down, her stomach protectively hidden under the table.

"He wouldn't give his name. He asked to dance with me again, but I said no. I didn't like him."

"Let's dance this fast number. It'll keep him from coming back," John said. Marietta looked around the room to make sure no one unusual neared. She took a sip of her water and closed her eyes wishing she could close her ears as well. The noise was starting to get to her. Thank God the baby lay insulated in her uterus, she thought. Suddenly she felt a hand on her shoulder. She looked up expecting it to be John's. Instead she faced a pair of sparkling green eyes on a very handsome face. His trim body was dressed in a white sailor suit. A navy man. As a teenager she'd stared at the sailors who often walked her neighborhood when they came to port at the Brooklyn Navy Yard. Now here was one staring her in the face.

"Would you care to dance?" he asked.

"No, thanks," Marietta said, as politely as she could, giving him a warm smile so he wouldn't take it personally.

"Aw, come on, just one dance. You remind me of a girl I knew back home in Iowa. I never had the guts to ask her out. Then I got shipped away. Last I heard she got engaged to a friend of mine. New York's a lonely town. What do you say?"

"Thank you, but I can't. I'm married."

"Well, that's the first time I heard that excuse." He scratched his head. "Can't you come up with a better one?"

"See that man, there?" Marietta pointed toward the dance floor. "That's my husband. He's dancing with my sister. I'm just waiting for them to come back."

"She's dancing with a married person. Why can't I?"

Marietta sighed. She pulled away from the table and exposed her swollen abdomen. "See, I'm also pregnant. You don't want to dance with a pregnant woman, do you?"

He rubbed his chin. "Well, it'd be a first. But since I asked you, I'm a man of my word. It's only a dance and I'd be real gentle not to press on the little one. It'd be as if I were dancing with two people," he smiled, amused with himself. "My name is Darren, by the way. My unit leaves tomorrow for six months in the Pacific."

"I'm flattered, Darren, but I really can't. I'm sure you'll find someone else among all these pretty girls to dance with."

"Well I see when I've lost." He tipped his hat and left just as John and Pia returned.

"Who was that?" John asked, annoyed. Did Marietta denote a trace of jealousy in his voice? He always claimed he wasn't jealous.

"A lonely sailor," she said. "Would you believe he asked me to dance? He wouldn't take no for an answer even though I showed him my belly."

John's jaw tightened. From the corner of his eye, he could see the sailor stare at him. "Let's go home," he said. "It's late anyway."

That night Marietta woke up with abdominal pains. The first one was mild. She gave out only a whimper of sound. A few minutes later, a second contraction came, this time stronger. It made her wince and groan loud enough to wake up John.

"What is it? Are you starting your contractions?"

"I think so. Here comes another," she said. John took her hand and held it in his. Marietta wondered what was going through his mind. Was he thinking what she was thinking? That she was terribly afraid? He looked at the clock on the nightstand and timed the length of the contraction. They waited for the next one. "That's three contractions in a row and they're about seven minutes apart. I'm taking you to the hospital," he said.

"Don't wake Pia. Let her sleep. We'll leave her a note," Marietta said. "But call your parents," Marietta grimaced through another contraction. She wanted a mother, even if it wasn't Stella. John's mother had been every bit a mother to her throughout the pregnancy. She taught her how to sew her maternity clothes, how to cook and how to take care of the house. She loved John's mother as if she'd been her own.

When they got to the hospital, her pains subsided. "I'm afraid you're not dilated." Dr. Kennedy said after examining her. "I'll see you in my office next week."

"I'm never going to have this baby," Marietta moaned when they returned home.

"Don't feel bad. Elephants take three years to give birth," Pia said, laughing, glad she was allowed to sleep during the false alarm.

"Bite your tongue," Marietta retorted, finally feeling free to smile. "You have no idea what it's like to carry another life that swells your legs, gives you heartburn and makes you feel warm all the time."

"The good thing about not giving birth today is that we can go to the beach. I'll make lunch and you can sit with your feet in the water and feel nice and cool," Pia said.

"And you can swim and be ogled up by all the boys," Marietta added.

"I can't help it if that's what I get for doing a good deed for my sister." Pia sashayed out of the room as if she were the most glamorous person on earth.

Later that evening Marietta went to bed early, eyeing the packed suitcase that contained clothes she hadn't worn in months. She made sure it was in easy reach. One thing she didn't want was to have the baby at home. It didn't matter that she was born in Nonna's house with Zia Maria as the midwife. Zia Maria wasn't here this time. Nor was Nonna who could make everything better. Marietta wanted her doctor, the nurses and all the hospital machinery to insure she had a safe delivery and a healthy baby.

The next morning she awoke early and startled. She had dreamt that Zia Maria had come to America and it was she, not her sister, who slept in the cot in the living room. She apologized for Stella's absence. "Your mother is not a midwife like I am," she said. "She was always afraid of blood. When you were born, she insisted on wearing a mask over her eyes until Nonna cleaned you. Then she took the mask off and held you."

"So it was Nonna who first held me," Marietta said.

"Yes, held you and loved you from the start... held you and loved you from the start... from the start." The words repeated over and over riveting Marietta into consciousness. She touched her abdomen. It was still there as high as a mountain peak. She would love her baby, she decided, the way Nonna had loved her. She'd be both mother and grandmother to it. Looking around her, she spotted the suitcase, ready whenever she was. She got out of bed and tiptoed into the living room. Pia lay on her side, her hands under her face with palms touching, as though in prayer, to support the giant curlers she'd rolled in her hair.

Marietta walked into the kitchen and was surprised at the energy she felt. She washed last night's fruit dishes left in the sink, made the coffee and started to prepare a batch of pancakes. She pulled the blueberries out of the refrigerator and added them to the batter. John and Pia walked in, one behind the other.

"Still here?" Pia teased.

"Still here and with bounce. I'm sick of moping and waiting. Anyone hungry this morning?"

"Always for you," John said planting a kiss on her lips. "But I'm late for work. I'll take a rain check on those pancakes, too."

"I'll take his portion," Pia said. Marietta knew she didn't mean it. Pia hardly ate. She watched her figure like a bodyguard.

"Somebody better eat them or I'm slaving for nothing."

"Now you sound like Mom."

"Speaking of Mom, do you think she'll come see the baby after I give birth?" Something in her still wanted Stella. She pictured her standing beside her in front of the nursery window admiring the baby, two mothers three generations together.

"Don't count on it. She hates New York. It has too many memories she'd just as soon forget."

"You mean me?" Marietta felt immediately threatened and vulnerable.

"No. Not you exactly. She doesn't want to meet our father or Uncle Paul and Aunt Teresa. I think they put the fear of God in her. She got as far away from them as she could. Every time I hear her speak about them, her voice gets low and gravelly and her face turns mean."

"Our father went back to Italy. You didn't know?"

"Really?" Pia said, surprised. "Mom still hates him and our aunt and uncle for what they did to her and to you."

"What do you mean? Do you know what they did?"

"I don't know fact from fiction any more. I was little at the time. I don't remember. Don't you know?"

"I'm not sure either. They may have done things behind my back."

"Do you see them much? Uncle Paul and Aunt Teresa, I mean?"

"Not often. They call every now and then. They know I'm pregnant and due any day. "

At that moment the phone rang. "Would you get that, Pia? It's probably John letting me know where to reach him in case the baby decides to be born today. I need to watch the pancakes so they don't burn."

"No, this isn't Marietta. It's her sister Pia." She cupped the phone with her hand.

"Speaking of the devil –it's Uncle Paul. He wants to speak with you. He sounds mad."

"Hello," Marietta said as her body tensed.

"Why didn't you tell me your sister was here?" Paul demanded.

Marietta ignored the question. "She came to be the baby's godmother," she said. "I wasn't sure you wanted any part of her or my mother."

"Your mother could drop dead for all we care. Your sister is another matter. She's Teresa's blood and blood sticks together. When can you bring her over?"

Now it was Marietta's turn to cup the phone. "They want to see you," she said to Pia. "They want to know when we can go visit."

"I don't want to see them," Pia mouthed. "I don't know them."

"Not even one visit, out of courtesy, since they're part of our father's family?"

"I hardly remember them or our father. I don't want to see people I don't know," Pia repeated.

"Are you sure you don't remember them? They remember you."

Pia walked out of the room to show she wouldn't change her mind. What excuse could Marietta give without hurting Paul and Teresa's feelings, without unleashing their anger? They wouldn't accept that Pia didn't remember them.

Marietta's motto had always been: keep the peace. So far it had succeeded. Her relationship with Paul and Teresa had been rather stable and smooth since the wedding. She and John worked and were too busy to visit. Teresa had become increasingly reclusive and Paul had to do all the food shopping and household errands now. It kept him busy and tired. Every few months, when he found occasion to be in Marietta's neighborhood, he stopped by.

"I came by to see how you were doing. Is John treating you well? Do you need anything?" Paul asked the same three questions in succession, his hand in his pocket, ready to dispense some cash in case she was short.

"We're fine. Thanks for asking," Marietta replied. "Can I get you coffee, a sandwich? Are you hungry?" He smiled and followed her into the kitchen, his hand coming out of his pocket happily empty. He would have been surprised if she'd accepted the offer. He believed relying on one's own resources as he did was the best way to live.

But now, phone in hand, Marietta struggled to deal with Paul's confrontation. She knew that Pia had every right not to want to visit with him and Teresa. But it left her in a bind. How could she break the news without hurting their feelings? She wanted to tell the truth but with them the truth always got her in trouble.

"Daddy, I don't have a car. John takes it to work," she finally blurted.

"Don't you think I know that? I'll come pick you up."

There was no escape. She braced herself for the full truth.

225

"Pia said she doesn't remember you and would prefer not to see you. I'm sorry." She hoped the "I'm sorry" would soften the blow.

"What the hell is 'prefer'? We're family, for Christ's sake! After all we did for that Duke-lazy father and no-good mother of both of you. Well, you both go to hell and don't come back," he shouted. He clicked the phone dead.

With the sound still ringing in her ear, Marietta felt the baby drop. She grabbed the back of the kitchen chair for support, leaned into it and sat down.

"Well, that's that," she said to the air. She wiped off the beads of sweat that had formed on her brow and then lowered her hand to her abdomen. She addressed the kicks that moved under her skin like pseudopods. "I want to spare you this," she said. "Ignore what just happened. I'll do everything in my power to insure it'll never happen to you."

Pia walked back into the room. "Was he very angry?" she asked.

"Angry is an understatement."

"I'm sorry if I upset you with my decision," Pia said.

"It is how you feel," Marietta shrugged. She felt drained. It wasn't just Pia's refusal that wore her down. It was the craziness of everything, going back to Paul and Teresa's inability to have a child. The mistake was in the timing, she thought. If she hadn't been born first, she would have stayed behind with Stella. How different her life would have been! But Marietta wouldn't have wished her fate on another, especially on her sister.

"You should lie down and rest for a while," Pia said. She saw how pale Marietta had suddenly become. "I didn't mean for you to have to shoulder this, especially in your condition," she added. She led Marietta onto the recliner in the living room. Pia tilted the seat back to elevate her feet. She opened the windows to bring in more air, but no breeze entered. She went into the kitchen and reached for the fan on top of the refrigerator. Positioning it in front of the window, she turned it on. When she looked up, Marietta was sound asleep. She sat on the couch, feeling responsible for her sister's exhaustion. She watched the swollen abdomen rise as Marietta breathed in and out. When she stirred, Pia was at her side in an instant.

"I have to go the bathroom," Marietta said. "Help me lower the recliner." Ten minutes later, she had to use the bathroom again.

"Did you break your water?" Pia asked.

"I go to the bathroom all the time. See, I have to go again."

"I think you need to call the doctor. If you broke your water, it means the baby's on its way."

"Let's wait. I want to be sure this time."

"I'm calling John," Pia said.

As soon as John heard about the frequent trips to the bathroom, he called Dr. Kennedy. Then he called Marietta. He told her he was leaving work early to take her to the hospital.

"They'll just tell me to go home again. I don't have any contractions," Marietta argued.

"It doesn't matter. If your water broke, you're open to infection. The doctor will induce you and the contractions will begin shortly thereafter. Then we'll have our baby. Be ready, Okay? I love you."

As soon as they arrived at the hospital, Marietta and John were escorted into one of the examination rooms. Pia waited outside. When Dr. Kennedy arrived he found Marietta lying on the table with John standing beside her, holding her hand.

"What a strong heartbeat the baby has. My guess is that it's a boy. Are you ready for a boy?" he asked, trying to calm his patient.

"I have no preference. I'll love and keep the baby no matter what," Marietta said.

"Of course, you'll keep the baby. Why wouldn't you?"

If only he knew, Marietta thought. But now was not the time to enlighten him. She needed him to concentrate on the delivery.

"Ha-ha. Just as I thought," he said. "There's a small opening in the amniotic sac. It's leaking fluid. The greater danger lies not in what comes out but in what goes in. Germs cause all sorts of problems. Looks like you'll definitely have your baby today."

Marietta was thrilled.

The baby was born August 15, at 8:32 P.M., a girl, healthy and crying, leaving Marietta feeling cold. After the attending nurse cleaned the newborn and laid her on her mother's chest and Marietta's arms circled the baby's tiny body, she was warm again. She placed her breast into the tiny mouth and the baby took it.

"Well, what shall we call her," John said watching his wife and daughter with admiration.

"Anna," Marietta said, "after Nonna – Anna, pure and simple,   full   of   goodness   and   peace."

"Wow, all that in four letters." He smiled.

"When can Aunt Pia see her godchild?" a voice chirped at the door.

"Right now," John said. "I have to go back to the hospital. I'll leave you three ladies alone. See you tonight." He kissed Marietta gently on the lips and the baby on the forehead before he left.

"Too bad Mom's not here," Marietta said. "It would have meant so much to me if Mom could have come."

"Yes," Pia replied. "Look what she missed, her first grandchild."

"Time for the baby to go back to the nursery," the nurse broke in.

"So soon?" Marietta said.

"You must rest. And the pediatrician needs to perform a few tests on her to make sure everything is okay." When the nurse left with the baby, Marietta realized how tired she was. She turned to Pia.

"It means so much to have you with me, not to be alone."

"But you're not alone. John's here and his mother and father are also. I can see how much they love you. No mother-in-law problems for you," she laughed.

"You don't understand. It's Mom I've always wanted. I wish she could love me the way John's mother does."

"Don't look back any more. You need to look forward. You have Anna. She and John are your family now."

Easy for you to say, Marietta thought. You were not the one given away, sent three thousand miles to live with strangers. Yet, Pia was right. Move forward. Don't look back. If only, she could. Marietta looked down her arm, picturing the warm bundle, the tiny face, the round lips suckling her breast that had been there minutes before. She would think only of this precious child, this gift from heaven who had been part of her body. She would never give her up. Not now, not when Anna turned ten or any other time. No one could take her away. They'd have to kill Marietta first, and then she'd come back from the dead to haunt them.

Chapter Twenty

Marietta expected to walk out of the hospital on her own two feet but the nurse stopped her. "Hospital rules," she cited, pushing the wheelchair under her. With John at her side, Marietta made a nest out of her folded arms and carried Anna close to her chest as though the two were still attached. In the car the three rode in silence, awed and overwhelmed by the change the baby brought. John pulled up to the curb and parked in the empty spot in front of their apartment. He walked to the passenger side, placed his hand under Marietta's arm for support and helped her out of the car. He didn't let go until they reached the apartment door where Pia, having heard their footsteps, stood waiting.

"While you two ladies tend to the baby, I'll fix us something to eat. I'm famished," John said.

"I've already made sandwiches," Pia said. "Just get them out of the refrigerator." She followed Marietta into the bedroom. Anna began to cry. She couldn't be hungry, Marietta thought. She'd nursed in the car. She laid the baby in the crib and stuck her finger inside the diaper. It was soaked. So was the undershirt. Everything had to come off. Once the baby was bare, she shielded Anna's face with her hand and poured powder all over the tiny body. She pulled out a new diaper from the box when suddenly her legs caved in. Pia caught her just in time. Marietta grabbed one of the spindles of the crib as sweat formed on her brow. Pia wiped it with the clean diaper and supported her sister onto the bed. She took off Marietta's shoes and propped her feet up so she could lie down.

"You rest for a few minutes. I'll finish diapering the baby.

230

"You make a better mother than I do," Marietta said wryly.

"I've been baby-sitting since I was eleven so I know a thing or two about babies."

"I never baby-sat. Don't you find that odd?" Marietta said. She wondered what else she'd missed besides baby-sitting.

"When they're ready for sleep, it's best to lay them on their side. If they throw up, they won't choke."

Marietta watched with the concentration of an apprentice. Once she was propped on her side, Anna closed her eyes and went immediately to sleep.

"If you two mommies don't come soon, I'm going to eat all the food," John called from the kitchen.

Marietta's nostrils caught the smell of rye bread and coffee traveling through the air and realized how hungry she was. Probably that was why she almost passed out. The two quickly tiptoed out and closed the door quietly.

"John, you can't scream like that anymore or you'll wake up the baby," Marietta warned.

"Sorry. I guess I have to get used to the fact she's here. Let's eat. I can't wait any longer." The three bit into the tuna salad sandwiches as if they had not eaten in days. Just then, the baby let out a piercing cry.

"I don't understand. I just fed her and her diaper was just changed," Marietta said. "What can possibly be wrong?

"Babies are unpredictable. They want things immediately," explained Pia. They waited a few seconds in case Anna fell back to sleep but she cried even louder. Pia brought her to Marietta who unhooking the flap of her nursing bra positioned the baby in the crook of her arm. Her nipple was slightly red. When she placed it inside the baby's mouth, she cringed momentarily as Anna's grip took hold. The child's face went wild with pleasure. A short pink arm wavered in the air like a thin tree branch, and then the tiny hand plopped on Marietta's flesh and clung to it.

John and Pia finished their sandwiches and drank the last sips of coffee. Marietta stared at hers with just one bite taken out of it. Her stomach growled.

"Use your other hand to eat," Pia encouraged.

"I won't spill on the baby?"

"You'll learn not to. It's called survival."

The rest of the week, Pia taught Marietta all she knew: how to burp the baby on her lap as well as her shoulder, how to support the baby's back and head in the bath, how to clip the tiny fingernails without catching the skin, how to slip those short restless limbs in the sleeves or pants of an outfit.

Although John had phoned with the news right after the baby's birth, Paul and Teresa had not visited or called or even sent a card. Not at the hospital, nor at home. She didn't know whether to invite them to Anna's baptism. It was scheduled ten days after the birth since Pia had to return to California for the start of her senior year of high school. A party would follow at John's parents' house. Would Paul and Teresa come? Would they cause a scene? How would Pia react once she found out they were coming? So many questions! In the end, she decided it was best not to send an invitation. She'd deal later with whatever problems resulted.

On the day of the baptism, John's parents' house filled with food, people and presents. A playpen, carriage, stroller, and highchair, took up a lot of room. There were also diapers, bath sets, bibs, blankets, sweater sets and frilly dresses in various sizes from newborn to two years. As Marietta opened each gift, she looked up, smiling in gratitude to John's family, friends and colleagues from the hospital. It saddened her that she could count only Pia as her family, and John, of course. After Pia left, there would only be John.

In the first three months the baby demanded a great deal of care. If Marietta didn't organize her schedule, nothing got done except tending to Anna. Time for reading or socializing didn't exist. It was a blessing she'd taken a leave of absence from school for the year. She couldn't imagine teaching or preparing lesson plans now. When someone stopped by to see the baby, the next day would be crammed with two days' work. Anna often insisted on being rocked in her mother's arms until she fell asleep. Feeding times blended with each other. Breakfast, lunch and dinner came and went too fast. Marietta had little time to eat or brush her teeth. She often skipped meals. She grew jittery and cranky. Frustrated at her inability to control the baby's eating and sleeping patterns, she felt lost, deep into a rut. Today: nurse, burp, bathe the baby and rock her to sleep. Tomorrow: nurse, burp, bathe the baby and rock her to sleep. Marietta often dozed off with the baby in her arms. When she woke up, it was time to nurse again.

One day Marietta looked in the mirror. Her pants looked baggy and her blouse hung loose. Her figure had disappeared. When she stepped on the scale, she weighed ten pounds lighter than before she got married. Good God, she thought! Her mind had gone downhill and now her body followed suit. She wasn't the only one with problems, though. After wanting to eat all the time, Anna now refused to nurse. She'd suck for three minutes and then lose interest, falling asleep as if she were drugged. As a result, Marietta's milk supply dwindled. She was beside herself with worry. Anna was her responsibility and she was failing as a mother.

"You can supplement with formula," said a neighbor. "It's no disgrace to bottle feed when a baby's not thriving at the breast." But John's mother encouraged her to check with the La Leche League.

"No formula." The woman on the other end of the phone was adamant. "Continue to nurse. Eventually the baby will get hungry enough to suck. The sucking will stimulate the breast and the milk will flow once more."

Marietta didn't know whether to believe her. She didn't want to take advice on blind faith. She wanted empirical evidence. She phoned John's mother again. "Have you heard of such a thing?" she asked.

"Sure, it happens. The best thing is to relax and keep breastfeeding. I think you'll see a difference in two or three days."

"Maybe you're right," she said. She'd been so stressed lately. She missed teaching and her students' reactions after class experiments, the adult banter of colleagues in the teacher's cafeteria, the feeling of getting up in the morning to go to work, of talking to adults and having a purpose beyond the house. As she reminisced, she heard Anna cry. Marietta hung up the phone and picked her up.

"Tell Mommy, what's wrong?" she said. "I love you. Why isn't everything all right?" The baby continued to cry. She didn't know what to do. She was tempted to call John's mother again, but the phone rang instead. Perhaps it was John wanting to check on her, she thought. He worried so.

"It's Linda. How's the little mommy?" she asked. She'd given up finding Mr. Right and had joined the Army. Already she'd moved up in rank. Was it Lieutenant or Corporal? Marietta couldn't remember.

"Linda! How nice to hear from you. The little mommy is worn out. It's more work than I dreamed. I don't think I'm very good at it."

"I've got a few days' furlough. Can I visit this afternoon? I bought the cutest little dress at the store. I don't want Anna to outgrow it."

"Come, by all means." Marietta perked up. A visit from a friend would do her good. She was hungry for another adult, especially a woman. Food shopping would wait until tomorrow. John could pick up pizza. Maybe Linda would stay, too. She made a mental note to dial John before he left the hospital.

The visit was nothing Marietta expected. Anna cried for most of it. Marietta and Linda could hardly talk. To soothe the baby, Marietta offered her breast but Anna, as usual, turned her head away. She wouldn't lie still in the playpen or the crib. Marietta finally picked up the baby and held her at arm's length.

"What's wrong?" she said, frustrated. "Mommy loves you. Don't you know that Mommy loves you?"

"Love isn't the only thing a baby needs," Linda said.

"It isn't?" Marietta was surprised. "I thought if a child is loved, it took care of everything." What else caused problems but an absence of love? Had Stella loved her, Marietta could have been so much more well-adjusted.

"Sometimes, the body has other needs. The baby could have pain, or gas or some other discomfort. They're just as important as love. Get her checked. And yourself too," she recommended.

"Yes, I have an appointment in a couple of days." Marietta acknowledged. "But if you had love, I thought all your needs would be met."

"They're not, though I will admit, love makes our problems bearable," Linda said.

"Aren't you the voice of wisdom today," Marietta teased.

"Did you forget? I practically raised my brothers and sisters."

The next day, when Marietta got on the scale, she'd lost one more pound. Could there be something physically wrong with her and Anna?

"Tell it to me straight," she asked Dr. Kennedy. "Why am I losing so much weight and the baby is not nursing the way she did at first? What's wrong with us?"

"I've checked all your vital signs. You're in perfect physical condition and so is the baby. You've been going at a rugged pace these last few months. It's normal to feel depressed after childbirth. As the baby sleeps through the night, you'll gain back the weight you lost. There's nothing to worry about. It's going to get better," he assured her.

She was relieved and encouraged. Then as if by magic, within a week, the baby nursed longer, both slept through the night and Marietta stopped losing weight. Soon rosy cheeks appeared on her face and she was buoyed with some energy. But she couldn't shake the melancholy feeling that settled in from time to time. It nagged at Marietta as if it were a heavy sac tied around her neck. After-birth blues, John's mother had called them. Why should she be blue, Marietta thought? She had a wonderful husband who loved her and whom she loved, a healthy child especially now that she was eating and sleeping longer. She did wish John's job was less demanding. He wasn't home enough to help her with the daily chores or with Anna. Or was it because Paul, Teresa and Sofia had kept their distance? They still hadn't called, stopped by or even sent a card for the baby's birth. Was that the emptiness she felt?

Some mornings, when John was at work and she lay in bed with the baby nursing, she could feel Anna's body react to her warmth. She felt Anna's heartbeat. Anna felt hers. Stella must have felt the same way with Marietta when she was a baby. She wondered: how can you give up your child after you feel her heartbeat? After you've given her life? After you've gotten to know her? When John came home that night, she shared these questions.

"Maybe you need to ask your Mom," he said. "She's the one who gave you away. She's the only person who could know the answer."

Ask Stella? She could be opening up a Pandora's Box. Marietta thought it strange her mother hadn't tried to explain why she gave her daughter away. You'd think Stella would want to exonerate herself in case Marietta blamed her. If she had given some reasons, Marietta would know why she was sent to America, and possibly all would be forgiven, even forgotten, like the pain of childbirth. But Stella had only cooked and talked of recipes. So the questions remained unanswered. Along with them lingered the familiar tug to ask or not to ask. Even if Marietta dared to pose the questions to her mother, the cultural difference between the two, to say nothing of the emotional toll it might have on each of them, was something to consider.

"All hell may break loose and I'll lose what I've gained," she said to John one evening. "But, I'm afraid I'll go out of my mind if I don't confront my mother."

"Funny you should say that," he said. "In light of what happened at the hospital, I mean." Marietta looked confused. How could what happened at the hospital have anything to do with her?

"I've been asked to attend a week-long medical conference at UCLA in the summer. I was going to turn it down thinking it'd be too much to go and leave you alone with the baby when I already leave you alone so much. But if you join me, you'd see your mother and she could see the baby. I know you want that. I wasn't going to mention it, but with what you've just told me, the trip might be the perfect opportunity."

"Then you think I should ask the questions? I'm not crazy or stupid for wanting to?"

"No. It's the healthiest thing you can do."

"But the baby – I don't want the baby affected by this."

"She won't be. All she wants is to be held, fed and changed. Besides, the baby is the one that really brought these questions to the surface. Maybe it's time to put them to rest."

"Do you think my mother will understand? Won't she get angry?"

"She might, at first, but if she loves you she'll understand. You're not seeking revenge. Just answers."

"How is it that you know me so well? You see my feelings through my flesh."

"I read once that flesh is transparent when you hold it in the light, but love can see through walls. I've never forgotten it."

Marietta kissed him gently on the lips. He had touched her soul, as he had when they first met.

As the winter and spring months went by, Marietta became adept at accomplishing more in less time. She could sit Anna in the playpen and surround her with toys while she exercised in front of her. She loved the way Anna's eyes followed her every move. When Marietta showered, she left the bathroom door open so Anna could hear her voice. When she shampooed her hair, she turned the water off in the middle so she could listen to any unusual sounds that might impact the child's safety. When it was Anna's turn to bathe, Marietta placed her in the sink every morning at ten, allowing her to play with the water and the yellow rubber ducky she loved to squeeze. They ate breakfast, lunch and dinner at the same time, Marietta alternating hands when Anna alternated breasts. Anna cooed, her eyes glued to her mother's face, the only world she knew, the only world she cared about.

Marietta often read to Anna. Most of the books were about animals. Anna giggled when Marietta mewed, barked or chirped like the creatures in the books. A favorite was <u>Are You My Mother</u>? By P. D. Eastman. It was a story of a little bird that, upon hatching in his nest, found his mother missing and went searching for her. Little bird posed the same question to every animal he met: "Are you my mother?" Each negative answer he received only made his longing for his mother stronger. Not until he was thrust back into his nest by accident and mother bird returned, did he rejoice.

It was difficult to tell who liked the book more, Anna or Marietta. When they heard "Are you my mother?" asked of each animal little bird met, both their eyes widened and

Anna's legs moved wildly. The question was haunting. Slowly Marietta realized how much the book and its recurring question was a metaphor for her own life.

"Next Friday is the big day," John said excitedly. He held up the plane tickets for their trip west.

Marietta paled. It had come too soon. Half of her wanted to ask her questions; the other half didn't.

"You could just visit," said John. "There'll be other opportunities. You haven't told anyone yet, not even Pia. No one would be the wiser if you waited to a time you feel more comfortable."

"I'll never feel comfortable and I did tell Pia. She's a nervous wreck. She's afraid of how my mother will react."

"Then wait until next year or a time I can be with you." he offered.

"No, I have to do this on my own. And if I don't ask her now, I'll never ask. I need to hear myself say the words. It'll never get easier. I'm terrified to ask, but I'm more terrified not to."

Chapter Twenty-One

Marietta awoke in the middle of the flight from New York to Los Angeles still in a daze from her dream in which Nonna offered her a slice of bread with olive oil as Lucia waved her orange peel in the air. She heard John's low snore as he slept soundly. Leaning down by her feet where Anna also lay sleeping in the cushioned box the airline had provided, she gently touched the baby's back with the palm of her hand. Satisfied that her hand rose with every breath, Marietta fell asleep again and continued dreaming. She was now at the Rome airport with a dish of steaming pasta in front of her. Nonna and Lucia were gone. Only Stella remained and the dreaded knowledge that Marietta would fly, alone, to New York to be adopted by an aunt and uncle she'd never met. She had left her beloved family in Castellaneta for a world she did not know, one she did not want. She would never see Nonna again. Her heart broke in two at the thought. Why, why, why, she screamed. But Stella didn't hear. She was too busy dangling a pair of gold earrings under her daughter's nose. Marietta woke up in a sweat, murmuring, "Why, why, why?"

When the plane finally landed and she and John were gathering all their belongings, she gasped. She thought she'd spotted Nonna standing by the cabin door with Lucia at her side. But no, it was another passenger with a child. It was her mind playing tricks with her desires.

Coming down the ramp John maneuvered the luggage they had brought by balancing the shoulder straps of the two totes across his back and pulling the handles of the two larger valises. Marietta draped the diaper bag over one shoulder and the strap of her purse over the other, leaving her hands free for

Anna to nestle snugly in her arms. In the distance they could see many arms waving wildly in the air.

"Over here, Marietta. Over here." The voice was distinctively Stella's but they were too far away to determine which face was hers. Marietta spotted Stella's blurred outline standing in an area sectioned off with rope. A few steps forward and the blur cleared. Suddenly Stella broke free of the ropes and ran forward against the flow of people exiting. Marietta's heart leaped at the welcome she felt coming her way. When they hugged, three generations would join, just as in Italy, albeit with a different configuration. Anna was the child instead of Marietta. Stella became her beloved Nonna and Marietta took the place of her mother. In anticipation, she shifted Anna to one side to accommodate the embrace. But when Stella arrived, out of breath, she snatched Anna out of Marietta's arms and pressed the child tightly against her chest, planting two loud kisses on the tiny cheeks. Anna let out a piercing cry, causing the people around them to turn to see what the commotion was all about.

"Anna, Anna. *Sei con Nonna.* You're with Grandma," Stella said. Anna continued to cry as if a pin stuck her flesh. It wasn't until Marietta pried the child out of her mother's arms that Anna stopped crying.

"She's afraid, Mom. She doesn't know you. You have to give her time." You should have hugged me instead, she wanted to tell her. Why didn't you hug me?

That evening Stella cooked enough food to feed a thousand. She prepared a giant platter of antipasto consisting of anchovies, large capers, aged provolone, soppresata, pitted green olives, roasted peppers and balls of fresh mozzarella in a carousel of milk as though the cheese were still lactating. A large pan of lasagna in a rich, red sauce laced with tiny meatballs followed. And in case John didn't care for the red variety, there was another pan of white lasagna drenched in béchamel sauce – a velvety glaze of butter and cream blended like silk. This was only *il primo*. Next, came *il secondo*: veal saltimbocca – thin, tender cutlets of veal, floured and spiced, sautéed in olive oil and covered with slices of provolone and prosciutto topped with a thick, gravy made from a roux of sweet wine, butter and cornstarch. The vegetables consisted of steamed Romano beans and sliced carrots marinated in oil, vinegar and oregano served at room temperature. There was also asparagus that had been previously rolled in egg batter, floured and fried. A salad of lettuce, tomatoes and cucumbers dressed in olive oil and lemon juice completed the fare. It helped digest all that went before, Stella said. Of course there was bread. A nice, healthy round loaf, crisp on the outside and soft on the inside, sliced from many angles as most Italians prize the crusted ends. The meal was not over until the espresso appeared together with *la torta*, a type of dessert baked with slices of fruit throughout the batter, resembling cake more than pie.

Early the next morning John left for his weeklong conference and Marietta reminded herself of the purpose of her visit. She wished her relationship with Stella could have been like the lasagna in béchamel sauce, an indistinguishable blend of love between mother and child, where she wouldn't have to ask such probing questions. She was afraid of her questions. After all, the relationship had only just begun. Would Stella be able to understand Marietta's hurt and why she had to address it?

Stella still couldn't approach Anna without the child crying hysterically. Thank God, Carl was wise enough to keep his distance, Marietta thought. Offers of lollipops, cookies and toys, which Stella passed to Anna via Marietta's hands, eventually began to quell the child's fear. On the third day, Anna accepted a lollipop directly from Stella. On the fourth day, she sat on Stella's lap as long as she maintained eye contact with her mother. Marietta felt relieved to have that tension end. She waited patiently, constantly on the lookout for the right moment when she would feel comfortable enough to broach the subject that tormented her soul. But that moment seemed elusive as friends stopped by to see Stella's long-lost daughter and granddaughter. There were trips to the grocery store. Anna's needs had to be met. Meals had to be prepared. And Carl was always home.

The kitchen became a magical place. When Stella cooked, she became a master artist. Marietta loved seeing her mother glow in her talent. She talked non-stop about the ingredients that went into the preparation of the food, their texture, origin and uses. At such times, Marietta again became Stella's apprentice rather than her daughter. With Pia gone for the day at work at her summer job, the two were lost in a world of culinary delights, flavors, spices, colors and scents. With the speed of a stenographer, Marietta wrote down every ingredient in each recipe just as Stella said it, half in Italian, half in English, and in measurements delegated by body parts. She took in every word and glance her mother sent her way. The familiar names and aromas of food bonded the two as nothing else had so far and Marietta wanted to freeze these moments in a fresco.

"*Cartellate* are a specialty of our region. Do you remember how much you loved them? Nonna made them *con il sugo dei fichi* – with fig juice – to give them that enchanting flavor." Marietta felt the timid voice of the ten-year old inside her shout, "I remember, Mamma. I remember. How could I forget? I can still taste them on my tongue." But Stella saw only the adult Marietta. She was oblivious to the child that was also there. Marietta feared that the questions she had to ask might taint the beautiful memories they now enjoyed. To spoil them with issues from the past was almost sacrilegious. She was tempted now to let them lie dormant, the way they'd been for more than half her life.

At the end of the day, Marietta brought Anna to every member of the family to kiss goodnight before bedtime. She laid her in the crib and covered her body loosely with her favorite blanket.

"Goodnight, Anna. Mommy loves you. I'll see you in the morning," Marietta said. If she could bring closure to her questions as easily as this goodnight, Marietta thought, she'd be free. She went to bed realizing only two days remained of the visit. If the right moment didn't appear, there was nothing she could do but postpone, maybe even abort her mission. The realization almost relieved her.

Marietta fell asleep resigned to whatever happened when suddenly she was awakened by moans. Why, they'd come from the back of her own throat, the recurrent dream, gripping her in fear. She was ten again and running as fast as her legs could carry her. Someone chased her. The person was gaining distance. The child ran faster but the faster she ran, the more ground she lost. She turned her head to see who pursued her. It was the woman with dark hair. Marietta looked down at her feet, now moving quicker, and realized she was running in place. The woman would surely catch her. She awoke moaning and afraid as she realized that the woman in the dream resembled Stella. Was Marietta trying to escape so she wouldn't have to leave for America?

"Marietta, did you sleep well last night?" Stella asked the next morning as they sat sipping espresso and eating the biscotti she had baked. Anna was safe in the playpen in the middle of the kitchen playing with all the toys Stella had given her. Carl went to the store on an errand. So it was just the two of them sitting at the table.

"Why do you ask?" Marietta said alarmed. Could Stella have heard her moaning? Could she have guessed her dream?

"Well, you have dark circles under your eyes, which you didn't have yesterday. Are you feeling okay? Maybe you miss John."

"I do miss him." Marietta said. She wished John would return. He'd shed light on the dream. She couldn't talk to her mother about it.

"*Vieni con me.* Come with me. Let me show you something. It'll pick you up." Stella motioned with her hands for her daughter to follow. Marietta glanced at the playpen and noticed that Anna had dozed off. Assured that the child was safe, she trailed her mother into the bedroom.

"Look at all these clothes, and this fur coat," said Stella, entering a large walk-in closet that could have doubled for a bedroom. Marietta's eyes widened. Eight or ten long gowns in every color of the rainbow faced her. Some of them were beaded. Others were interwoven with silver thread or lace. All were elegant. To the right were several dozen skirts. Twice as many tops and silk blouses lined the wall as did a handful of suits, tailored with varying lapel styles. On the floor, boxes of shoes were piled high, rivaling sections in a shoe store. "We've come a long way from Italy where we had only two or three outfits each," Stella said.

"Are all these yours? I mean, do you actually wear them?" asked Marietta.

"I've worn every one once, except for those that have the price tag attached." Stella's hand passed across a dozen hangers, making an arc, the way a farmer might when pointing out the expanse of his fields and glowed. Marietta recognized the glow. She'd seen it on her mother's face the day they'd shopped for clothes for her to wear on her voyage to America.

Stella pointed to a drawer full of perfumes, soaps, shampoos and creams. "If you want to use any of them, feel free," she said. Marietta had no idea why her mother needed them. Her skin was flawless.

"*Ma vieni. Guarda qui.* But come. Look here," she motioned, coaxing Marietta to kneel beside her. Stella knelt on the floor of a deep closet in front of what looked like a large square box covered with a plaid blanket. Stella removed the blanket and revealed a small, black, metal safe. "It's bolted to the floor so no one can steal," she explained. Reaching for her glasses, she placed them on her nose. Then she cupped her fingers on the dial of the safe. With a few turns to the left and a few to the right, the metal door clicked open. Stella's hand entered the safe withdrawing a plastic bag of gemstones. There were jades, opals, amethysts, sapphires, emeralds and diamonds which sparkled like stars under the closet light.

"These are the rarest and most expensive," Stella said. Her face was as radiant as the stones. "I kept them all these years in the hope of someday giving one to you. Which one would you like? Choose and I'll have it made into a beautiful necklace or ring."

"I...I don't know. They're all so beautiful," stammered Marietta, dazzled by such luster. Realizing they were both genuflecting to pieces of metal, she gave a muffled laugh. What irony, she thought. Why hadn't Stella *kept her* as closely as she had kept her jewels? Wasn't she as precious?

"Take this one," Stella offered. She removed an amethyst from the pile and held it in the palm of her hand. "It's the most expensive of all of them. I'll make it into a heart – from me to you."

Marietta took the jewel out of her mother's hand and looked at it. She didn't want it any more than she'd wanted the ring and earrings her mother had given her at the Rome Airport years earlier. She wanted Pia, Nonna and Lucia. She wanted the years she lost without them. Had she been Stella, she would have traded all the precious stones in the world to keep her family intact.

She laid the amethyst gently on the nightstand. She decided if ever a moment would be the right time, it was now. If she had the courage. Mustering all her strength, she rose, took a deep breath and faced Stella who, too, had risen from her knees. One adult to another.

"Mom, there's something I need to ask."

Stella turned tenderly toward her daughter. "Anything, darling. Is there something else I can give you?"

Marietta watched a smile cross Stella's face as her eyes fell on the jewelry once more. She recalled the power possessions had on her mother. Some things never change, she thought.

"It's not things I want, but questions answered."

"What kind of questions?"

"Questions about the past," Marietta declared. Stella's face froze. She'd gotten comfortable living in the present. A grand house, expensive clothes, a husband who loved her and didn't beat her, friends and neighbors surrounding her in idyllic California. Now an earthquake had come to shake it all up.

But Marietta was undeterred. Her voice was calm, unwavering. "Mom, you know I love you. I never wanted to leave you and Pia and Nonna in Italy. But I have this question that torments my soul."

"*Si, dimmi* – yes, tell me."

"Mom, why did you give me away?" There! She'd said it – finally.

Stella's lips began to quiver. Her eyes brimmed with tears.

"I trusted you. I thought you loved me as much as you love Pia," Marietta continued.

"I do love you. I love you more than my life. You don't know how much I suffered without you."

"Then why didn't you keep me the way you kept Pia? Was there something wrong with me?"

Stella instantly shook her head. Marietta didn't know whether her mother was answering her question or denying the scene in front of her, but it didn't stop her from continuing.

"Do you know how betrayed I felt when you sent me away? Rejected by my own mother? You threw me out. You discarded me like an old rag."

Stella's body grew rigid. She stared wide-eyed into space, almost turning white. Then her body shook as if the earthquake had actually taken place. Marietta panicked. Oh no, what had she done? Would her mother die on the spot?

"I'm sorry. I didn't mean to hurt you," she cried. "Please understand. This question has haunted me my whole life. I want to be free of it. I have to ask it."

Then, just as quickly as they came, Stella's tremors ceased. Her body relaxed and she recovered, smiling as if nothing had happened.

"I don't understand how you could give me up. At ten years of age? They'd have to kill me before I'd give up Anna at any age," Marietta explained.

"I never wanted to give you away," Stella cried, embracing her. "I thought it'd be only for a short time. I thought I'd get you back. By the time I knew what I had done, it was too late." Stella's tears ran down Marietta's back. She could feel her mother's hot breath on her neck.

"What happened? What had you done?"

"Your no-good father, he wanted to give his sister a child ...because they couldn't have any. Meanwhile it was God who made them barren... to punish them for their evil ways. Look what they did to you. They made you stay away from me all these years."

"My father?"

"It was your father's idea all along. He said it was our chance to go to America. I could be a movie star. He promised me I'd get you back."

"Why did you agree? You knew he never told the truth."

"I'm sorry," she sobbed. "I didn't know what I was doing. I was young. But he threatened me, that no-good scoundrel. He said he'd kill me and all my brothers with me... if I didn't sign the adoption papers."

"Why didn't you call the police?"

"I was afraid. Your father was violent."

"But why did you give *me* away? Why didn't you give away Pia? Not that I wanted you to, but why me over Pia? She was younger, a baby. Most people who adopt prefer babies instead of older children. What made you choose me to give up?"

"I made a mistake," Stella said, disengaging from Marietta. She moved further into the closet. It enclosed her like a cave. She was hardly breathing now. Her eyes looked away as if she could see through the threads of her gowns, through the walls. Her spirit had been transported to a different time and place. Marietta, too, felt removed from her surroundings, as if she'd entered her mother's womb again, knowing she'd be ejected violently not once, but twice.

Then Stella's eyes darkened. It seemed as if an evil spirit had entered her body. Marietta feared her mother would lash at her, but she wasn't afraid. She stood tall, ready for whatever came. Then, in a rush, Stella embraced her again. She latched on so tightly that Marietta could feel her mother's heart pound. Tears streamed down Stella's face as Marietta cried, too.

"Talk of adoption began long before your sister was born," Stella admitted. "In fact, it began right after you were born. If it weren't for Nonna, you would have come to America much earlier. She stood up to your father every time he came near. She fought for you like you were hers. It was just a matter of time when you would go. I had already signed the papers releasing you."

At the mention of Nonna, Marietta felt a giant weight lift. She knew that Nonna would be on her side. How grateful she was for that! If only Stella had fought for her, too, she could more easily forgive her. But then Stella had been a

249

child herself, wild and selfish. Motherhood had done little to tame her, to mature her. You can't draw blood from a stone, a friend had once told Marietta. How could she expect her mother to give what she didn't possess? To blame her father Antonio was pointless. She had never been attached to him. It was her mother whom she'd always wanted, who linked her to Nonna.

Both exhausted now, standing face-to-face with each other, Marietta noticed for the first time that she stood taller than her mother. In the past, Stella had always seemed larger than life.

For the next few minutes they stood silently, each lost in their own world. Marietta was engaged in a scene that seemed to play in front of her. When it was over, she turned to her mother and said, "I should go check on Anna."

"Yes," Stella agreed. "Let's make sure she's okay."

"What happened? You seem like a different person," John said that night, after returning from the conference. They were getting ready for bed.

"I feel like the weight of the world has been lifted off me."

"Do you want to talk about it?"

Marietta recounted every detail. "Wow," he said. "And Nonna remained loyal to you 'til the end."

"I wish my mother could have fought for me the way Nonna did. She says she loves me but it's not the way I love Anna."

"Do you believe your mother told the truth?"

"I don't know. So many years have passed. Why she sent me away no longer matters. All that's important is that I asked why. I finally stood up for myself, for the little girl I used to be."

"Can you forgive your mother after all she's done to you?"

"I suppose so, if I want to be free. Strangely, I forgive her more for my sake than for hers." She hesitated. "And you might think me stranger still if I tell you what else happened."

"Nothing you say or do is strange to me, mysterious yes, but not strange." He pecked her on the cheek, wanting to soothe the pain he knew she'd endured. But she was somewhere else, unaware of his tender touch.

"When we were done talking, the image of me as a little girl appeared. She smiled as though she were thanking me. Then she waved goodbye and skipped away."

"Where do you imagine the girl went?" John was curious.

"Back to Castellaneta, I would think. It's where she always wanted to be."

"And you," John said. "Where do you want to be? Would you prefer to stay here with your mother and sister?"

"My family is with you and Anna now. It's where I belong," she smiled. John smiled back, relieved.

"I do have one request, though," she said.

"Oh?"

"I want to go to Castellaneta. The three of us, I mean. To see Nonna before it's too late. And Lucia and all my cousins. I want to walk the ancient streets and once more feel the cobblestones under my feet," she laughed. "And I want to go in spring when the geraniums bloom."

EPILOGUE

The roar of the plane's engines reverberated in Marietta's ears. She and John sat in the row above the wing with two-year-old Anna strapped in the seat between them. Looking out the window, Marietta smiled as she spotted the clouds that passed below her. She would make new memories for them to hold. She was flying to Rome, then to Bari where her cousin Peppino had promised to pick them up with his car for the hour's drive to Nonna's house in Castellaneta.

Marietta had no idea what she'd find as she set foot on the cobblestone street. Would it have the scent of orange peels? Would Lucia recognize her? And what of the other cousins? They were no longer children but adults like the aunts and uncles she'd left behind. Most of all, how would she feel once she climbed the stairs and entered the house she loved, once she set eyes on Nonna and Nonno and they on her? Once she was in their open arms?

She couldn't contain her excitement. Marietta's world was coming back full circle. It was the first day of spring – *la primavera* – the first truth.

Discussion Questions for ORANGE PEELS and COBBLESTONES

How would you assess each of the main characters: Paul, Teresa, Stella, Antonio, Nonna, Marietta, John? Which one touched you or appealed to you the most and why?

Did Stella do the right thing by sending Marietta away? What do you think were her motives?

Which particular scene was your favorite or touched you the most? Why?

There are three pivotal scenes that frame the book. Which three do you think they are?

In the scene in the principal's office, did Marietta do the right thing? Did Stella? What would you have done if you were Marietta, or Stella or the principal?

How would you answer Marietta's question: How can a mother give up her own child?

Should Marietta have forgiven or not forgiven her mother? Why?

Did the ending satisfy you? Why or why not?

What is the significance of the title? Why do you think the author chose it?

Did you like the book? Why? Would you recommend it to others?

Orange Peels and Cobblestones